As the girls lifted their bags, T-Rex's gaze landed on Remi.

Her hand was raised, shielding her eyes as she gazed into the morning sun. Something about her posture tightened T-Rex's muscles. He scanned to see what she was looking at, but from his vantage point, all he had was a strip of mown grass that dipped into a runoff pond.

T-Rex turned to Ty. They'd been Unit members together for long enough that when T-Rex bored his gaze into the back of Ty's head, he turned.

As T-Rex lifted a hand to signal, Rory gave a low growl from the back of his throat. Hackles up, he gave an aggressive bark, pulling to the end of his lead.

T-Rex strode toward his principal, so he could cover her no matter the disturbance. If his face was caught on camera, he'd just have the photographer delete those frames.

Ty reeled Rory back, but Rory was lunging aggressively.

Eyes scanning the horizon, T-Rex still couldn't find anything amiss.

And that's when all hell broke loose.

Fiona Quinn is a six-time *USA TODAY* bestselling author, a Kindle Scout winner and an Amazon All-Star.

Quinn writes suspense in her Iniquus world of books, including the Lynx, Strike Force, Uncommon Enemies, Kate Hamilton Mysteries, FBI Joint Task Force, Cerberus Tactical K-9 Team Alpha and Delta Force Echo series, with more to come.

She writes urban fantasy as Fiona Angelica Quinn for her Elemental Witches series.

And, just for fun, she writes the Badge Bunny Booze Mystery Collection of raucous, bawdy humor with her dear friend Tina Glasneck as Quinn Glasneck.

Quinn is rooted in the Old Dominion, where she lives with her husband. There, she pops chocolates, devours books and taps continuously on her laptop.

Facebook, Twitter, Pinterest: Fiona Quinn Books.

A GUARDIAN'S STRENGTH

USA TODAY Bestselling Author

FIONA QUINN

Previously published as *Danger Zone*

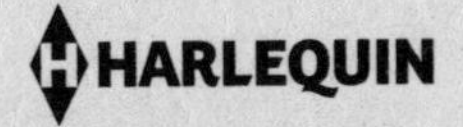

This book is dedicated to Blythe ~
who inspires me with her strength of character,
creativity and curiosity.
And to those around the world whose lives
turn upside down without a moment's notice,
may you always find loving support and kindness.

Recycling programs for this product may not exist in your area.

ISBN-13: 978-1-335-45510-9

A Guardian's Strength

First published as Danger Zone in 2021.
This edition published in 2023.

For questions and comments about the quality of this book, please contact us at CustomerService@Harlequin.com.

Harlequin Enterprises ULC
22 Adelaide St. West, 41st Floor
Toronto, Ontario M5H 4E3, Canada
www.Harlequin.com

Printed in U.S.A.

A GUARDIAN'S STRENGTH

Acknowledgments

My great appreciation

To the real world Christen Davidson for our decades of friendship.

To my editor, Kathleen Payne.

To my assistant, Margaret Daly.

To my friend, M. Carlon, for helping me find the story.

To my Beta Force, who are always honest and kind at the same time.

To my Street Force, who support me and my writing with such enthusiasm.

Thank you to the real-world military who serve to protect us.

To all the wonderful professionals whom I called on to get the details right. Please note: this is a work of fiction, and while I always try my best to get all the details correct, there are times when it serves the story to go slightly to the left or right of perfection. Please understand that any mistakes or discrepancies are my authorial decision-making alone and sit squarely on my shoulders.

Thank you to my family.

I send my love to my husband. Every day I wake up grateful that you grace my world. Thank you.

And of course, thank YOU for reading my stories. I'm smiling joyfully as I type this. I so appreciate you!

The Teams

Reporters

FR-13

Jean Baptiste Rujean

Éloïse Marquette

Marie-Claude de Nimoux

Washington News-Herald

Remi Taleb—war correspondent

Liu—Editor in Chief

Jules Edwards—photojournalist

Jasmine Tremblay—White House reporter

David Puck—covering the DOJ, Washington, DC

Iniquus's Cerberus Tactical K9

Tripwire and K9 Valor—Team Alpha

Bear MacIntosh and K9 Truffles—Team Bravo

Bob Palindrome, logistics—Team Alpha

Military

Soar 160th—Night Stalkers

D-Day Rochambeau

Nick of Time

Delta Force: G Squadron (clandestine), Echo (reconnaissance)

Lieutenant Colonel Burnside—G Squadron Commander

Josiah Landry (T-Rex)—Echo Actual

Tyler Newcomb (Ty)—Echo Two, K9 handler for Rory

Jeopardy—Echo Three

Nitro—Echo Four and Laurel, his wife

Havoc—Echo Six

Carlotta Hill (Winner)—logistical support

Government

US Senator Barb Blankenship (Texas)

Diamond Johnson—senator's aide

Chapter 1

Remi

Monday, Washington, D.C.

Horror wasn't a new sensation for Remi Taleb. In fact, it was kind of her go-to emotion.

After a while, she'd learned even horror could feel banal.

This…*uselessness*.

This *incapacity* to help in any way at all.

Fear and panic pumped through her system as Remi stood in front of the wall of television monitors here in the D.C. newsroom.

Jean Baptiste, look at him!

News stations around the world all played the same reporter telling his story.

His clothing, shredded. Dirt and what looked like an

oily substance covered what scraps still clung to her dear friend's wiry frame.

The haphazard bandaging that wrapped Jean Baptiste's head and left eye seeped with blood, drying around the edges to rusty black splotches.

His arm hung bizarrely twisted and limp at his side.

It was surprising that Jean Baptiste could stand at all. He was almost unrecognizable to Remi, though his face had been a constant in her life ever since she signed her first contract, climbed in the back of her first armored vehicle, and began her career as a war reporter.

Troubled spots were Remi's home turf. Just like the other misfits that called themselves war correspondents.

They were Remi's kind of people—folks with the ability to hold both compassion and emotional distance, at the same time maintaining—or feigning—an indifference to the steady blast from their internal adrenaline hose.

Her job was to traipse the cliff's edge, summit the mountain of human depravity. One either found their balance, or they crashed to the valley floor.

Jean Baptiste Rujean was one of the best combat photojournalists around. His high wire tricks were legendary. He'd been behind his camera, focusing his lens on the worst atrocities found in the far reaches of the world. Not only had he succeeded at gathering his reports, but he had emerged from the jungles and deserts, the urban guerrilla fights, seemingly unscathed.

His luck had finally run its course.

In this story, horror had become personal.

The wall separating journalism from the reported event had dissolved.

Unwilling to take her eyes off the screens even to blink, Remi stood, hands on hips. Piking forward, with her shoulders arched back, she tried to get space in her lungs for air.

She aimed her mouth vaguely over a colleague's trash can in case she needed to puke up this morning's bagel with lox and the large coffee that was churning around her insides.

The room held still in stunned silence.

The journalists and news staff, like Remi, stretched their eyelids wide. Hands covered mouths and suppressed gasps. They pinched at their lips to hold back expletives so that they didn't disturb the newsroom's silence and everyone could focus on the wall of televisions.

The only sounds came from Jean Baptiste, the French reporter reporting on the reporters.

That sentence became an earworm. A stupid alliterative sentence that would get Remi an eye roll from her editor, but this was no time for elegance of phrase.

This was catastrophic.

Two of them. Marie-Claude and Éloïse. Colleagues. Friends. Held hostage.

Only Jean Baptiste made it over the Syrian border into Lebanon.

Jean Baptiste, Marie-Claude, and Éloïse working for FR-13, a French television station, were fellow travelers in this crazy-assed job.

Remi had been trading war stories with them at the hotel bar in Addis Ababa, Ethiopia, where they were covering the coup attempt. The general at the head of the effort had been captured and killed.

The following day, Remi leaped on a plane back to D.C.

And her friends had flown on to Iraq, jumped into an

SUV heading over the border into Syria. Into the arms of ISIS.

Thirty-six hours ago.

Crap.

Another wave of horror washed over Remi, threatening to drag her into the bottomless gulf of self-recriminations.

I was supposed to be with them.

The FR-13 team had invited Remi to join them on that very assignment.

And Remi agreed to go.

Logistics planned, bag packed, ready to climb on her flight with Jean Baptiste and the others, when her boss, Liu, had nixed the trip. He'd called her back, ostensibly to be part of some discussion about another hot spot he wanted covered.

Remi had assumed that was a ruse to force her back to D.C. where Liu could compel her to attend the National Journalism Awards Ceremony and accept her applause for her reporting on SEAL Platoon One. Sure, it was a prestigious award, but Remi didn't care about honors. They weren't a motivating factor. If anything, accolades were disincentives. She was always uncomfortable with praise and personal attention.

Remi wanted to put her head down and get the job done.

Liu had other things to consider in asking her to attend the award ceremony, like the newsroom's stature and consumer engagement.

Though Remi had made solid arguments why she should be allowed to go with the FR-13 team, Liu had insisted she fly back immediately.

In so doing, he had probably saved Remi's life.

Remi scraped her bottom teeth over her lip as she absorbed the unfolding story on the TV screens.

Jean Baptiste should be in the back of an ambulance, not swaying on screen telling this story.

While fluent in English, Jean Baptiste was slurring out the timeline of his capture, torture, agreement, and release in his native French, with English subtitles racing across the screen. He explained that Marie-Claude and Éloïse would pay the price if he didn't record and air this story immediately.

Jean Baptiste was obviously in shock and in need of medical attention as he rambled through the description of the atrocities he'd endured.

From his pocket, he dragged a scrap of paper. He tried to read it, turning his head this way and that.

Jean Baptiste didn't have his glasses on.

Someone off-camera pressed a pair of half-moon reading glasses toward him.

Then there was the fumbling as Jean Baptiste tried to figure out how to maneuver one-handed. He put the paper between his lips, flicked the glasses through the air to get the earpieces to extend, and tried again. This time, he was able to read down the list of points the terrorists wished to convey:

ISIS knows that these three held fabricated press credentials.

These three are not French nationals but Lebanese with connections to the West.

The three crossed from Iraq into Syria not to report on the ISIS victories at providing food to the town but to gather data for an attack.

ISIS is not comprised of fools. Spies are rec-

ognized when they present themselves. The three are CIA.

The West should not allow Syrians to find shelter within their borders, or they will face consequences again. Be aware, ISIS can unleash terror anywhere at any time.

Jean Baptiste concluded his report by explaining that, as an elder, his captors didn't believe he would survive long enough to be of use to them.

The terrorists blindfolded him and took Jean Baptiste to the border, where they spun in a U-turn, tossed him from the moving pickup truck bed, and roared deeper into Syria.

Jean Baptiste signed off as he collapsed.

A professional to the outer edges of consciousness.

Remi blinked for the first time as the station anchors came onto the screen to reiterate the highlights and pull in experts who answered questions via video connections, adding their punditry to the circumstances.

A warm hand on her shoulder made Remi jump and spin.

"Sorry. I didn't mean to startle you," Liu said. "Come on." Liu turned, assuming Remi would fall in step.

As he strode past the newsroom staff, he held his hand bladed by his face to indicate he wasn't available for conversations.

Hoping Liu wanted her to go to Beirut to report this story out, and so she could be of some support and solace for Jean Baptiste, Remi scampered after him.

Chapter 2

Remi

Monday, Washington, D.C.

Liu had dressed his slight frame in trousers with sharply pressed pleats.

His dry cleaner stiffened his ubiquitous white button-down shirts with extra starch. Remi always thought that if Liu were to bend over, he might just snap in two like a cracker.

As always, Liu had loosened his tie, unbuttoned the top button, rolled up the sleeves, giving him the look of a doer and a shaker.

He maintained a whirl of energy about him.

Rounding into his corner office, he moved behind his desk. Avoiding his captain's chair, he leaned forward, pressing the length of his fingers onto the cluttered surface. "Sit down."

Remi could barely keep her body still. Sitting would be torture. She held up her hands to ward off the invitation.

"Jeezis, Remi." He caught her gaze. "I'm sorry."

Her head bobbled in tight, quick nods to accept the words. The corners of her mouth grew heavy, dragging her expression into a dramatic frown. She blinked away the tears, wanting to be away from this professional setting before she allowed herself the indulgence of sobbing out her frustration and anger at what had happened to her friends. Opening her mouth to speak, nothing came out. She sniffed, cleared her throat, and tried again. "I have to get to Lebanon."

"No way." Liu walked the three steps over to the office door and pushed it shut with a bang.

"Liu—"

"Stop." He held up a hand as he made his way back behind his desk. "You heard Jean Baptiste." Liu's hands came back down on the desktop. "They were there to gather information on the food situation."

Remi scratched at her face. "I'm aware. You remember, I was supposed to be with them. We were invited by the leaders. Perhaps—"

"They took the FR-13 folks deep into Syria. Éloïse and Marie-Claude aren't held along the border."

"I don't—I have to get to Jean Baptiste. Talk to him."

Liu quirked a brow. "What good would you do over there?"

Remi shrugged. "I could make some phone calls. Pull some strings."

"And you can do this better than the French government? Better than the U.N.?"

"Yes." Remi pressed and rubbed her sweat-slickened palms together. "Yes. I've worked in the region on and off for over a decade. I've got contacts others may not have."

"Better than the CIA?"

"No." Though Remi thought of a black ops guy named Angel with whom she had a mutual aid relationship. She also knew two other CIA officers, one named Grey, the other Red.

Those three often worked behind Syrian lines. But Remi didn't have contact information for them. When a need arose, the CIA would reach out to her, not the other way around.

While Remi wasn't sure where Red exerted her energies other than "regional," Angel and Grey seemed to target women under duress. Remi understood that while saving females was partly humanitarian, from a practical point of view, women were great sources of information for the CIA.

ISIS fighters thought of females as rocks in the garden, furniture, not sentient, intellectual beings, so the terrorists felt free to talk in front of the women.

If only Remi knew how or where to catch up with Angel and Grey. They showed up when they needed something. They traded news stories for information.

It was fair.

Yeah, that wouldn't work. Those connections weren't readily available. Though in Remi's mind, she was flipping through her files, trying to figure out just whom she could ask, pressure, or coerce into helping her save Marie-Claude and Éloïse.

It gave Remi zero relief to know that these two women were whip-smart and athletic. That would do little to help them survive this situation.

While ISIS thought little of females, they knew the West was different. Holding and torturing women would hit the western countries much more profoundly than if they had captured a man.

Jean Baptiste said he was released because he was old.

Remi would guess he was let go because he was an unattractive male and wouldn't garner the same level of sympathy. Of the three, it made sense to Remi that it was Jean Baptiste who was released to play the mouthpiece.

Two fit and attractive women being held—yeah, that would impact the West differently, right or wrong.

And the bile that burbled along Remi's esophagus reminded her that if she hadn't been called back to D.C., she, too, would be held captive.

Liu clapped his hands. "Focus," he said sharply. "I know you're in shock. I know your mind is going warp speed trying to figure this out. You need to stop. You can't go find them. You can't even run through your vast contact files. Why?" He leaned back, tucking his chin and crossing his arms over his chest. "I'll tell you. You'll step on toes."

Remi shot Liu a snarl that said she couldn't care less if she did.

"You never know if you'll be saying the wrong thing in the right ear. The thing that will get your friends moved. Get your friends hidden more deeply. Or just get your friends' necks under a jihadist sword for a snuff film. You're a reporter not—*hear me*—not a hostage rescue professional."

Remi slid her splayed fingers into her hair, fisted her hands, and bent at the waist as a strangled noise crawled out of her throat.

He was right.

Of course, he was.

Cooler heads prevailing…it was a thing.

Typically, she was a cooler head. Today… Today, she was horrified.

"You're home, I will remind you, to receive the Excellence in International Journalism Award. It's a big deal. For you. For our news organization. You could mention your friends from FR-13 during your acceptance speech, bring attention…" He lowered himself into his black leather captain's chair.

Remi wasn't giving up. "Liu, you could go for me, stand in my place. Shoot, I'll even lend you my gown. We're about the same size-ish. You'll be gorgeous."

Liu rolled his eyes at her. "Be serious. This is a big deal. You deserve to stand there and receive your applause.

"It's *Jean Baptiste.* What do you think is more important to me, applause or Jean Baptiste?" She sidestepped, sliding into the guest chair in front of Liu's desk so they'd be eye to eye. "Please, Liu. If I swear that I won't try to save Éloïse and Marie-Claude, if I promise to just go and kiss Jean Baptiste and support our staff, can you find me a way over there?" She pitched herself forward. Her gaze was beseeching.

Liu locked his fingers behind his head and pressed back in his chair, leaning back to the full extent of its springs. He focused unblinkingly on the ceiling.

Remi knew better than to push. She wanted to talk her way forward; it was what she did for a living, talking her way into situations. Or out of them.

But here, she knew that would be counterproductive.

She had to physically bite into her tongue to hold it in place, letting Liu have a moment to see that she was sane in the face of this evil. In control of her emotions as much as one could be.

"All right. Fine." He came upright again. "To get you into Lebanon with a quick visa turnaround, we'll need a reason, preferably diplomatic…government involved…" Liu swung toward his computer.

Remi sat quietly as Liu scrolled and tapped.

"Here!" Liu put his finger to the screen, then angled his head toward Remi. "Do you know of a woman named Barb Blankenship?"

"U.S. Senator representing Texas. I only know the name and background basics. I've never reported on her specifically."

Liu balanced his reading glasses on his nose. Leaning forward, his fingers blazed over the keyboard. "Okay. I can pull Jasmine."

Jasmine Tremblay? She's a White House reporter.

Remi didn't move a muscle; she just held her breath and waited for more information.

"America hosted an international girls' robotics competition. Texas Senator Barb Blankenship will be flying two groups back to their homes and giving a string of speeches over a few days. First London for an Oxford speech. Blankenship was a—"

"Rhode's scholar, yes."

"Then to Iraq for a brief touchdown to deposit the Iraqi girls' team." Liu used his index finger to trace down the schedule of events listed on his screen. "Then on to Lebanon to give a speech about women leadership at the American University of Science and Technology in Beirut. A meeting with the embassy and representatives for the Lebanese government."

Remi leaned forward. "About?"

"The U.S.'s ongoing commitment to Lebanese security and to truss up relationships," he lifted his gaze to catch on Remi, "in that ISIS in Syria is a major threat to Lebanon." With his chin dipped down, Liu squinted over the tops of his glasses at her. "You actually have to do the job. You have to shadow the senator and write the article. But at least it will get you back to your friends so you all can see each other. Check-in for support. There should be downtime for you to do that. If not, I'd be okay with your tacking a few days onto the end of your visit and flying commercial home to the States." Without waiting for her response, Liu focused back on the screen. "It looks like Blankenship will mostly be doing photo ops. The photographer is Jules Edward."

"Jules?" Remi wrinkled her nose and instantly regretted it. "Cool. *Love* Jules. Jules and I will be *awesome* together."

Liu paused, assessing her. "Promise me a story. A *good* one."

Remi held up her hand as if taking an oath. "I swear on my mother's grave."

"Your mother's in good health. I saw her at Barney's two days ago."

"Figure of speech." Rocking forward in her chair, Remi shuffled her feet over the oriental rug, anxious to get moving. "How soon until I can be in Lebanon?"

"You're always so eager to take a bite from the apple."

Sucking in a breath, letting her chest expand until it lifted her shoulders up to her ears, Remi exhaled with extended lips, not even trying to hide her impatience.

"I can forward these background notes Jasmine submitted," he said, turning away from the computer screen to focus back on Remi.

"Thank you. Okay." Remi scooted forward to the edge of the chair. "So Blankenship is flying the girls' teams to England and Iraq." She paused and tipped her ear toward her shoulder, furrowing her brow. "There's a girls' robotics team in Iraq?"

"They're in an internationally run refugee camp that works at bringing the girls' literacy rates up to be commensurate with the boys'. You won't be going to that camp. The charitable group is sending a bus to pick up the girls at the airport. Eventually, I guess…they aren't releasing information about the time or place where the senator will set down. Security, I assume, is going to be tight. And I suppose that touchdown will be brief. My guess is fifteen-twenty minutes. Dump the kids off the plane, throw the luggage onto the tarmac while the senator says, 'Huzzah for the girls!' Back on board and take off. They'd want to get the senator in and out as quickly as possible. If anything happened to Blankenship in Iraq, we'd be right back at war. Iraq, then a quick hop over the border to Beirut. I'm assuming that's where they'll take Jean Baptiste to get medical help. Though it could be that they'll medevac him to France."

"No," Remi said with a shake of her head. "His family's in Beirut. He'll want to stay there with his wife. Thank you," Remi reached out to grip the edge of Liu's desk, "for finding a story. When does Blankenship leave?"

"Wednesday, so you have tomorrow to rest up and read through your mail pile. Do some advanced research. I need to check with Blankenship's office to make sure they'll accommodate you on the plane…" He leaned over and wrote himself a note on a yellow sticky.

Though upside down, Remi could make out "Pull Jasmine from London trip," written in cramped script.

"It shouldn't be a problem," Liu said. "Having you along is a feather in Blankenship's cap. It gives her speeches and action not only visibility but the power of your byline."

"You're spreading it on a little thick now." Remi raised a single brow.

"I'm perfectly serious. I'll reach out to Blankenship's office and let them know we've changed journalist assignments. I'll make sure there's room on her plane. If not, that might complicate things in terms of the fast turnaround on getting your visa. But I'll do my best. I'll email you logistics."

Pressing to her feet, Remi put her hand on her heart. "Liu, I could kiss you."

"You're not my preferred gender," he deadpanned.

"Figure of speech, and it would be in the vein of a daughterly kiss on the forehead. Not sexually." She squished up her face in exaggerated disgust. "Ewww."

"And thanks for that." Liu stood.

"Seriously, Liu, it's a big favor. I'll owe you."

"It's not a bad story. Feel good. Forward-looking. Hopeful at a time when we could all use it. It's a spin on what you normally do. But *if* it's done right, we can make this an important glimpse into the struggles of womanhood and what the next generation is doing to overcome despite the horrors of the girls' pasts. Pay me back by making it worth our while to send you."

"Yup. Got it. I can do this."

"Uh-huh. Well, try anyway." He tipped his head. "Remi, go home. Get yourself a massage or whatever you do to help yourself unwind. Pack. And we'll keep our fingers crossed that I can make this a go."

With a curt nod, Remi started for the door.

"Oh, and Remi, the senator will be escorted by a military personal protection team. Just a reminder," he pulled his reading glasses off his nose and jabbed them toward her, "the operators will safeguard the senator. They won't do jack shit for you. As the operators like to say, watch your six."

Chapter 3

T-Rex

Monday, along the Niger border in west-central Africa

Delta Force Echo ran full tilt for the Black Hawk heli with their commander, Master Chief T-Rex Landry, bringing up the rear.

More mule than man at that point, T-Rex was laden with equipment. The hundred and fifty pounds of banging, clanging, bruising packs strapped over his body armor felt twice as heavy to T-Rex. His thigh muscles quivered, and his butt cheeks cramped from exertion.

He'd pushed his forty-year-old body to the breaking point.

Echo hadn't stopped, let alone slept in the last thirty-six hours.

They hadn't even paused to heat and eat an MRE.

They simply ripped the packages open and threw what calories they could down their gullets.

As master chief, it was on T-Rex to grit his teeth and plow on, setting an example for his men.

Standing six-feet-seven, three hundred pounds of lean muscle, T-Rex sank up to the tops of his boots in the monsoon saturated clay with each stride. That clay sucked at his feet, trying to hold him prisoner, trip him, take him down.

T-Rex bit down hard, his nostrils flaring as he sucked in oxygen and powered forward like a locomotive.

From previous experience, T-Rex knew that when he finally shucked the boots after this mission was over, there would be a ring of blisters encircling his ankles. The clay slime made its way past his boot laces, into his socks, and between his toes. With each step, T-Rex could feel the grit cutting tiny nicks into his feet.

Ground moisture wicked up the length of his pants to his hips. The fabric rubbed against his thighs. Rug burns and chafing lit his skin on fire.

Bonus, the night air was only ninety degrees, much cooler than when the sun burned bright. The humidity, though, continued to hover around one hundred percent. It was like running through soup.

Hounded by intermittent bullets buzzing past them, knowing the enemy was regrouping and coming after their team, every step getting themselves out of this mess was life or death.

This exfil had been nuts.

Navigating the terrain with night vision, the eerie green landscape created by the vegetation was dappled in the warmer spectrum of reds and oranges. The body heat of animals sleeping under branches lit up their lenses and drew the operators' attention away from their trajectory.

With speed as their priority for this run, T-Rex just had to pray that none of those red circles was the head of an enemy peeking up from a shooter's hole or a machete-wielding tribesman ready to amputate a limb.

His teammate Ty, their team K9 handler, had given up trying to run his Belgian Malinois, Rory, over this terrain. Rory had floundered in the muck and couldn't keep up, his fur matted with the thick clay. Not willing to risk an injury, Ty had handed off his rucksack to Havoc. Now, Ty was running with Rory draped over his shoulders.

Rory's tongue lolled out, panting in the heat, his saliva dripping in long frothy strands down Ty's back.

Havoc and Nitro each grabbed a strap of their brother's pack. It swayed between them as they added that weight to their burden.

They pushed to their limits.

The labored breathing of the Delta Force Echo teammates fell into a machine-like cadence.

Completing this mission had been much more complicated than they'd planned. Or contingency planned.

Their window to get to the landing zone was counted down by the TOC—tactical operations center—where the unfolding mission was monitored in Djibouti.

The problem was: The Black Hawk could only hold so much fuel, and, with engines running, their pilot was counting every drop, staying on the ground as long as she could before she had no choice but to bug out.

D-Day Rochambeau was a special forces pilot with the Soar 160th—a Night Stalker. Their task was to put special forces where they needed to be, when they needed to be there. D-Day was precise to within thirty seconds on any given mission. So when she said, "T-Rex, your team has twelve seconds to get on my bird," it was an exact number, and then she'd be gone.

There was a timer tick-tick-ticking on her control panel.

Man, as they came over this last berm, seeing the black outline of the helicopter against the night sky felt like a miracle.

As they reached their landing zone, the men threw themselves onto the waiting heli with groans and heaving gasps. Rolling to the side to make room for the next teammate to leap, their limbs quivered with overexertion.

Jeopardy stood outside the door opening, slapping each man as he piled in, counting off, making sure that each of his Delta Force brothers made it onto the aircraft. He squeezed the shoulder of the last man, Ty Newcomb, as he bounded on with Rory. "All accounted for, Master Chief."

Swiveling, T-Rex planted his hips on the deck, grabbing at the strap and attaching it to his D ring, securing himself in place as he did his own head count. Double-checking. It wouldn't be unprecedented to make a mistake with this level of brain haze. Forty miles, it had felt like he was back at the Delta Force "Long Walk," but they'd only been expected to carry seventy pounds back then.

Sleep. It was the only thing that was going to defog his brain.

Nick of Time, the co-pilot, swiveled forward and signaled to D-Day that they had indeed gotten every last man.

She maneuvered them up into the sky, over the terrain, and onward to base. T-Rex closed his eyes and let the adrenaline slide from his system.

He knew D-day had it handled.

The men on this flight were silent.

Exhausted.

They'd accomplished their mission. Even with things turning sideways on them, they could land with their heads held high.

Right now, everyone needed a long shower, a hot meal, and sleep.

T-Rex pressed his finger into his ear as he listened to the TOC.

"Change of plans." Their commanding officer, Lieutenant Colonel Burnside, bellowed into the comms, loud enough that T-Rex could make out his words.

T-Rex toggled his mic. "Echo Actual, copy."

"D-day's racing the clock to get you here in time. We have a transport willing to wait a short while. You, Havoc, Ty, and K9 Rory are heading to Washington D.C. The rest of Echo will return home on the previous timeline."

"Understood."

"We're handling logistics on your personal gear. The rest of the equipment can head back with Echo."

T-Rex turned to scan over his brothers' faces. They'd all fallen into an instantaneous and profound sleep. Everyone except for Ty and K9 Rory, who focused on T-Rex expectantly. Ty was his number two. "Copy," T-Rex bellowed past the sound of wind and rotor.

T-Rex knew that their logician would have everything squared away when they landed. The three-man team could jump off the Black Hawk and jump right onto their taxi stateside.

"You'll get cleaned up once you're back home."

T-Rex looked down at his mud-caked clothing. TOC had no clue what they looked like.

If the three-man team didn't have time to change, they'd at least have to find a water hose to spray the clumps off their boots and to clean Rory up.

Burnside's gravelly voice rumbled past the whistle of wind. "I'd pop some Ambien and do what sleeping you can on the transport."

T-Rex looked across at his men. Typically, T-Rex and the team were read into a program, they did their homework, and T-Rex assigned the roles. "Who chose the team?"

"That comes from up the chain."

"Good copy." T-Rex called into his mic.

"Three things went into the decision making. One, your team is fresh off operations simulation."

Because The Unit often did close protection for vulnerable VIPs, the men did a rotation in major cities worldwide, learning the layout of the cities, learning the mass transportation systems, the rules of etiquette. More importantly, they trained on negotiating the various countries' traffic, practicing their protective maneuvers in cars with left-side *and* right-side steering wheels.

"Once Echo was chosen, they pared down to you three because of language proficiency and because Rory is a bomb sniffer."

T-Rex glanced toward Ty then Havoc, scrolling through the languages his men spoke, trying to weed out where they might be headed.

All Delta Force operators did a stint at language school to develop their fluency, depending on needs. Everyone on his team had some Spanish, some Arabic, and Russian. They had a smattering of other languages that they'd picked up from deployments.

French was a common denominator for Africa, and his men could all get through the basics—Stop! Hands in the air! Do it now!

T-Rex, Ty, and Havoc shared the same language fluency. He tried that on for size. "So Arabic and French?"

"Bingo. You're headed to London, then Iraq, and Lebanon. You'll be escorting U.S. Senator Barb Blankenship."

"Numbers that we'll be guarding?"

"You'll be on a private jet. Blankenship is escorting two robotics teams home after competing in a U.N.-sponsored competition in Washington. These girls' teams are both comprised of refugee teens. The team from London is a mixed bag of Syrian and Afghan girls. Once they're deposited, Blankenship is flying the Iraqi girls home. There is a quick stop in Trebil on the border to let them off the plane, then Blankenship has a few days of speeches planned for Lebanon. I've already uploaded a file with the information. We've been working on getting your threat assessment together. We won't have time to send a forward team to scope out the situations, so the CIA and the State Department are handling that for you."

"Copy. Numbers traveling with us?" he repeated his question.

"Slim if you don't count the girls' teams. They left four seats for security personnel on the jet. The three of you and Rory. Media includes a pool journo and a photographer. We'll get those names nailed down and backgrounds run. Then the senator and one support staff. Compared to where you've been and what you've been doing, this'll be a vacation. The primary is your *only* concern."

"This isn't what G Squadron Echo normally does."

"The senator asked for you specifically, T-Rex," Burnside said.

Okay, that was number three on the list of reasons Echo was tapped for this VIP protection task: recent training, languages, and the principal's finger pointed his way.

Me? Specifically? How in the heck would Senator Blankenship even know I exist?

Chapter 4

T-Rex

Monday, Camp Lemonnier,
Djibouti, Africa

Hurry up and wait. It was a military truism. A way of life. Bursts of adrenaline followed by long stretches of… crickets.

It worked in T-Rex's favor this time.

D-Day landed the heli at the right place and the right time for the three men tapped for the Blankenship assignment to jump and run.

But their transport aircraft was still fueling.

T-Rex, Havoc, and Ty beelined for the showers.

Their logistics specialist, Carlotta Hill, had three rubber bins waiting for them. She must have rifled through their personal gear to grab their shower kits and a change of clothes. "It's too long a flight to be caked in mud," she said, handing the top bin off to Havoc.

"Amen to that." Havoc accepted his bin and jogged the few steps to the showers.

Ty, juggling Rory's lead, accepted his bin that had equipment for cleaning Rory up, too.

T-Rex didn't mind the intrusion into his personal space. He was appreciative, in fact, that he wouldn't have to claw around in his pack. Clay was almost impossible to get out of anything, T-Rex had discovered in his two decades of military life.

Carlotta Hill was a competent logician. Lotti was her nickname heading into her military career, which was changed to "Lottery" in boot camp. Then she was quickly re-labeled "Winner" when her fellow boots discovered she had strategic skills that put her team at the top of the scoreboard.

Those skills had played well for Delta Force Team Echo.

With his rubber bin balanced on his palm, and a first-aid kit dangling from his other hand, T-Rex headed to the showers hoping he'd find an open stall.

"I had Private Mason in there saving you all spots," Winner called after T-Rex.

T-Rex raised his arm as a way of acknowledging and thanking Winner. That was the kind of attention to detail that was expected at Special Forces Tier One level.

Seamless action.

Emerging from the showers, changed into gym shorts, T-shirts, and shower Crocs, the men would rest much better on the long-haul flight from Africa to Andrews Air Force Base in Maryland and a rental car over to D.C. to meet with their primary, Senator Blankenship.

Nitro's wife, Laurel, was packing bags for the three

bachelor operators and driving them up from Fort Bragg. This wasn't her first time stepping in with an assist, and most likely, it wouldn't be the last.

Sometimes, it takes a village, T-Rex mused. *Speaking of which…* He strode toward the transport plane to thank D-Day.

Making his way to D-Day, T-Rex spotted Ty out in the field by the runway, throwing a ball under the stadium lights that turned the area from night into day. Ty would try to wear Rory out before they got on the plane. When Ty took his Ambien, he'd also medicate Rory.

Twenty hours was a long time for Rory to be confined to his crate. He'd usually let everyone know, vociferously and constantly, that he found his confinement unacceptable.

D-Day stood there, with hands on hips, watching the Malinois sailing six feet into the air to catch his ball, then hightail it back to Ty so Ty could throw it again.

Havoc and Nick of Time each balanced a foot on a storage box as T-Rex arrived beside them.

All three of the operators heading home had tended their open injuries. White taped gauze covered their newly cleaned wounds. Each had popped a prophylactic dose of antibiotic. Who knew what microbes were multiplying in that primordial soup they'd slogged through on the way to their exfil? It wouldn't do to be a walking biohazard around the senator.

T-Rex held out his hand to shake with D-Day and Nick of Time.

"Another successful mission on the books," she said. "Glad you had time for a rinse. You all smelled like something that crawled out of the swamp," she said. "It's going to take some doing to get that stench out of my bird."

T-Rex offered a nod, stroking a hand over his still damp beard. His brown hair hung down to his shoulders, ending in curly waves. He'd have to make sure that he and Havoc got to a barber as soon as they deplaned.

Ty had just come off an assignment that required him to be spiffed up, so he was good to go with his western-style grooming.

"Good to see you whole and healthy." D-Day stepped onto a box, so the two were eye to eye. She was a tiny little thing to have such titanium-plated balls.

"Good to see your time off for honeymooning didn't affect your flying skills," he replied.

D-day flashed a smile.

"Ty told me your wedding was a blast." Havoc snorted, then ducked as D-Day feigned a swipe.

"You can read a paper, can you?" D-day's expression didn't change.

It didn't look like she was going to give that conversation any oxygen.

But they'd been filled in.

The low down: D-Day came from a billionaire family, the Davidsons. That was billions with a capital B. Money like that meant rules were considered for fools. They got what they wanted when they wanted it, no matter the morals or ethics.

D-Day's mom had pulled her away from all that, and D-Day was antithetical to her family of origin. A complete 180.

Her dad, William Davidson, had been playing footsie with a terrorist that had been on Echo's wish list for seven years, Omar Mohamed Imadi.

Tracking Omar, the CIA discovered two things: Kira had been college roommates with London Davidson and had introduced London to her Uncle Omar's friend,

William Davidson, in a May-December romance. Omar had been invited to the Davidsons' compound in Tanzania for a secret meeting. Kira would be there to see her friend London.

Echo had had to get into that compound, plan a way to capture Omar, and bring him to the CIA for interrogation.

The way in had been through Kira.

That mission had required that Ty get a spa makeover. He'd been assigned to work with the CIA to develop Kira as an asset. Getting behind those thirty-foot security walls by hell or high water was Ty's directive.

Kira was an innocent in a den of thieves.

On assignment, Ty (and Rory, for that matter) had lost their hearts to sweet, intelligent, gentle Kira.

The mission was successful, Omar Mohamed Imadi was dispatched. But when a local guerrilla force showed up, Kira had nearly lost her life in the incident.

Spin forward a couple of days from that mission, and Kira was in Washington helping her friend, London, host a pre-wedding cocktail party for D-Day and her fiancé Gator. That cocktail party was "the blast" that Havoc was teasing D-Day about.

D-Day's brother thought he could take out the family and clear his father's last will and testament of extraneous names, hiding their murders behind a fake terrorist attack.

Lives were lost.

London was shot in the head and was comatose, last they'd been updated.

Ty had been in the room when the terrorists flooded in.

Maybe the bad guys didn't do their due diligence. D-Day was marrying Gator Aid Rochambeau, a retired

Marine Raider. He now worked for the world-renowned group Iniquus Security, staffed by ex-special forces professionals. The golden boys with sterling reputations.

Gator's teammates were all in that room. Ty joined their ranks to save their women.

Ty got Kira out safely.

Iniquus stomped the terrorists into the ground.

Since Ty was there, he was able to give Echo a blow by blow.

D-Day had left the building at the time of the attack to go pick up her in-laws. She and Gator missed the fireworks.

They married without further incident. Left for their honeymoon. And now D-Day was standing there, taking the ribbing that Havoc was offering up.

If you didn't come from a military special forces family, Havoc's joking might have seemed insensitive, but terror was part and parcel to their daily lives.

If you're breathing, you push forward. That's the only way this worked out okay.

That the terrorist attack was incited by D-Day's family caused D-Day no end of grief. She got pulled in to revamp her clearance levels and to prove that she was estranged from her family. She nearly lost her position with the military. And she had fought and trained hard for over a decade, working her way up the male-dominated world of special forces to earn her place as a Night Stalker.

That a mere familial tie with someone, whom she hated and had shoved out of her life, threatened her work and aspirations was total crap.

Because Ty had fallen in love with Kira on that assignment, he, too, had to jump hoops to maintain his clearance. There was always the risk that he'd been compromised.

Not in T-Rex's mind. But on paper.

This was why you don't fall for your asset. You don't fall for your principal. You just *don't* fall.

Workspace was workspace, and personal space was… limited. Better to wait to find love once you'd retired from your post and no one had the right to scrutinize your relationship.

That was T-Rex's philosophy, and he'd tried to make it Echo doctrine.

They didn't need to lose a team member to a soft heart and hard choices.

Ty and Kira, D-Day and Gator were prime examples.

Ty looked up, caught D-Day's gaze, and jogged over. A tip of the head. A question in his eyes. He wrapped an arm around D-Day's waist and spun, then set her on the ground. "Welcome back to the wild west, Mrs. Rochambeau."

"Yeah, I would have married most anyone to get rid of my family name."

"I hear ya. But in the end, Gator's a good guy."

She batted a hand through the air. "Yeah, yeah, Gator did you a solid. Echo owes him. I'd still like to know what that's all about." She tipped her head.

"You'll have to wait for the movie." Havoc reached down to give Rory a scratch behind the ears.

D-Day balled her fingers into a fist and crossed her hands over her chest.

T-Rex could tell she was itching to pet Rory, too. But only Rory's team could touch him. He wasn't a pet.

D-day kicked Ty's boot. "You grew your beard. Does Kira like it?"

Ty dipped his head by way of response.

"Is Kira still in the picture?" D-day asked, "or were we too much for her?"

Ty looked off at the horizon, where the first flames of a new day scratched at the sky. "We're trying to get our sea legs. She's been having issues with nightmares and panic attacks. She's hooking up with doctor's support. I'll join in when I'm around."

"Which isn't much," Nick said.

"Roger that. And Kira has to weigh that in with everything else…see if our relationship can handle the distance."

T-Rex saw D-Day had touched a nerve on Ty.

She caught Ty's gaze. "I'm sorry. I really am. Kira did a beautiful job planning that party. She's a really kind person from what I saw. I hope she gets the help she needs. Sometimes I forget what I was like before I joined the Army. Civilian life. It's a luxury to have avoided violence and pain. We learn to detach, but that's a skillset."

"Yeah, well, Nitro's wife, Laurel, and the other Echo wives took her out and had a heart-to-heart with her." Ty put a hand to his chest. "I asked them to. Like you were saying, I've been at this game my whole adult life. I can't imagine it from the outside looking in like the other wives can. I wanted them to spell it out—the good, the bad, and the ugly. Marrying an operator isn't for the faint of heart." He pressed his lips together and shook his head. "Wrong words. Marrying an operator isn't for everyone. I want to bow out if I'm hurting her. She's had it rough enough."

D-day pulled a worried brow. "Are you giving up on her?"

"Me? No way. But I'm not pushing an agenda. We're

taking it slow. Right now, I just want her to be able to sleep."

T-Rex listened with a master chief's ear. He needed his number two squared away. Ty couldn't be distracted by the doings back home. He needed to compartmentalize.

Home was home. Work was work.

Not the easiest of tasks to separate the two out.

Ty was right. In their chosen profession, you needed more than love in a spouse to make a go of it.

T-Rex had met Kira. She was soft-hearted, an innocent. On the Echo mission, where she was labeled an asset, she was front and center of an attack on their compound. Kira might have handled that okay, but she'd stepped from one terror attack into another within the same week, and that was hard on a civilian.

Unless you played in the world of war, you had no idea—*none*—about how to navigate the emotions.

Heck, back when his wife, Jess, was still alive and working a cop's beat, she had had a hard time when violence was packed too closely back-to-back.

Jess had told him that she couldn't reach out for support because she was the only female on the force.

So she sucked it up. And that had created its own problems. For her. And for them.

Anxiety. Depression. Drinking.

T-Rex was never a hundred percent sure that when Jess showed up the night of the domestic dispute that took her life, that the guy wasn't looking for death by cop—a form of suicide. And that maybe…just maybe, Jess liked the idea herself. Death by criminal. Lauded and remembered as a hero.

The question was there in the back of his head.

He'd never get his answers.

So when the idea showed up like it did now, he gently put it back in its box and put it on the shelf of unknowns.

"Gentlemen load up," a voice bellowed.

"That's us." T-Rex was glad for a distraction. "D-day, your skills today were much appreciated."

She pointed a finger at each of the three operators. "You stay safe."

"Back at ya."

The three-man team, along with K9 Rory, climbed on their ride home.

After their two-day mission with no shuteye, high temps, high humidity, and mosquito swarms, the cold air in the cargo hold felt like heaven.

The rumble of the engine noise was just what they needed to drown out the memory of the sounds of the screaming villagers, the bleating livestock, and the rebel rifle pops.

Echo claimed their space, hung their hammocks, popped their pills, and crashed hard.

Sleep was a requirement. It helped insulate the special operators from PTSD. It gave their bodies a chance to heal.

They needed to be at 100% over the next few days. While Echo was trained and ready to handle VIP security. It wasn't an assignment that was a walk in the park.

Everything that possibly went sideways while they were protecting Senator Blankenship would reflect badly on The Unit.

T-Rex couldn't let *anything* go wrong.

Chapter 5

Remi

Tuesday, Washington, D.C.

Remi sat cross-legged on her living room floor in a pair of yoga pants and an oversized T-shirt. A towel wrapped the damp strands of her ebony hair in a turban. With her back pressed against her couch cushion, Remi made neat piles of notes beside her as she researched Senator Blankenship. Her goal was to discover an angle for this "feel good" piece. What was Blankenship's motivation for flying these girls home?

There had to be a get.

That's the way it worked once you hit that level of power.

Always a get.

Remi was scrolling through YouTube videos of the

senator. This one was from two years ago. Remi tapped the screen.

There was the senator in all her glory. She wore a white suit with a Christmas red cowboy hat and rhinestone-encrusted boots, standing in front of a castle in Ireland.

The press pooled around her.

The buzz and click of camera apertures were like a swarm of pesky mosquitos. But Blankenship took it in stride. She smiled to the left then the right. She sent her smiling face in a slow arc so everyone could get her best side.

"When I was a little girl, I always wanted to come to Ireland and spend some time in our city's twin. Y'all know how that works, right? Two places pick each other and work on things, almost like pen pals. As a matter of fact, when I was a little girl, there was a show on PBS called the Big Blue Marble that introduced kids to other children around the world. Not only did they do shows about other countries, but they wanted to encourage people to chat, ya know? This was long before there was the Internet. I got tickled with the thought that I could be a pen pal with someone in our sister city. So, I wrote to the address they put up on the screen, they wrote me back and said that they had someone right up the road a piece from here in Cork. Molly was my pen pal's name. My correspondence with her was magical. She told me all about the Blarney Castle and the gift of gab. I set my sights on coming here since I was, oh, right about nine years old."

"This way if you please, Senator."

Blankenship angled toward the voice.

"Now, I'm a considerable bit older than I wanted to be on that adventure. Had no idea what I was gettin' myself messed up in. When you get up there to the top of the tower, it's kind of harrowing. I'm sayin' that for all of my Texas brethren who might want to make the trip. The trip is worth it—but you need to come prepared. First, you've got to get yourself up there." She pointed to the top of the tower. "*All* the way up there. Then," she crouched and spread her arms wide, "you lay down on your back, and you kind of scooch up toward the hole in the ground."

She pointed at the tower again. "The hole's up there at the top, and it goes all the way down to the ground below. So hold on to your chompers if they're like to fall out on ya." She wiggled her hips as she stepped back and squatted a bit as if acting out the event. "Once you're in position, hovering over that hole, lying flat out on your back, mind you. Well then, you do a back bend into the hole, and you reach your lips out as far as you can get them. And you kiss the stone." She put her hands on her back and said, "Oof." Then raised her brow and nodded.

The audience chuckled.

"Well, anyway, it took three nice tourists to pull this old gal back up onto her boots. When I was standing there, putting my hat back on my head, the attendant asked me if now that I'd kissed the Blarney Stone if I felt more eloquent." She sent the audience a long look.

Remi had discovered that Senator Blankenship knew how to work a long pause.

"I said, 'Eloquent? Hell, honey, I've always dressed nice.'" She offered up a broad wink.

The crowd roared with laughter.

"So, I'll leave you with this. We are all eloquent when we speak to each other with open minds and respect. Ever since I was a little girl and watched The Big Blue Marble, I thought that as we speak to each other, as we learn from each other, as we lift each other up, we will only make progress. When we make progress together, we all prosper. So let's all stand shoulder to shoulder, and let's move toward a brighter future. Thank you for your kind hospitality."

The audience burst into applause and whistles.

Senator Blankenship punctuated her speech with a bit of Texas-style boot shuffle, raised her hand to say goodbye, and walked off.

The Big Blue Marble, huh? Interesting, Remi thought as her phone pinged. She glanced at the screen, then swiped to answer. "Hey, Joli. Any word?"

"About—?"

"Éloïse and Marie-Claude?"

There was a long pause.

"Remi." She stopped.

Remi felt cold wash through her system. She waited…

"Remi," Joli finally said, her accent thicker than normal. "There will be no quick answer. You've reported on this type of thing. You know what Éloïse and Marie-Claude are caught up in. This is a long road. Years. Decades. Sometimes never. Yeah…sometimes never…" Her voice sounded like it had fallen off a cliff. Remi couldn't make out the end of her sentence.

Remi swallowed. She had no words.

A Canadian colleague of Joli's had been kidnapped in Syria. Put in a hole in the ground for over a month, she was eventually sold to ISIS. An Arab businessman bought her and returned the reporter to Canada. It had taken almost three years.

Others weren't as lucky.

"Okay then, were you calling for some other reason?" Remi tried to pull out of the fog that wrapped her.

"I was wondering if you'd heard about the Pegasus Project?"

"Doesn't ring a bell..."

"My newsroom just sent out a warning. A private group out of Israel developed spyware that they were licensing to various governments."

"Okay..." Remi reached for a pad and pen in case she needed to jot notes.

"It has to do with military-grade spyware originally developed to track terrorists—but get this—the governments were using it to track journos."

"Wait. Someone's hacking our phones? Tracking us? Who found this?"

"A Parisian non-profit and international watch dog groups. There's a group here in Toronto that's been following Pegasus for a while now. They're looking through the data that showed up—sent by some whistleblower. It looks bad. Human rights groups, politicians, as well as journalists, are being monitored. They got hold of some of the phones on the whistleblower's list, including thousands of phone numbers. Each phone that they analyzed was infected by the Pegasus program. My number was on the list. They think it's because I was working over in Hungary."

"Didn't you have security on your phone?" Remi doodled question marks onto her pad next to the word Pegasus.

"This program can break through anything. Anyway, since my phone was on the list and I speak to you at least once a week, I thought you might want to check on yours."

"Should I just toss my phone and start again?" Remi asked.

"Maybe? I think knowing if you were being surveilled is an important question."

"Yeah, yeah, do you have a resource?" Remi scratched the pen back and forth over the pad.

"I'll text you a number. Ask for Jean Marie. Tell him we're friends."

"Yup, thanks," Remi said. "I'll do that. *Thank you.* Are you safe?"

"Are any of us?"

And that's how Joli left the conversation. Remi stared at the phone. Was it corrupted?

A moment later, there was a ping as Joli dropped a text with a number and no message.

It was too late to call a stranger tonight. Remi put it on her mental list of things to do in the morning.

The phone rang again. Liu.

"Hey, I was just about to reach out to you." Remi twiddled her pen nervously. "Have you heard of the Pegasus infection?"

"Yeah, actually. We have our lawyers checking on all of our journalists' phone numbers. In the meantime, we'll be sending out letters suggesting you get new phones and new phone numbers."

Remi moaned.

"I know it's a pain. But no one's going to talk to you if they think the connection is compromised. Also, not why I'm calling. Turn on CNN now." He ended their connection without a goodbye.

Remi reached over to her coffee table for her remote and pressed the buttons to get the news channel playing.

A journalist stood in front of a courthouse building, the wind whipping her hair across her face as she spoke into her hand-held mic. "We're at the courthouse in Sacramento. We've just been told that the judges have reached their decision on the Spencer Ackerman case. Spencer Ackerman is a retired SEAL."

Remi looked at the time, eight-fifteen in D.C. It was just after five in Sacramento. Remi's phone pinged with a text.

Greg: They let the SEAL off. I'm sorry. You tried.

The reporter on CNN said, "Last year, Remi Taleb, reporting for the Washington News-Herald, broke a story about Navy SEAL Ackerman that led to charges being brought by the Navy. It began with a Memorial Day cookout in Afghanistan that involved allegations of sexual assault." She pulled the strands of hair from her mouth, then simply gripped her hair in her fist and continued without missing a beat.

"Taleb reported out about a string of incidents that had involved the elite special operators' team, not just Ackerman. This came on the heels of the Secret Service incidents that included drinking to inebriation and engaging prostitutes while out on assignment protecting the president. The Navy didn't want to tarnish the SEALs' reputation in the way that the Secret Service brought public scrutiny and condemnation to their organization. In an unprecedented move, the Navy brought the entire platoon back to the States, citing leadership failures."

Remi leaned forward, listening, knowing that Greg would have the inside scoop. They were letting Ackerman get away with it. *Unfathomable.*

"This was the same platoon that had been led by Special Warfare Operator Chief Stanly Gotwald," the reporter continued. "He was charged with taking pictures with the corpses of Islamic fighters, shooting civilians, and rape.

"In Ackerman's case, he has been charged with intercourse without consent. As described to this reporter, in the military justice system, sexual assault has to rise to the level of 'life-threatening' for the victim in order for the crime to be classified as rape. According to the allegations, the victim was penetrated *against* her consent while she fought to get free. However, her bruising and lacerations were not deemed to be life-threatening. Therefore, according to the military, she was not the victim of a rape."

People started to pour out of the courthouse doors.

The reporter was focused and undaunted by the stampede. "Ackerman's lawyer insists on his client's innocence, though the victim, Jane Doe, went immediately to the hospital where they obtained a sample of semen, and it was positively identified as Ackerman's DNA. The trauma nurse photographed Jane Doe's bruising, including the bruises that encircled her neck. Ackerman maintains that the victim enjoyed rough sex. He was, according to Ackerman, engaged in a consensual role-play with the victim."

As if. Remi blew out hard. That poor woman. This would retraumatize her, knowing that the guy did this to her and yet walked away a free man on this count.

"This case comes on the heels of other high-profile rape cases such as the case in Minnesota where the judge ruled just yesterday that a man could not be charged with felony rape because the woman he raped had done vodka shots and passed out in his apartment. He had sex with her after she blacked out. She never gave her consent to have sex with the man.

"According to Minnesota law, 'Mental incapacity'

to give consent only applies if the perpetrator gave the substance to his victim without her knowing about it, such as date rape drugs. However, if a person chooses to drink, then that law cannot be applied. The Minnesota man was cleared of wrongdoing."

Can you imagine that? Remi thought. You drink, you get drunk, a man finds you, rapes you, and it's all hunky-dory.

Her phone dinged. Without taking her eye off the news stream, Remi answered, "Hey."

"It's Tony. You in Ethiopia still?"

"D.C., heading to London tomorrow."

"Pshhhhh… All righty."

"Why?"

"America just did a drone attack in Somalia against Al-Shabaab. I hoped you could pop down."

"No can do. Pedro's in the area, though."

"Good. Thanks." And he disconnected.

Remi put her phone under her thigh and reached for her mug of lavender tea in the hopes she could soothe her nerves.

Remi refocused on the television.

"Women's groups are watching the outcome of this case," the reporter was saying. She hadn't yet confirmed what her friend Greg had texted about Ackerman walking away a free man. "Texas Senator Barb Blankenship has been working across the aisle with Michigan Senator Margaret Tallow to develop new regulations for sexual misconduct in the military. Their aim is to take rape reporting out of the victim's chain of command, among other measures, to make military life safer for both women and men."

The reporter then cited the incident where two Marine Raiders and two Navy SEALs broke into a Green

Beret's room in Mali, tying up the Green Beret. The assailants had hired a local man to rape the Green Beret as an act of hazing. The Marine was all set up to film the rape. However, the Green Beret died of asphyxiation before that could happen.

"Blankenship and Tallow want to end these assaults," the reporter concluded.

Remi quickly scribbled notes to talk to Senator Blankenship about the Ackerman case and the two female senators' progress in the reforms. Would the male senators prevent the legislation? And if so, why?

Okay, maybe there's a story worthy of writing on this assignment.

Though, her main aim was to get to Jean Baptiste and offer what support she could.

Chapter 6

T-Rex

Tuesday, Washington, D.C.

"Hey, look at this," Ty called out, lifting his phone.

Echo Force had commandeered a meeting room in their hotel to do their prep work for this assignment. It was out of the way and big enough that security shouldn't be a problem if they kept their voices down.

Dressed in BDUs—battle dress uniforms—they'd pulled from their packs that Winner had loaded onto their transport plane yesterday. They were waiting for a more appropriate set of clothes to arrive.

Nitro's wife, Laurel, was now in her car, making the six-hour drive from Fort Bragg with close protection clothing and equipment.

"When I took Rory for his jog this morning," Ty said, "we ran past a doggy day care with walk-in hours at their dog paddle pool. We were the only ones there." He held up a video of Rory dropping his ball into the water.

In a low crouch, eyes on the prize, Rory dramatically stalked to the other side of the pool, froze, then leaped into the water, as if surprising his prey, to grab the ball and swim to the end with an exit ramp. He did it over and over again.

The men chuckled at Rory's antics.

Rory laid under the table at the men's feet, his chin resting on his paws, lifting his brows and looking from man to man.

Ty stopped the video replay and attached it to a text message. "I'm sending this on to Tripwire."

"How's he doing?" Havoc asked.

"Health-wise? About the same. I try to send updates on Rory to Trip each week, make things a little easier on the guy. Tough break getting medically released from his SEAL contract and their reassigning Rory to Echo. As tight as Tripwire and Rory were, it must have felt like losing a limb."

"He still going to adopt Rory when Rory is retired from service?" T-Rex asked.

"That's the plan." Ty bent to look under the table at Rory. "Not that I'm not going to miss you like hell. But they'd never let me adopt you since I'm never at home."

"He's still with Iniquus?" T-Rex asked.

"Yeah, their Cerberus Tactical K9 team. He's working a dog named Valor. Search and rescue. Since he doesn't need to pull off an exfil like we had in Niger yesterday, he's able to keep up with that workload."

"Good gig," Havoc said. "Great organization."

"Yep." Ty looked through his phone's photo album for a good action shot of Rory to send Trip also. "They'll be over on the eastern Mediterranean Sea about the same time we are. They're heading to Israel. Tomorrow, I think they leave out."

"Cerberus?"

"Yeah, both their Alpha and Bravo teams are cross-training with Israeli and European rescue for urban disasters." Ty leaned forward, elbows posted on his thighs as he scrolled when his phone pinged. "Ha! Speak of the devil, Trip sent a picture of Valor." He held up the photo for Havoc and T-Rex to see.

A beautiful female German Shepherd was whole-body hugging a woman with curly brown hair.

"Who's that?" T-Rex asked, taking the phone. "She looks familiar."

"Dani Addams. Military vet. She took care of Rory when he got injured."

"Yeah, I remember now." T-Rex handed it back.

"There was a search and rescue mission where Trip and Valor found Dani. She'd been on a path along a cliff that collapsed in a storm," Ty said. "Trip and Valor dug her out and saved the day. Everyone got home safe and sound. It looks like Trip and Dani are going the distance. They're engaged."

"Well, hey now," Havoc said. "Good things can come from bad circumstances."

"Yeah." Ty tipped back in his chair. "Something about bad circumstances can make things spark. If you ever want to hear the psychology behind it, CIA Officer White filled my ears with that crap. I can tell you all about it."

"Worked for you and Kira, though," Havoc said. "Where's Dani stationed now?"

"Maryland. Still doing military veterinary care."

Havoc kicked his feet up onto a nearby chair, crossing his ankles, getting comfortable. "Has Dani met Kira?"

"After the terror attack at D-Day's party, Dani came over to help calm Kira down. I thought, another woman, you know? I had just met Kira, and though we both had feelings… Yeah, I just thought it needed a woman's touch, and Dani was the only woman I knew in the area."

"It help?" T-Rex asked.

"Dani was able to calm Kira down a bit." Ty scrolled quickly through his pictures and held up a photo of Dani and Kira lying on the floor holding hands with Rory and Valor draped over them.

"Hell of a thing." T-Rex could see Kira heading Ty in one of three directions. Kira could be a stabilizing influence as Ty continued his job. She might be a distraction. Or, she could be a reason to not sign his re-up contracts and maybe try to get a gig with Iniquus, so he could stay closer to home with a better work-life balance. Only the first option was okay with T-Rex. "Then she gets involved in not one but two terrorist incidents in a matter of days."

Ty seemed to pick up on T-Rex's concern. "We're working through it. It's good for Dani and Kira to have made friends." He swiped his phone closed and laid it facedown on the conference table. "I think it's the dogs that brought them together. All's good."

T-Rex nodded and turned to his computer. It was time to get on the video call with Burnside and Winner.

He tapped the last button and waited for them to log in.

While Ty was exercising Rory that morning, T-Rex and Havoc had headed to the barber shop. Their hair was now cut to military specs, their faces clean-shaven.

T-Rex kept painting a hand over his jaw. It felt strangely naked, like running to the coffee shop without his pants on. At least his neck didn't itch anymore. And his hair wouldn't blow into his eyes and distort his vision.

T-Rex preferred this look. But he worked in Africa and the Middle East, so safety often came down to how well he could blend. Though, at his size, he stood out no matter where he went in the world.

"Gentlemen." Burnside's voice pulled all eyes to the screen.

"Sir." T-Rex sat up straight, shoulders back, chin tucked.

"Have you received and reviewed your advance prep packet?"

"Affirmative, sir."

"Then you'll have found the maps of each debarkation location with various routes mapped out. The blueprints for each location. The Embassies in London and Beirut will provide you with three armored cars. Before you go, your team is to head over to the vehicular training course—Winner, you put the address into their info?"

"Yes, sir." Winner had slicked the black strands of her usually curly hair into a neat bun at the back of her neck. She'd left her face make-up free. "It's twenty-five minutes from their hotel. They have the course reserved for fifteen hundred hours."

"Copy," T-Rex said with a quick glance at his watch. They didn't have long until they needed to head out.

"I want your driving skills in England to be perfection," Burnside growled. "Go through all of the maneuvers driving on the left-hand side until you've refreshed your muscle memory. I will not—hear me clearly—*not* have an incident like we had when our diplomat's wife admittedly killed that teen with her poor driving skills. If that goes down—which it will *not*—I will be first in line to kick your can down the street, then hand you over to their police for a proper trial. You will *not* shame America."

"Sir," T-Rex said.

Burnside looked at Winner.

Winner sat up a little straighter. "Once you get to Lebanon, things will be more stressful. You should be aware that three French journalists, following a story at the Iraqi-Syrian border, were captured. ISIS tortured the three then released the male at the Lebanese border crossing. He's in the hospital in Beirut. Jean Baptiste Rujean. His colleagues, Éloïse and Marie-Claude, remain hostages. From our CIA contact, we've learned that this has heightened the stress levels around the city. There was a major influx of Syrians into Lebanon as ISIS expanded its territory. Now, the populace is concerned that ISIS is growing bolder and might test the border, possibly expanding into Lebanon. One of the reasons that Blankenship is going to Beirut is to reassure their government that America is their ally."

"That influx, how is that affecting Beirut?" T-Rex asked.

"Electricity in the area doesn't meet demand. There are frequent blackouts, and they depend on diesel generators for backup. Lebanon is considered a 'Threat Level Three—reconsider travel.'"

"What are the reasons listed?" Ty asked.

"Crime, terror, armed conflict, civil unrest, kidnappings—obviously," Winner said. "The American Embassy in Beirut has only a limited capacity to support U.S. citizens if they run into issues. Of course, the senator is a VIP, so that doesn't apply to her."

"Do you have background on the journalists traveling with us?" T-Rex asked.

"The photographer is Jules Edwards," Winner said. "He's followed along on VIP trips before. He's there to take photos, not have a personality. He'll keep up and won't add or subtract in any way. The fly on the wall, if you will."

The three operators nodded.

"The journalist was traded out last minute. That might be a problem. You should be aware of her at any rate. Remi Taleb."

"Taleb?" Ty cocked his head to the side. "I thought she was a war correspondent."

"Interesting, right? White House journalist Jasmine Tremblay was originally on the list. She's been bumped."

"Why?" T-Rex leaned back in his chair, crossing his arms over his massive chest.

"Best guess? Remi pulled strings to get back over to Lebanon," Winner said.

"More?"

"Jean Baptiste et al. were pals of hers. I did a bit of research, and they've shared bylines for over a decade. I'm sure she wants to go and offer what support she can to Jean Baptiste."

"Is she the type to pull some crap, try to jump off and go find the missing reporters on her own?" T-Rex asked.

"She's got a reputation for being brazen and fearless. But in this case," Winner shrugged, "I don't see it happening."

"Regardless," Burnside said. "Taleb isn't our principal. We're tasked with keeping the senator safe. Period. Let's stay mission-specific."

"I'm putting links to a couple of articles that might have bearing on your conduct during the mission." Winner looked down as her finger flew over the keyboard. "I'm going to be honest. Remi Taleb looks like she's a one-woman wrecking ball for the special operations community."

"All of us?" Ty asked.

"SEALs," Winner said, wrinkling her nose. "You need to watch your backs."

T-Rex leaned forward. "Why?"

"Remi Taleb is the reporter who broke the story on Ackerman that ultimately sent their whole platoon home."

T-Rex processed that for a moment. "My reading of that story was they needed to be brought home and disciplined. Granted, an operational element that large—fourteen enlisted and two junior officers—takes two squads off the grid. That makes an impact. But they were starting to act like some of the lesser appreciated contractors like Omega. Their conduct was criminal."

"Have you had the news on today?" Winner asked.

"No." T-Rex stared into the camera.

"Ackerman was let off."

"From the rape charges?"

"Non-consensual sex charges. Yes. All of it. Every last thing he did over there."

T-Rex's face hardened. It wasn't often that T-Rex showed emotion, but this news made him seethe.

"So I guess he was innocent of the allegations, then?" Havoc asked. "Her reporting was wrong?"

"Let's put it another way. He wasn't proven guilty." Winner sighed. "But DNA, lacerations, and bruises around the woman's neck? That sounds like a technicality cut him free, not innocence." Winner turned her focus from Havoc to T-Rex. "You were in the SEALs with him. What do you think really happened?"

"I kept my distance from Ackerman. He smelled

like trouble. I moved on to SEAL Team Six before he started to become a SEAL problem."

"Remi also broke the story of the snuff photos and trophies that led to the other arrests," Winner said. "Hell of a hit for that team."

"Accurate." T-Rex let the emotions slide from his face, and he was back to his seemingly unperturbable self. "Still. We should be policing ourselves. News like that gets sucked into the propaganda machine overseas and puts us at higher risk—makes it harder to gain the trust of locals. Let's move on from her reporting to the personal. What are we dealing with here? Does either Remi or the photographer have habits that can compromise the mission?"

Ty leaned over and pulled the piece of paper that Rory had snatched back out of his mouth, shaking a disciplinary finger at him. "Anything in their background about drugs or alcohol abuse? That would be some pretty serious lack of self-awareness if Taleb's bringing down men's careers over something she's into herself."

"I'm not worried about that," T-Rex said. "We're not babysitting them—we don't have responsibility."

"If either of them gets coked up around the senator..." Winner made a face. "That can lead to issues."

"You kick her out of the car if it leads to issues, Master Chief," Burnside said.

"Yes, sir."

"We've had Jules Edwards out with us before. Unless things have changed," Ty said, "Jules is benign. Solid family guy. Two kids in college, so he keeps his head down and pays the bills. Is Remi in a relationship that's concerning? Anyone she might be passing Iraqi landing schedules to?"

"Nothing I can find on a romantic partner at any point. If someone's in the picture, not even the CIA knows about it."

"Remi is usually working hot spots," T-Rex said. "Why's she here in the United States now?"

"She was up for an award. The Excellence in International Journalism Award for her article on…us. Well, the special forces community."

T-Rex let out a low whistle. "That's an impressive award. You sent me that newspaper article?"

Winner nodded. "I did. It's in the links section."

Looking down at his watch, T-Rex said, "Okay. We need to get rolling if we're going to make it to the track and get our practice in. I'll go over the files on the plane. Tomorrow is go day."

"Remember, gentlemen," their commander said, "you are the shadows that keeps the senator nice and safe. You will not stumble. You won't give this Remi Taleb one iota of a reason to pick you apart in her article. Keep your noses clean and stay out of that woman's way."

Chapter 7

T-Rex

Wednesday, Washington, D.C.

Havoc rolled through the empty parking lot toward the private hangar owned by Senator Blankenship's first cousin. The cousin was lending Blankenship her long-range jet that seated just the right number of people for this trip: Senator and staff member, 2 journos, 4 security, 1 flight attendant, four chaperones, and forty-eight students; two dozen on each team.

Rory had his head hanging out the open window of the SUV, sniffing the air. Hot macadam and jet fuel in the morning.

It was five a.m. Eastern Standard; they weren't flying out for another hour yet.

T-Rex felt rested after sleeping nearly all the way home from Djibouti on Monday. Tuesday, his team had worked out their stiff muscles with massages and some time in an infrared sauna along with haircuts and training.

Now that Wednesday was here, his three-man team was primed and ready to go.

Fortunately, there was little chance that the level of "go" would surpass heads on a swivel and holding doors. It was all good.

"Hey, let me out here," T-Rex said as they approached the glass door to the hangar. "Let's drop the equipment."

The unloading didn't take long. Each man's suitcase was packed with the specialized suits they wore in public while performing personal protection duties. Shoulder gussets, Lycra in the material, and extra support stitched into the waistband to help support their duty pistols meant their movement wouldn't be constrained. Today, the team members were each dressed in a pair of pressed khakis and a black polo shirt, professional, casual wear for the trip. Was it weird for Laurel to go into their houses and pack them up?

Sure.

T-Rex was a private person.

But Laurel was a nurse, so for some reason, less uncomfortable than someone else doing it.

Echo's standard weapons weren't allowed in England. They'd be kitted up by the CIA when they reached Iraq, and they'd take those weapons with them into Lebanon.

Rory was the prima donna, needing the most equipment and space. Ty held Rory's lead while Echo and T-Rex pulled the collapsed dog crate from the trunk, setting it next to the rest of their bags just inside the hangar door.

"Ty, go ahead and let Rory do his business in those woods over there. Havoc, you return the SUV to the rental office. I'll wait here with the equipment and see if our VIP shows up."

"Wilco," Havoc said, rounding back to the driver's seat.

Ty glanced down at Rory, tapped his leg, and they took off at a jog.

As his eyes acclimated to the dim interior, T-Rex found a group of girls in the far corner, sitting on the cement floor in conversation circles. They were playing string games and cards. Women with hijabs and long dresses stood against the wall chatting with half an eye watching to ensure the teens behaved.

As his gaze scanned the rest of the space, he caught sight of a figure dressed in black with a rose-colored scarf looped around her neck. Women in Lebanon often wore their scarves like that, readily available to drape over their hair if they needed to. European women also wore scarves that way. T-Rex hadn't seen any women in America do that.

Though still far away, T-Rex would guess that that was Remi Taleb.

His first thought was, *"We are at our best when our paths cross."* It was a quote by Nemr. That thought startled T-Rex. He wasn't sure what to make of it.

As the figure drew closer, T-Rex was sure he'd been right. This was the famous Remi Taleb.

Remi moved forward with a long stride that belied the length of her legs. Though she was a tall woman, she walked with the kind of gait that someone develops when they walked next to someone much bigger over a long period of time.

She had an assertiveness about her, a steely but understated aggression in her look. Hard-assed, if not badass, like she could cause problems.

As she got closer, he assessed her physical qualities. He needed to know at the outset if she could hold her own on this mission. Keep up. Not that he had any plans to slow down for her. His duty was specifically to Senator Blankenship, and he couldn't let either his men or him get pulled away because the journo needed a hand with her bags.

Remi wore two backpacks with cross-body straps. They overlapped in the front between her breasts, making her double D boobs jut out. Not provocatively, the look was more "warrior princess."

He noted that this configuration allowed Remi to maintain her movement hands-free. If this was her only luggage, then she traveled light.

Stopping at the wall near the office door, Remi pulled one pack off, then the other, leaning them beside the bench there.

She'd spotted him, he was sure.

Of course, she had.

But Remi ignored T-Rex and the fact that he boldly stared at her.

She was close enough now that T-Rex could see the details.

Full lips, dark eyes, long lashes, tanned skin, slightly lighter around her eyes where her sunglasses would rest.

Her hair was black, appeared to be straight and silky. She cut it at a length that was just long enough to pull back into a ponytail at the nape of her neck. The ponytail was maybe two inches long, not enough for someone to be able to grab and manipulate her hair or head, long enough that she could keep it back and out of her face, feminine enough to… She was a very attractive woman.

T-Rex had had trouble winding down to sleep last night. He'd been caught up by watching Remi's reports on YouTube and doing searches on her articles. He was curious. T-Rex could admit that to himself. Like everything T-Rex had learned last night from watching videos of her reporting, even her haircut seemed to have been given thought and attention beyond her physical appearance. Pragmatic. Rational. Disciplined. All qualities T-Rex respected.

When she did an interview dressed in a dress and heels, he'd seen scars on her exposed legs. Where did they come from? How bad had the events been that marked her for life? That she was often right there smack dab in the middle of dangerous events was evident in the footage.

He'd thought of Ty's new love, Kira. How tender she was, how affected she'd been by the events that had unraveled around her. These women were from different ends of the spectrum.

Pulling her phone and pen from the thigh pocket of what looked like tactical tights, Remi reached under her tunic, produced a pad, and then sat.

The cover on the pad he recognized, waterproof paper.

The pen, too, he recognized. It was a tactical pen. He, Ty, and Havoc all had them on the inside pockets of their suit jackets. They could write at any angle—wet weather or dry, hot or below freezing—without worrying about ink flow. And they served as a make-do kubaton—a pressure point weapon that was helpful in venues that didn't allow his standard tactical weapons.

She had chosen the tactical pen with sharp ridges scalloping the end. Stabbed into the skin and twisted, not only did it leave a painful wound that was slow to heal, it left a unique injury, one that was readily identifiable by law enforcement. The pen would also collect DNA on its ridges, again for the identification of a perpetrator.

Did she know how to use it properly? Or was she a poser?

He glanced down at the thigh pocket where Remi had pulled the pen from. Two other clips stuck out. Judging from the rounded length inside the pocket, T-Rex would say that she had a tactical flashlight and a multitool with her. If that flashlight was high enough lumen, then that too could be an effective weapon or at least a discouragement in the dark. And any woman who carried a multi-tool was the kind of woman that he'd…

T-Rex found himself cutting off that thought before it could form whole and problematic in his mind. *This assessment is professional; that's all*, he disciplined himself.

Remi ended that call, and she accepted another one.

Her pen landed back on the pad, and she was nodding as she scribbled her thoughts.

Since journalists can't carry weapons, a pen that wrote under adverse conditions was an implement for her job, not a weapon. A flashlight, the multitool, they were all everyday devices that wouldn't necessarily be explicitly categorized as a weapon.

Smart.

The level of excitement streaming through his circuitry shocked T-Rex. It was a sensation that he hadn't felt in a very long time. Not since… Jess.

T-Rex dimmed the switch as soon as that light came on.

He looked away, but his attention was drawn immediately back.

It was an interesting outfit she wore. Her shoes looked like European walking shoes. That was good, no clattering of high heels and moaning over sore feet. She was a tall woman. He'd guess five foot ten, maybe five-eleven. Even so, the tactical tights seemed to rise up higher than was typical. He knew that they probably came up to her bra line because her tunic split up the sides to that point. The tunic had a Middle Eastern, maybe East Indian, cut. That made sense. That region from the horn of Africa to India seemed to be Remi's beat.

Remi definitely had the look of someone who was undaunted by danger. Capable. Strong.

T-Rex had met his share of badass women like that before.

D-Day Rochambeau was like that…

Storm Meyers was like that. Storm was a soldier who had often attached to Echo when T-Rex was new to The Unit. On missions where they needed a female to interact with the local women, go in and do things that men weren't allowed to do in the Middle Eastern culture—speak to the women, pat them down for weapons or suicide vests… Because she was female, Storm hadn't been allowed into the training courses like the men. Special Forces trained her on the fly. After all, their team was only as good as their weakest link. And she was good. Storm had deserved the same level of opportunity and distinction as the men on his team.

Yeah, Remi had that Storm Meyers kind of energy about her. Capable and unafraid.

As he thought that, Remi turned her head and locked eyes on him.

T-Rex didn't look away. This was part of his job as far as he was concerned, assessing those in proximity to his principal.

Remi stood, slid her pen and pad away under her

tunic, and answered another call. With a finger stuck in her ear to hear, or maybe for focus, she paced the length of the bench and back.

As she turned, he noticed that her waistline was thicker than he would have expected. Given the apparent strength of her thigh muscles and the roundness of her deltoid, Remi lifted weights. Heavy ones.

Could she be pregnant?

Doubtful. Surely that would have been a known that would be part of the team's prep package. Traveling with a pregnant woman wasn't something that Winner would have missed.

T-Rex turned a quarter turn. This was getting out of hand. All he needed to know was that she was fit and capable of holding her own on this trip.

He didn't stare at Jules and dissect him.

What the heck was he thinking, ogling the woman like that?

From her vantage point, that probably felt predatory, a man as big and lethal as he was staring at her that way.

All he needed was to have her see him lick his lips to make him come off as a first-class perv.

T-Rex didn't need her to start interpreting his behavior that way. His insensitivity to her private space might become part of another "Special forces operators are jackasses" article. Though the ones he'd read were all accurate and fair, as far as he could tell.

The girls in the corner of the hangar stood and bounced with excitement as a jet taxied toward them.

It turned and parked as a backdrop.

Through the window, T-Rex could see a lectern and chairs. Obviously, the senator was planning a speech before they left.

It wasn't on the itinerary. T-Rex would have to speak

to the senator's aide, Diamond, about giving the team plenty of time and heads up if they changed their plans.

The senator walked in, and T-Rex snapped to attention.

T-Rex wanted to know how Senator Blankenship knew his name and why she'd requested him on this duty.

Maybe now he'd get his answers.

Chapter 8

Remi

Wednesday, Washington, D.C.

The guy in the khakis and black polo, who had been staring at her, suddenly snapped to attention. Military, obviously.

Remi's gaze slid in the direction he was focused.

Senator Blankenship pushed through the door in her signature cowboy hat and boots.

Ah, the guy was part of the senator's protection unit, just as Remi had guessed.

Hmph. Staring at her like she was a monkey at the zoo. What was the man thinking? You don't observe people that blatantly.

He didn't seem predatory, though. And he hadn't seemed hostile. He seemed…curious.

And huge.

She'd watched him duck as he came through the door. How did this man crawl under the barbed wire in the obstacle course in training?

His whole persona was something out of Hollywood. Broad-shouldered, tight hips, soft-looking ebony-brown hair cut short, but not so short that she—that someone—couldn't run their fingers through it.

His olive skin was warmed to a tan by the sun. Across his cheek, cuts and abrasions looked fairly new.

Remi would bet he came in from an assignment in the last couple of days.

Hazel eyes drank everything in. Full lips that looked so kiss— Remi cleared her throat as if that would clear those thoughts from her head.

He sent a shiver through her system, a tingle of excitement.

Interesting, since this assignment was anything but exciting. Remi was slogging through this story to get to Jean Baptiste. That was it.

The senator looked over her shoulder, saw the guy, and startled.

Placing her hand over her heart, she gasped and laughed. Senator Blankenship leaned her head back, her hand crushing the top of her signature red cowboy hat onto her head. "Whew! They made you big."

"Ma'am," he replied. The non-answer answer of the military.

"But there you are in all your glory, Josiah Landry, right? She told me you were a big 'un, but her words didn't quite convey the reality."

"Senator Blankenship, I'm Master Chief Landry. I prefer to be called T-Rex to keep my identity private. It's a security issue."

He spoke softly—on-brand for a special operator.

Remi hadn't quite landed on the reason why special forces used that caliber of voice. She'd speculated that the men trained to speak in a way that their voices didn't carry—though that was rather moot here in the echoing expanse of the empty hangar.

Remi also had thought that odd tone they used was a way to exercise dominance.

It wasn't the screaming rabid dog voices that showed power. The growly, spitting, angry voices always made Remi think of the phrase "all bark no bite." No, this "special forces tone" was controlled and unaffected by emotion. The men spoke so softly that one had to bend in to hear clearly—to strain. Remi mostly found it obnoxious.

"Got it." The senator bobbed her head. "Thank you. So it's you, huh? When I was told that the president's office wanted me to have security with me, I thought this might be my opportunity to meet you. I wanted a chance to see you in action."

"Hopefully, ma'am, the opportunity to see me in action won't present itself."

"Well, you've got that right. We don't need anything spectacular happening on this trip, no razzmatazz." She shuffled her boot.

Remi thought that was a quirk that the senator had developed for showmanship. It was an "Aw shucks, pour me a whisky, why don'tch yah?" kind of move.

Blankenship's personal popularity always superseded her job performance numbers.

People voted personality. It worked for her.

"Your wife." The senator reached her free hand out, laying it gently on T-Rex's forearm.

T-Rex's body stiffened from its already formal stance

when he heard the senator mention his wife. "I'm sorry, did you say my wife? Ma'am, I'm here as security."

Wife. Okay, Remi could acknowledge that disappointment rippled through her system.

Wife. Good. Remi didn't need the distraction of curiosity about this guy on a personal level.

"I well understand the importance of a separation between your work and your home life," the senator said. "I apologize for blurring those lines. But I knew your wife a while back. Liked her a lot." The senator rolled her lips in and nodded her head. "During our time together, she told me good things about you. She guarded me while I was on the campaign trail, supporting our president during his last campaign. Jess said at the time you were down range, so she might not have told you about me."

"No, ma'am."

"I was giving speeches around North Carolina, and Jess had been guarding me not three days before… Tragic. Just a surprising, horrible tragedy. There are no other words for it. During the time I knew her, Jess was a skilled, professional officer. I know you're proud."

"Ma'am."

"Ha! Jess said you weren't a big talker." The senator turned her head, and Remi caught sight of her big toothy grin. "So I'm gonna tell you this here story, so you know why I requested you to be my protection." She patted his arm, and Remi read that as an invitation for T-Rex to walk with her.

Jess (possibly) Landry, Remi noted. Out of curiosity, she'd look up the name. Tragedy?

T-Rex and the senator started across the expanse of the hangar toward the open bay door. Remi followed along.

Remi was a tall woman, just like the senator. She'd

found that when she was interviewing someone much taller than she was, the dynamic of looking up at their faces shifted the energy between them. Remi liked equal footing. She'd often sit on the arm of a chair or on an adjustable stool so she could get her interviewee eye to eye. If that wasn't possible, she'd do what the senator had just done; Remi would encourage a walk and talk. That way, they were parallel, looking forward. Besides the psychological dynamic, it was easier on her neck.

"I had gone to North Carolina to stump for our party, supporting folks up and down the ticket. My ideas weren't necessarily well-received in the run-up to those speeches. I'd gotten some threats, along with the president. Since I'd need to go to the ladies' room—you know, to freshen my lipstick and try to tame the wild tumbleweed on my head—seems to be what happens to hair in high humidity—they gave me Jess as my close protection gal."

There was a moment of sudden noise as a woman in a blue suit was getting the teens up and guiding them to the seats outside.

Remi missed a bit of the conversation between the senator and T-Rex—great name. Remi wondered if he got a lot of short-arm jokes.

She picked back up on their thread when the senator said, "Jess was amazing. Quick with a smile. Quick with a sarcastic remark. Just bright as a new penny. Why, there were a couple times when I thought for sure that things were going to come to blows, but, nah. Jess talked her way out of every situation."

Blankenship poked T-Rex in the side. "I'd imagine that she had you wrapped around that little finger of hers. Big as you are, and as little as she was." Blankenship put out the flat of her palm to indicate about how tall Jess stood. "I hadn't thought she was much protection when I first laid eyes on her. But you know, that taught me a lesson that I thought I had learned. You can't judge a book by its cover. Well, unless it's a Stephen King book. You see his name, and you know that whatever is between those pages is going to haunt your dreams with terror."

She smiled at T-Rex. "Me anyway. I can't imagine you being afraid of anything." Stopping, Blankenship turned and extended a hand toward Remi. "You must be my reporter gal."

"Remi Taleb, Washington News-Herald," she said, accepting the senator's two-handed shake.

A fly buzzed between the two women. Remi's hand shot out, catching the pest in her fist. Her other hand slipped behind the high side slit on her tunic, and out came a tissue she used to squish the bug. "I'll be shadowing you on this trip." With another reach under her tunic, Remi produced a small bottle of Purell.

Remi cleaned her hands while Blankenship chuckled. "She's like a magician," Blankenship said to T-Rex.

Jules hustled through the open bay door, sidling past the students, then stood there disoriented in the shift in brightness, camera in hand.

Another plunge under her tunic put the bottle of hand sanitizer away, and she reemerged with a tiny digital recorder.

"Ma'am, permission to record?"

"Of course."

She pressed the button. "Remi Taleb speaking with Senator Blankenship. Wednesday, August twenty-fifth. Senator Blankenship, members of the Senate aren't usually afforded a security detail. You have three members of the United States military with you." Remi had only seen the one, but that's what Liu's notes had indicated.

Blankenship's demeanor micro-adjusted from the friendly warmth she'd expressed to T-Rex. Her posture read much more senatorial now. "It's an inopportune time for me to be traveling, according to the NSA. Granted, it's rare for a senator to be given any kind of security. But it was insisted upon. I guess things are at a flashpoint in the Middle East. When in my life hasn't that been the truth?"

Remi pulled the recorder closer to her mouth. "But you're going anyway?"

"'Course I am. Do you know what happens in conflict? Women suffer. Always. When women suffer, children suffer. I'm not sitting back and waiting. I'm pushing for women to come into the government. I believe that when there are more women—hear me when I say, I'm not trying to displace men, simply trying to climb the mountain to stand beside them. When we do, I think things in the world will improve. A bias of mine that I fully own."

"Security?" Remi redirected the senator back to the topic she'd asked about. Remi well knew how politicians started off a sentence as if they were going to answer a question, then they'd pivot hard to make whatever point they'd had queued up.

"There was some concern from the White House that my stopover in Iraq—no matter how brief—and then in Lebanon might stir up some issues. They didn't want any blowback in this news cycle. It's all in keeping the focus on this legislation that they're trying to ram through lickety-split." She smiled. "My thinking, candidly, is that they're afraid of my presence being an opportunity to smack the United States in the face and start a bar brawl. We're stepping off the plane in Iraq—"

"Don't print that until we've left Iraq," T-Rex interjected.

Remi nodded.

The senator hadn't stopped talking. "—fifteen minutes and right back up in the air. In Beirut, there are long memories of what happened to America when we were there trying to keep the peace." She patted Remi's arm. "Long before you were born, I'd assume."

"Are you referring to the attack on the U.S. embassy?"

"And our Marines." Her lips dragged down in the corners, and she stared out the open bay, out in the distance. Took in a breath and focused back on Remi.

It was widely known that Senator Blankenship's brother had been one of those marines who perished in the attack on the Marine barracks in Beirut. Remi wondered what this trip was going to be like for the senator. "Have you been there before, Lebanon?"

"Never. A first for me." Blankenship popped her eyebrows.

"And you think this is a security risk for you?"

"I think it's a security risk for *everyone*. I don't believe the risk will be specific to me. I was asked to let a security detail come along. I have a distant association with T-Rex, so I requested him."

"Military, not Secret Service?" Remi clarified.

"Military. Trained by Secret Service, though. And the FBI and CIA," Blankenship tossed in.

What? "So they're Delta Force operators?" From Remi's reporting on special forces operators, Delta Force was a clandestine group who tried to wipe their existence off public records and were the only ones that Remi knew were trained that way. Delta Force and CIA were often fluid. Delta Force operators could be brought in and made temporary CIA officers, so they could navigate the various laws.

Okay, Delta Force and the senator, *that* was big.

"I can't say for sure." Senator Blankenship sent a furrowed brow T-Rex's way. "And wouldn't if I knew." She spun her attention back to Remi. "And you should be extra careful about speculation." Blankenship's face was reinforced concrete, rigid and inflexible.

"I understand," Remi replied, taking that admonition as a confirmation. "I can be discreet."

"See that you do." Blankenship gestured toward T-Rex. "I don't mind having someone at my back. And since I sit on the Defense Committee—a huge industry and a resource flow for Texas—I like to see our men and women in action. It helps me make those numbers less bureaucratic and more personal."

"Did you personally choose not to be protected by Secret Service?" Blankenship hadn't agreed that this guy was special forces. Remi would try getting that answer by hitting it from a different, albeit speculative, angle.

"The Secret Service, like the special forces operators, are stretched mighty thin. Too many hours. Too little in return. Wears a soul down. I didn't want to tax their systems further since they're busy with the president's barnstorming tour to gather energy around his initiatives."

Remi pulled her recorder closer to her mouth as she asked, "The Secret Service has garnered bad press lately for an abundance of alcohol, partying into the wee hours instead of resting in preparation for the next day of work, strip clubs when off duty, and sex workers who went unpaid. Did you perhaps choose a military escort so that you could avoid having your name attached to such behaviors should they occur while you are out of the country?" Remi pushed the recorder back out to capture Blankenship's response.

The Senator focused on T-Rex, their eyes held, then she turned to Remi. "Off the record?" She raised a single eyebrow at Remi.

Remi tapped stop on her recorder.

"I'm interested in self-preservation, both of my person—though I don't think that's an issue on this trip—and my reputation. Woe be it for any man who creates a stink and bad press in my sphere. I am the golden gal on this trip. I'm to look shiny and fresh, a leader on the world stage. I don't cotton to folks who create roadblocks to where it is I want to go."

"Where is that, Senator?"

"Forward. Now on the record." She paused to let Remi click her digital recorder back on. "I would say that I'm grateful for these proud and highly accomplished military men to be by my side as I deliver my message of hope and strength to the women of the world."

"Thank you, ma'am." Remi cut off her recorder and slipped it under her tunic as Blankenship turned toward the woman in the blue suit rushing their way.

"What is it, Diamond?" the senator asked.

"It's time for your welcome speech. The photographer said the angles with the lights were bad for filming. Rather than trying to turn the whole setup and lose the backdrop of the jet behind you, I got him one of those roller stairs to stand on, so you'll look your best. He's all set up if you're ready. Then we'll get the girls loaded on the plane and head off on our adventure."

Blankenship looked up at T-Rex. "You just make sure it's not too much of an adventure, you hear?"

Chapter 9

T-Rex

Wednesday, Washington, D.C.

As T-Rex emerged from the hangar with the senator, he scanned the area.

The girls and their chaperones sat politely in the metal folding chairs.

Ty and Rory were climbing on the plane to give it a search before boarding. Havoc wasn't back yet. T-Rex glanced at his watch.

The photographer, Jules, was posted just to the side of the chairs. He stood above their heads on a set of stairs that could be rolled up to a commercial jet for passengers to load.

Diamond had angled the steps so that one of the two sides with safety bars faced the lectern.

Jules was adjusting his video camera on its tripod.

With its huge lens, his still camera dangled from a blue strap Jules had looped around his neck.

T-Rex turned to the lectern and saw that two professional mics were angled there to capture the senator's voice. Remi made her way over to the mics and tested the system, using hand signals to confer with Jules.

The heat of the day hadn't quite risen to the point of discomfort.

The light was still the milky yellow of an August morning.

No unusual movement in the area.

No extra eyes.

Diamond nodded at Remi, and Remi moved off to the side. Her micro-recorder lay on her open palm.

T-Rex guessed that was backup, or maybe she just liked to have her own copy for quick reference when she was writing a story. The SEAL mantra "one is none, and two is one" flashed through his mind. A reminder that even the best-laid plans often went awry, so you'd better back up your systems.

Tugging at the bottom of her suit jacket, wiggling her shoulders, then squaring off in front of the mic, Diamond spread a professional smile across her face and stilled, waiting for the audience to clue in and quiet themselves.

"Good morning, ladies. Welcome. It's an honor to be here with the brilliant minds that will lead the world into the future. So many of you will make a real difference. Now, more than ever, science will lead the way as humanity deals with our various crises. Keep powering forward." She paused, her smile frozen on her face. With a nod, she began again. "My name is Diamond Johnson. I'm assistant to your host, Senator Barbara Blankenship, whom I will present momentarily. First, let me introduce you to our flight crew, then I will be going over some housekeeping topics."

She held her hand out, indicating the pilot, co-pilot, and flight attendant who stood to Diamond's right.

T-Rex noted their names.

The crew nodded graciously, raised their hands in a wave, then pivoted and headed back to the plane, passing by Ty and Rory, who re-emerged in the doorway.

Ty gave T-Rex a thumbs up and stood to the side of the stairs.

The pilot boarded; the flight attendant stood at the bottom of the stairs at attention.

Neat and orderly. T-Rex just needed Havoc back on site, and they'd be off to a good start. T-Rex pulled his cell phone from his pocket and sent a quick text: ETA? We're getting ready to board.

"One last check before Senator Blankenship welcomes you," Diamond said.

Senator Blankenship stood to Diamond's left. She adjusted her cowboy hat as Diamond ran through her list.

"In the information packet, we let you all know that we have drinks on board, but we won't have food service since there are a number of you with allergies and special meal preparation requirements. I need to make sure, though, that no one is going to go hungry. Do you have your lunches and snacks? Hold them up so I can make sure each girl is prepared."

The girls all leaned over their backpacks, unzipping them and rustling around.

T-Rex was keeping an eye on the adults' hands as they dug in their packs to ensure that only food items emerged.

The Echo team hadn't been warned about the no-meals situation, but he and his team always had a couple of MREs thrown in their packs, and they kept their camel water bladders full. They were good to go.

As the girls lifted their bags, T-Rex's gaze landed on Remi. Her hand was raised, shielding her eyes as she gazed into the morning sun. Something about her posture tightened T-Rex's muscles. He scanned to see what she was looking at, but from his vantage point, all he had was a strip of mown grass that dipped into a runoff pond.

T-Rex turned to Ty. They'd been Unit members together for long enough that when T-Rex bored his gaze into the back of Ty's head, he turned.

As T-Rex lifted a hand to signal, Rory gave a low growl from the back of his throat. Hackles up, he gave an aggressive bark, pulling to the end of his lead.

T-Rex strode toward his principal, so he could cover her no matter the disturbance. If his face was caught on camera, he'd just have the photographer delete those frames.

Ty reeled Rory back, but Rory was lunging aggressively.

Eyes scanning the horizon, T-Rex still couldn't find anything amiss.

And that's when all hell broke loose.

A flock of birds with their broad, powerful wings and ugly, heads swooped. They were enormous and determined as their talons spread, reaching for the girls' lunch bags.

The girls were screaming. Their chairs tipped and banged to the ground as they leaped and ran for the bay, covering their heads with their arms.

Senator Blankenship clutched at her hat as a bird winged its way in her direction.

T-Rex was at her side, wrapping an arm around her

shoulder, leaning his body over the top of her to protect her from the sharp talons, semi-lifting and dragging her toward the building.

Diamond was racing as fast as her pencil skirt and heels would allow toward the hangar, forcing T-Rex to swerve around her.

As he made his way past the door, T-Rex spotted Ty working to control Rory, who was in protective mode, snarling and chomping at the birds.

The girls already inside, T-Rex hit the button to lower the bay's automatic door, sealing out the birds. As the door crunched and ground on the pully system, he asked, "Senator, were you injured?"

A man hollered, then was shrieking.

Senator Blankenship pressed on T-Rex's back. "Go. Go. I'm fine."

T-Rex didn't bother taking the time to raise the door. He simply dove under its descent, rolling as its heavy length slammed shut just behind him.

In his mind, he was weighing his duty to stay with the senator and his duty to follow her directive.

T-Rex couldn't imagine that was Ty or Havoc screaming like that. It had to be Jules. Where was Remi?

Rolling to a stand, T-Rex arrived at what could easily be a horror film scene.

He'd never seen so many birds of prey at once. And having spent his share of time on the African planes, that was saying something. T-Rex's gaze landed on Ty, who was hauling Rory up the steps to the plane.

Rory was excellent at following commands under even the most harrowing of circumstances. Something about this scene made him break his training.

Ty lifted a hand and pointed. T-Rex followed the direction but couldn't see past the flapping wings.

It was like swimming through the sea in the black of night and accidentally swimming into a feeding shiver of sharks.

Bending his elbow and resting it on his brow to protect his eyes, T-Rex kicked his way through the heaving mass of gorging birds.

He aimed for the shrieks. Those were female and young.

T-Rex lifted a folding chair and used it like a riot shield as he slogged forward, looking under the birds' wings, searching for any girls that might not have made it to safety.

There was Jules, dangling from the stairs. His elbow encircled the rail, and his hand clung to his shirt. He was a heavy-set man, and T-Rex couldn't imagine that he'd hold there long.

The drop was enough for an untrained man to break his legs.

His camera was in the bird's talons and it was trying to fly away with it. The strap encircled Jules's neck, dragging his head backward. With his free hand, Jules was trying to make space for air to pass down his throat. His mouth open and soundless. Blood dripped from gashes on his head.

T-Rex prioritized the girl over Jules. If Jules would just let go of the stairs, he'd fall, he'd be hurt, but he would be free.

T-Rex caught a flash of Remi through the black storm of wings.

Remi had wrapped her rose scarf around her head, so only a slit in the fabric allowed her to see, protecting her eyes and skin. In one hand, she had her high lumen flashlight that she was shining into the birds' eyes, making them scatter. In the other, she had a folding chair just like T-Rex had.

Remi disappeared from T-Rex's view behind a screen of feathers as several of the birds rose into the air.

T-Rex beat his way through the wake, hoping that Ty was securing Rory and coming to assist.

Where was Havoc?

Having battled blindly through the riot of birds, ecstatically screeching over the bounty of food they'd discovered, T-Rex's hand landed on Remi's calf. He followed it up her bent thigh to her hips. She was on all fours with a folded metal chair across her back—a turtle's shell of protection over her.

A bag open on the flat surface of the metal seat, the bird was devouring the meal, pressing the chair down on Remi.

Beneath Remi, a student cowered.

"Remi," T-Rex yelled, swatting at a bird that had caught Remi's head scarf in its beak.

"Get her! Get her!" Remi screamed back.

T-Rex reached under Remi's body and caught hold of a blood-covered sleeve. He dragged the girl out from under Remi. "Come on. Let's go."

He heaved the girl over his shoulder in a fireman's carry so he could keep the chair-weapon flailing in front of him to clear a space. He saw that the girl was holding pieces of a ripped sandwich.

"Drop the food," he ordered as he slogged toward the side door, hoping it was unlocked.

The girl didn't comply. T-Rex didn't know if it was because she was in shock or if she didn't speak English.

He dropped the chair and reached for the doorknob. Locked. He lifted his foot and push kicked just below the knob. The door moaned. He kicked it again, splintering the wood. The door flew back and banged into the wall.

A woman screamed and ran forward, reaching for the girl draped over his back, the sandwich still in hand.

T-Rex handed the child over to the women's care while he ran back out to see what could be done for Jules.

The bird still clung to the camera strap and was still powering forward.

With each downstroke, Jules's body shifted forward then fell back with each lift of the bird's wings.

Remi was lying on the top of the stairs, her feet dangling out the side. The folded chair covered her back once again. Her strobing flashlight lay at her side.

As he closed the distance, T-Rex recognized the multitool in her hand. She sawed at the strap, which confused T-Rex.

"Hold on, Jules! Hold on!" Remi hollered. "I'm almost through. I'll get you free. Hang on!" She yelled the encouragement.

T-Rex wondered why she didn't just drag the camera out of the bird's talons, crash it to the ground. With a plastic bag held tight in its talons, the bird flew by him, and T-Rex took a swipe from the wing. T-Rex hadn't been prepared for the massive power that the bird delivered.

Remi seemed safe under her chair shelter.

T-Rex wondered under what circumstances Remi had learned to behave that way. She was making do with what was at hand. Maybe she'd picked up a thing or two as she covered the special forces community.

T-Rex rounded the steps to find Jules's flailing legs. "Remi, pull your hands away," he bellowed up at her.

"Away!" she yelled. Just enough information repeated back so T-Rex knew she'd understood and would comply. Not a word too many. Good.

"Jules, on the count of three, let go. Jules, do you hear me?" There was no way for the man to signal, no free hand, no breath for words. "On three, *let go*. One—" T-Rex squatted. "Two… Three!" T-Rex sprang up.

Stretching his arms, T-Rex caught hold of Jules's ankles and tugged as T-Rex dropped back to the ground.

As Jules crashed down, T-Rex made a circle with his arms and turned his head to look over his shoulder to protect his nose from being broken. As Jules brushed through T-Rex's arms, his descent slowed enough to reach the ground with no broken bones.

Now, T-Rex could understand the scene better.

Remi hadn't frightened the bird away because the talons had pierced the canvas of the strap, becoming ensnared.

The bird had been dragged to the ground with Jules's weight and was fighting for its life.

Protecting his eyes behind an elbow, T-Rex reached under the beating wings, grabbed the leg that had been caught. T-Rex dropped his elbow from his brow just long enough to grab the strap and jerk it free from the talons.

As soon as T-Rex released the bird's leg, it took off flying.

Jules was in bad shape. His neck was encircled with a rug burn. He was making strangled sounds as his chest heaved.

If Jules's throat was swelling from the assault, Jules could still be strangled to death.

T-Rex pulled him over his shoulder and once again was racing toward the hangar.

A siren was close.

T-Rex hoped that 9-1-1 had dispatched the fire fighters to the scene. They'd have a paramedic and the equipment to handle this event.

T-Rex laid Jules on the cool cement floor as Blankenship and Diamond rushed forward to help.

T-Rex stood to go after Remi, but she walked in on her own steam.

Pressing her back against the wall, fist clutching the fabric over her heart. She looked at the floor, panting from exertion.

T-Rex scanned down her body. No visible blood or wounds as she unwrapped the scarf from around her head. He noticed that she'd put on a pair of ballistic glasses, the same kind his team used. Made of polycarbonate plastic, the lenses were thick enough to protect her eyes from most projectiles, even bullets. A clever use of what tools were at hand.

The first responders burst through the door, observed, then split into two teams, one headed to the bloodied student, the other toward Jules.

The senator and Diamond had crouched to help with Jules. T-Rex extended his hand to help the senator and her aide to their feet then guided them out of the responder's way.

"Well done, T-Rex." The senator's hair was a wild tangle of curls. "You know," she said as she bent to swipe up her cowboy hat and set it back on her head. "Maybe I jinxed us when I brought up Steven King." She adjusted her suit jacket. "Looks like I conjured our very own scene from The Dark Half. I won't be doin' nothin' like that again."

Chapter 10

Remi

Wednesday, Washington, D.C.

"Hey," Remi said when Liu answered his phone.

"How is it that you're calling me right now? Aren't you supposed to be winging it over the Atlantic?"

"Things didn't get off to a very good start."

"With the senator? I talked to their office. It was all arranged. We agreed on the cost of your seat, the money was forwarded to them. What's the issue? Did she leave you behind?"

"We're still at the airport. There was a bird incident. Jules is in an ambulance heading for the hospital." Remi watched the first responders wheeling Jules from the hangar to the ambulance. The white bandaging that covered his scalp was slowly turning red as it absorbed his blood.

Head wounds, even when they were superficial, tended to bleed profusely.

She felt her stomach wobble.

"Is this a joke? The hospital? Did you say bird incident?"

"Yeah." Remi pulled the rose scarf from around her neck, trying to relieve the sense of claustrophobia that lingered from being under the beating wings of the birds. "It was like something out of a sci-fi show. I've never seen anything like it. One of the birds tried to drag Jules off the stairs. Jules was beaten to hell and back."

"By the birds."

"Yep. Let's see—head lacerations, a nasty cut by his eye. He was squeezing his lids shut. I hope they didn't get his eyeball."

"Remi, this isn't funny."

"I'm not kidding. I'd send you the video, but Jules's video camera is in a million pieces. So head, eyes, he pulled his shoulder out of the socket when he was dangling from his elbow."

"His elbow...?"

"He's not a light guy. That was a lot of weight to hold. And the paramedic put an intubation tube down his throat. The responder was worried that Jules's airway would swell shut."

"Because?"

"The bird got its talons caught in the camera strap and freaked out, trying to fly away. But the strap was around Jules's neck. So basically, the bird was strangling Jules."

"Strangling... Remi—"

"I swear on my mother's grave, Liu. Why would I make something like that up?"

"What hospital are they heading to?"

She put her hand over the phone. "Hey!" she called out. "What hospital?"

"Suburban. They have an ocular trauma doctor on call today."

"Thank you!" She raised a hand. "Suburban," Remi repeated into her phone.

"Yeah, I heard."

"I don't have a photographer. Can you arrange for a photojournalist to add on when we arrive in London?"

"Do you have your camera?"

"I do, but it's not the same quality." Remi noticed that the student she'd shielded until T-Rex could scoop her up and run her to safety was now bandaged. She sat with her head on a chaperone's shoulder, gripping the woman's hands. She wasn't heading toward the ambulance for a checkup at the hospital. Remi imagined that the chaperone just wanted to get her home where the girl could see her regular doctor.

Remi glanced around the hangar and decided that folks weren't gathering their things up to get on the plane yet. Remi thought she had time to slip into the ladies' room and splash some water on her face…try to regain her professional demeanor.

She started for the white sign with the blue woman's symbol.

"Remi, I'm going to be honest with you," Liu said. "The senator will make the papers with the feel-good underdog story about the girls and the robotics. That's great. But this speech she's giving in Lebanon? Not interesting to our audience. I'd say a good ninety percent of our viewers couldn't find Lebanon on the map. Most people will only remember Lebanon for the 1983 attack on our embassy and the attack on the Marine barracks that same year."

"That attack was the biggest attack and loss of U.S. military lives in a single event since World War II and Iwo Jima. People *should* remember it. And remember that those Marines were on a peace-keeping mission. But yes, the generation that would recall that incident with any kind of grief or interest is thin. I have another angle." She pushed through the door and caught sight of herself in the mirror.

Not great.

"Two angles. No, three. One, Ackerman wasn't convicted."

"I heard. I'm sorry. You did outstanding journalism on that piece."

"Thank you. But it didn't accomplish much. So angle number one: Blankenship is working on a bipartisan bill to reform how sexual assault is dealt with in the military. I could work with her on that?"

"As a follow-up, that's not a bad idea." Liu fell silent.

Remi knew to give his wheels time to turn while he sifted through all the articles that other journalists were reporting out and making sure that this wasn't a story that someone was already digging into.

Finally, he said, "You had a second angle?"

"Yeah, I just talked to Gretel from NTL München TV before the bird incident. She said that word in the diplomatic pockets is circulating new fears of Havana Syndrome. Gretel said that symptoms that were seen in Havana are now showing up in Vienna. Rounding numbers, about two dozen diplomats and CIA are reporting the same symptoms that the embassies in Russia and Havana had. They think there's been another attack."

"You're nowhere near there, but I can check in with Keith. He's in Bratislava writing about the Zoric family."

"What's going on with the Zorics?"

"A couple of their female family members, the ones who were transporting the girls into America for prostitution, are about to be released from prison, good behavior and diplomatic pressure is popping them free. They'll be deported as soon as they walk out of the prison gates."

"Yeah, Keith would be a good person to write about Havana Syndrome. He has a scientific background. But I was thinking about Lebanon. What about we hit it from the angle of that sound scientist—rogue DARPA scientists. One of them is still there. I'm not recalling the name. I can look it up."

"The DARPA guy was arrested."

"One of them. The one that was doing the memory experiments on PTSD. I'm talking about the guy who was DARPA adjacent. He worked for Montrim industries. If I'm not mistaken, he's still in Lebanon since there's no extradition treaty. As a matter of fact, I believe that George Mathews—yup, that's his name—Mathews is still teaching at the American University where Senator Blankenship is scheduled to give her speech on women's education and world contributions."

"Take me on the ride. What are you thinking?"

"I'm wondering why the president was pressing Russia on Havana sickness. Why did the U.S. take it up with Russia and not China, since most of the intelligence community believed that Havana Syndrome was a Chinese plot? Why wasn't Mathews arrested and brought back to the U.S.?"

"No extradition, you just said that."

"Right, but we give Lebanon billions, you'd think... Well, I don't know the ins and outs of international law. But Mathews is a U.S. citizen. They could revoke his visas and send him home." Remi tilted her phone on top of the hand dryer so she could hear over the speaker. She pushed her sleeves up to her elbows.

"Anti-U.S. is my guess," Liu said. "And it's not a bad story to follow up on now that the topic is getting a little sunlight from the White House. The third idea?"

"A personal impact story, Senator Blankenship's older brother was a Marine killed in the attack on the Marine barracks in Beirut. It's got to have something to do with her wanting to go to Lebanon. We're approaching the fortieth anniversary of the strike and his death."

"I like it." Liu's voice echoed against the ceramic tile. "Yeah. Okay. But one story at a time. Your plate is full. Maybe we can keep you over there, when the senator flies home, to work the other angles. You follow the senator, and you hand me a feel-good piece. You give our regards to Jean Baptiste and show him our support. And sorry about this, but, as we've been talking, I've been searching my list of field photojournalists, and I don't have anyone to send you. You're on your own with this story."

After Liu severed the line, Remi washed her hands and arms with copious amounts of hot water and soap. Bird germs, she thought with a wrinkled nose. Splashing cold water on her face, then toweling off with the rough brown paper from the dispenser, Remi looked herself over in the mirror. Front. Back. She picked off the pin feathers and searched for any bird poop.

Outside there was a whistle and a pop.

To Remi, it sounded like the kind of dispersal explosives that cops used as a warning during protests. The police were most likely getting the birds to fly on.

What would the girls do for food?

No one had warned Remi to pack her lunch, but

from experience, she learned to always carry at least two days of food and a full camel water pouch in her pack. And, of course, she had at least a day's worth of calories in her supply belt under her tunic.

Pulling the elastic band from her stubble of a ponytail, Remi leaned back and gathered the strands into a sleek fistful, then wound the band around them. Finally, she arranged her scarf around her neck.

Remi had found a scarf to be one of the best tools around. Everything from protecting her head from bird attacks but also from any debris that would fall after an explosion. A first-aid tool—blood staunching or tying up a splint. It was also a weapon. More than once, she'd wrapped it around her knuckles as she punched her way through a situation—breaking a window or breaking a bad guy's nose. She'd also wrapped it around a guy's neck and choked him out, giving herself enough time to run. Her scarves allowed Remi to be culturally appropriate when needed and gave her the simple clothing choices—the tactical tights and tunic that she wore as a personal uniform—a bit of flare. Yup, Remi was a fan of the Middle Eastern-sized scarf. It was called a shemagh when worn by the men; hers measured slightly more than three-foot square.

Feeling human again, Remi went in search of the senator to see how she was handling the crisis.

As Remi walked by the door T-Rex had kicked in while rescuing the student, she stopped to look outside. The birds were gone. There was the stench of sulfur in the air.

The girls were outside gathering their bags.

They were visibly shaken by the event. Remi wondered if the chaos of the last few minutes would trigger any of them. All of these girls were refugees from war-torn areas.

As Remi rounded into the open expanse of the hangar, she noted that Blankenship was thanking the last of the first responders, flashing a brazen, toothy smile.

Blankenship wore too much blue eyeshadow for today's standards. Her high-dollar suits were made bourgeois by the cowboy hat and boots—if one could call a cowboy hat and boots bourgeois… Larger than life.

Remi went to stand with Diamond and the senator.

T-Rex and two men in the same black polo and khaki attire stood behind Blankenship.

One of them had a K9 with him.

Interesting.

Big men. All of them. That was kind of unusual. Remi had been in the world of destruction and combat since she'd earned her diploma. On the job, she'd brushed past more than her fair share of special operators. Typically they were little. Surprisingly small. Her height—five-foot-ten—seemed to be about their norm. And wiry more than bulky. They were the kind of bodies one saw watching extreme sports on television.

But here were these guys, blowing the norms.

"Remi Taleb," she said, looking at the dog handler.

"Ty, ma'am. My K9 Rory." When he said the dog's name, the K9 looked up to see what Ty wanted him to do. When no command followed, he lowered his chin and looked around the room, his tongue hanging long.

"Quite the excitement for Rory with the birds," Remi ventured.

"Yes, ma'am. Just a heads-up, Rory isn't a pet. We don't allow anyone to touch him or any of his things."

"Thanks for the warning." Remi had seen birds of prey in Africa rip dogs apart. She thought Ty's choice to protect Rory on the plane had been a practical one. Military K9s had about a hundred grand in training under their collars. They were force multipliers, but only when correctly deployed.

Remi turned to the other man.

"I'm Havoc."

Remi gave the man a quick nod before focusing on the senator. "Are you okay?"

"I was just about to tell Diamond that back, oh a little over a decade ago, I had a friend, Bubba, who was flying his Cessna. It was a Citation 500 business jet, so it was considerably smaller than the jet we're taking. Off he flew out of a little airport from a stopover in Oklahoma. All of a sudden, the damned jet went into a nosedive, straight into the ground."

Remi's gaze drifted to their jet as a wave of cold doused her system, sending a shiver through her frame.

She could feel T-Rex's eyes on her, assessing.

"Yep, his wife Millie said there hadn't been any warning at all. Weather was good. Plane checked out." She used her hand to mime the plane's actions. "The guy in the control tower, he had instructed Bubba to climb and turn, but no one answered. He kept trying to raise Bubba on the radio but got nothing. A moment later, some guy goes running into the control room, hollering that he'd just watched a plane fly into the ground and explode. The forensics guys said it was birds that brought it down." She stuck her tongue up in the space between her lip and teeth, making her lips bulge out, then gave a little sucking noise.

She stared out at the jet. "You know, I think about that story every time I get on a plane." She dragged her gaze away from where the girls were filing on board and let her focus land on Remi. "Here's hoping the birds felt like they did enough damage for today and will let us get in the air without our becoming a fiery ball of hell."

Chapter 11

Remi

Wednesday, Washington, D.C.

Remi was waiting until the last possible second to board. She wasn't great on planes or any small, confined areas that she couldn't easily leave.

Since it was part and parcel to her job, she'd come up with some tips and tricks that helped her, this side of prescription anxiety meds. Over the counter Dramamine took the bite out of her anxiety by making her too tired to care. The package told her to put the patch behind her ear in advance of boarding to avoid travel sickness. Remi's reticence wasn't about travel sickness but rather a lifetime of incapacitating anxiety over being trapped.

Once she tapped the patch behind her ear, she'd become sleepy and incapable of functioning in work mode.

Remi wanted to get on the plane and get the vibe of what would come next. If the senator were to sleep or be otherwise busy, Remi would allow herself the relief.

If Blankenship were talkative, Remi needed to be ready. Her job, after all, was to collect stories like a child gathers fireflies in an open field during summer twilight, to look at them and share them with others before releasing them out.

One thing Remi had noticed over time was that boarding early was not a perk. Sitting low as a parade of humanity pressed past her, looming over her as they got stuck in the aisle waiting for their fellow fliers to lift their travel bags into the overhead bins, increased the claustrophobia and the sense that Remi was a sardine plastered into a can.

Getting on last or near last was the ticket.

Remi stood to the side and used the time to do a quick search for "Jess Landry, North Carolina, police" on her phone. A distraction. The articles populated her search filter. Grabbing one from her paper, Remi scanned the basic information.

Officer Jessica Landry had been killed responding to a domestic violence call. She shot the guy who shot her back. They both died at the scene.

Well, shit.

Four years ago…

Not married, widowed.

Four years was a significant amount of time.

T-Rex came into her line of view. He was sexy as all get out, in a physical way. Mentally? Remi wasn't that into soldier-boy types.

She also wasn't considering him for a relationship, Remi reminded herself.

But since he wasn't the subject of her reporting, he wasn't off-limits to her.

Yeah, she wouldn't mind bending over for him as long as he didn't turn out to be an egomaniacal pain in the—Remi stopped herself as that thought bubbled into her consciousness. Well, honestly, what red-blooded, straight woman could be around T-Rex and not have her libido kick into gear?

T-Rex turned to find her with that question in her eyes, cutting her off from that line of thought.

Remi saw his body react to whatever he read there. It was kind of a jerk and hold. Oddly, he asked, "Where did you come from?"

Was it a filler question? It seemed disingenuous of T-Rex. Surely, his team checked everyone's background who would be in contact with the senator on this trip. Maybe she startled him with whatever energy she was giving off, and that was the question that would help him to decipher what he read in her eyes. Which honestly was a hodgepodge of emotions—concern about her friends, anxiety about boarding, and the distraction of sexy thoughts.

He raised his brows and repeated himself, "Where did you come from, exactly?"

Still…might as well tease the man.

"Are you serious right now?" Remi lifted her brows to match his. "No one ever told you this? Okay, look." She paused and drew in a breath. "When two people love each other very much, they get a special tickly feeling in their bathing suit area."

T-Rex turned and strode away.

And a little smile played across Remi's lips.

As soon as Remi boarded, she felt the jittery vibration glistening the air with sharp edges. The girls were still riled from the bird incident.

Remi's whole body fought against her walking down the aisle.

She worked on a breathing pattern, trying to ignore the voice in her head screaming at her to jump off the plane and run for her life. Certainly, Senator Blankenship's merry little "bird crashes plane" story wasn't helping.

She *could* do this.

It was eight hours in the air, then this flight would be over, just like all the other flights she'd powered herself through. Flying was part and parcel to her job; Remi wouldn't give in to her fears now.

She found that the only seat left on the plane was the window seat on the inside of where T-Rex was taking up space. Taking up lots and lots of space. His long legs didn't fit behind the chair, so he stretched them out along the aisle, tucked to the side as much as possible.

Across from them, Blankenship sat on the aisle, and Diamond was next to the window.

As Remi lifted her two backpacks into the overhead bin, her hands visibly shook.

The air left her lungs.

Having a man as big as T-Rex blocking her into her seat...that was more than she thought she could handle. She couldn't ask him to be at the window...his legs. Besides, he needed to be at Blankenship's beck and call.

Remi wasn't sure if the senator was astute enough to sense the problem or if this just turned out to her benefit, but Blankenship tapped Diamond's arm. "You go sit at the other window. I'm going to scootch over and have a chat with Remi."

It took a little bit of doing for Diamond to displace to the spot that was supposed to be Remi's.

Remi didn't even try to hide her gratitude.

The aisle was much more doable, sanity-wise.

She sat, buckled, and leaned her head back, not watching out the window for birds. Why had the senator planted that vivid picture of a crash in her head?

The take-off was fine.

It was *fine.*

She was fine.

She was even more fine when the flight attendant came by with alcohol. Remi accepted a rum and coke.

Diamond and Blankenship both had whisky, neat. "I have a splitting headache. This is just what the doctor ordered," Blankenship said as she closed her eyes and took a sip.

"Are you unwell?" T-Rex asked, accepting a bottle of water. He was working, though what security might be needed on the plane wasn't readily apparent.

Blankenship kept her eyes shut as she took in a long breath and released it through her pursed lips. "Nah, I've had a lot on my mind lately. I've had a bout with insomnia that I'm just about fed up with. I'm planning on a chat with my doc when I get back. See what she thinks might help."

After a long stretch of silence, Remi turned to T-Rex, regretting a little her answer outside, and by way of being conciliatory, she said, "I heard the senator speak to you about your wife's death. Please accept my condolences."

He nodded.

"I read the reporting from my newsroom. Your wife was a brave woman. Those children will grow up knowing that someone cared. She saved them. Remarkable and admirable."

T-Rex nodded.

Personal life is not allowed. Got it. Okay, well then…

"Congratulations on your position with The Unit. Well-deserved by all accounts." That last compliment was fishing. T-Rex hadn't confirmed that they were from a Delta Force team.

T-Rex didn't answer in any way, just lifted his plastic bottle and swallowed the contents down.

He takes the concept of "the silent professionals" to the extreme, was her first thought. Her second was, *if we run into danger, I'm probably on my own. He doesn't seem to like me much.*

Senator Blankenship patted Remi on the knee. She was obviously the touchy-feely type. Remi bet Blankenship liked to give hugs.

Remi, on the other hand, preferred physical distance unless the person was one of her tight circle of friends and family members. Like many of the special forces operators she reported on, Remi liked at least an arm's length of space; it offered her reaction time.

"Well done indeed, little lady," the senator said. "I pulled T-Rex there off to the side and asked him what happened out there with them damned birds." She batted her hand through the air. "I liked what he told me about your actions. Clever, brave. Yep, I like that, sets a good example for other women to stand up and not be the shrinking violet type. These girls saw a woman running into the fray instead of just men-folk. 'Course you'd have to be courageous to be out there reporting under fire the way you do. Rare bird, if you don't mind my play on words."

"Thank you, ma'am."

"You're not my usual gal."

"No, ma'am, I was assigned because I'm familiar with Lebanon."

"Remi Taleb." The senator elongated her name as far

as she could, stretching each vowel out like a rubber band. "Yep. I know you by way of reputation. Taleb—seeker of knowledge. Seems like an apt name for someone in your profession. Out of curiosity, how much do you make putting your life on the line like you do?"

Remi hitched a thumb toward T-Rex. "Oh, about as much as your security guys but without the added perks." She caught his eye.

"Perks?" T-Rex asked.

"Housing. Shopping in the PX."

"You want to stock your cupboards with MREs?" Diamond asked.

"They're expensive on Amazon." Remi shrugged. "I eat them all the time. I have cases of them in my apartment. When I get an assignment, I shove some in my backpack, fill my camel water bladder and head out."

"Moment's notice," T-Rex said.

Remi thought she might start counting the man's syllables and see how high he could get in a single sentence. So far, four was about average, she'd guess. Maybe fewer.

"When a story strikes, it's not going to wait around for me," Remi explained. "I have to be there. It's grab and go. No event is going to wait patiently while I take my sweet time."

"You know," Blankenship said. "I think you're the right kind of gal to be on this trip with me. I've read one of your pieces. You're the reporter that brought the boom down on that Ackerman fellow."

"I tried. Ackerman was found not guilty."

"Don't get yourself down on account of a military tribunal. Your work had its impact. It made me sit up and take notice. When I found out you'd be on this trip with me, I thought, I'd like to buy that gal a drink if it were allowed. I know how you journalists are sticklers for ethical conduct. Just know, I read that article, and it got me to thinkin' about how I could help my fellow women bypass the crap and reach their potential. I've put together a proposal that I'm working to gather bipartisan support—it's an everybody issue. Who could possibly be pro-rape? Actually," she paused to wrinkle her nose, "a surprising number of my male senators seem to shy away from anti-rape legislation. Makes you wonder... Anyway, I need to get the word out because there's a SEAL in Texas, not going to name names, but he thinks he's all that and a bag of chips, as they used to say—can't keep up with the lingo, I shouldn't even try. It's like my grandma trying to wear a ruffled bikini to the beach. Not a good look." She gave Remi a broad wink.

Remi was a little confused by the senator's disordered ideas. This wasn't linear conversation but a scramble of connected thoughts. It's not how the eloquent senator had spoken on tape.

The plane jostled and dropped, then lifted again.

Remi squeezed her eyes shut.

The pilot came over the speaker, "Ladies and gentlemen, please remain seated with your safety belts on. We're going to be flying through turbulence for the next, oh, twenty minutes or so. I hope to get us above this air current and get you more comfortable at that point."

At that point. Ugh. Remi's whole body felt clammy and overly hot. She unwound her scarf and put it in the seat pocket in front of her, then reached up to adjust the air so it would stream toward her face.

"T-Rex." Blankenship leaned across Remi, taking up Remi's personal space and making her claustrophobia that much worse as the plane slid down another gust and back up again, roller-coaster-like. Remi had to focus hard so she didn't do something outlandish in a bid at self-preservation, like punch the senator in the nose.

"Yes, ma'am?" T-Rex said.

"Which branch of the military brought you to your present duty? Master Chief. You came up the ranks through the Navy?"

"Navy SEALs, ma'am."

"When you were a SEAL, Master Chief, were you a number or a color?" Without her cowboy hat on her head, the senator had an interesting look. Her hair was plastered down at the top, ringed by a wreath of wiry grey curls.

"I started off in SEAL Platoon One, Bravo, ma'am."

Oooh, eleven syllables. A personal best.

"And from there?" Blankenship asked.

"From there, I advanced, ma'am."

Blankenship chuckled. "That answer has the makings of a future politician."

"That's not something I'd be interested in pursuing, ma'am."

"No? Tell me, what do you envision in your future?"

"Tomorrow, we'll be escorting you to your speech in Oxford. The day after, we'll deliver the young women to Iraq, and then we'll move on to Lebanon."

Blankenship nodded. "All the makings of a politician." Blankenship leaned even farther across Remi's lap. "So you knew Ackerman, did you, T-Rex? That's where he's from, Platoon One, Bravo."

"We went through Hell Week together."

"He caused quite the stir in my committee meeting. That kind of behavior is reprehensible." She lifted her brows and dropped them. "Now, don't get me wrong, I liked to kick up my own heels from time to time. In terms of the alcohol, I get that. Finding a warm body to give a soul some comfort. That's human, isn't it? It's not like I'm a prude." She caught and held T-Rex's gaze. "I think if a man has a lot of testosterone, it has to get released one way or another. Consensual sex. I'm all for that. Even the naked dancing around the campfires? Psh. No harm, no foul as far as I can tell."

T-Rex locked his muscles into a form of parade rest. This was a conversation that he, obviously, didn't want to have.

"The other stuff, though, is mighty disturbing. Drug abuse, violence, murdering Afghan citizens? The dehumanization of our fellow man. And women. And children. Granted, most of us only know about SEALs—you're not with the SEALs now—but The Unit scoops from the same pool. I'm sure it's just more of the same."

T-Rex swung his head around to see if anyone around them was listening.

Remi did the same. Thankfully the girls around them looked engaged in their own conversations.

"Pressure to be super-human. I don't see a cure for that. Hollywood makes y'all out to be infallible. But in the eyes of God," Blankenship pointed toward the heavens, "we are all his children, and children are known to mess up a time or two." She stuck her pinky in her mouth and dug something from her tooth. "I'm forgiving, as I said, about drink and fornication as long as it's kept personal, not public." The senator stopped, shifting her gaze to Remi. "It was you who wrote that article that got SEAL Platoon Bravo recalled home. The one that got our boys in a twist with the law."

"I wrote an article about the incidents, yes, ma'am." Remi thought that question had already been asked and answered…

"You'd be wise to keep your nose clean with this

little gal running at our heels." Blankenship raised her brow toward T-Rex.

Before he could slip in his "Yes, ma'am," the senator was back focused on Remi.

"Good job. Better out than in is what I like to say. Well, that's usually when a friend has had too much to drink." She laughed. "But better for an American to police their own rather than have this mess splashed across some less than advantageous news headline. Moscow or Turkey. China. People who could make hay of this."

Remi shifted her weight from hip to hip.

"Don't get me wrong. The press is in our Constitution because they play an important role in a democracy. I'm glad you wrote that story up. With you coming out with it first, it looks like we're vigilant and hold our soldiers to a high standard. For the sake of our reputation, I had hopes that Ackerman and the other one..."

"Gotwold?" Remi offered.

"Yep, that one. I had hoped they'd spend some time in the brig. And because they're heroes, they deserve psychological support along with that punishment. Yep. Eyes of the world on our special soldiers." She turned to face T-Rex. "Good thing you're so good looking, T-Rex. You're standing behind me in the photos means we can perpetuate that Captain America crap and broadcast it worldwide."

T-Rex looked uncomfortably at Remi.

The senator noticed.

"Mmmm hmmm." Blankenship pressed her lips together as she quirked the corner of her mouth up into a half-smile. "I can tell, this is gonna be a humdinger of a trip."

Chapter 12

Remi

Wednesday, London, England

"Thank god," Remi said aloud as she dropped her hotel key card on the table and her backpacks on the floor.

She turned around backward and flopped across the bed. She'd made it. They were in London.

Tomorrow was the speech in Oxford. A second night here at the hotel, then on to Iraq and Lebanon, where she'd get to see Jean Baptiste.

Remi pulled her phone from her thigh pocket, ready to call one of their friends to see if there was an update on anyone from the FR-13 team. Scrolling through her texts and missed calls, Remi discovered that an overwhelming volume of communications had come through while en route. Remi figured if she called one, she'd have to call them all.

She was just too tired for that.

Remi set her phone on airplane mode.

She'd start returning messages tomorrow.

Exhausted from holding her muscles braced on the plane for eight hours, then the extra scrutiny paid to her when she was moving through customs because of the kinds of stamps she had in her passport, Remi had been left behind by the senator's team.

She made it to the hotel on her own.

Noted: Keep up or adios.

Remi was relieved, actually. She needed a little space to decompress.

Having dragged her tunic over her head, Remi unclasped her "utility belt" before she forced herself up and to the bathroom. She wanted to get cleaned up before she fell asleep there on the comfy mattress.

It was luxurious to pull off her shoes and tights and just let the cool air brush over her bare skin.

She stood there in her panties while she drew a bath, looking in the mirror.

Thinking back over her flight, sitting across the aisle from T-Rex—he was the epitome of the strong silent type. She'd gotten nowhere in learning about him. She bet he wasn't thrilled to be here. A lot of travel without much adrenaline. It didn't seem like his kind of gig.

She bet he was magnificent in action.

And then a vision of him in bed, sheets draping over his muscular thighs as he pumped his tight hips. *Whew.* Not the action Remi had originally been considering—running through the jungle Rambo-style. But yeah, she bet he was magnificent doing the horizontal rumba, too.

When was the last time she'd made love to a man? Remi tried to remember. It was August now…months?

Yeah, back in May. She'd been assigned to Cairo.

That cute Egyptian studies grad student from Berkeley was there. Excited about life. Clean cut and innocent. That had been nice.

He was twenty-three years old and never seemed to tire in bed.

Remi traced her hands over her breasts, turning this way and that in the mirror. Almost forty…not bad. She was holding it together pretty well. She lifted her breasts and let them go, testing the effects of gravity. Hmmm. Not much of a change from her own graduate days. This was one of the benefits of having an active job. Lots of hiking, hefting equipment, running for her life…

She turned and looked at her butt. She liked the cut of these panties; they made her legs look long and seemed to give her curves a little extra oomph.

Things were still toned, her skin still tight. Stomach flat.

She slipped her fingers under the elastic on her panties, letting them slide down her leg. She used her big toe to work them the rest of the way down past her ankle, so she could step out of them.

When she climbed into the tub, she lay back against the ceramic, her shoulders curved forward. Brrr.

The water was cooler than she wanted it, too. Remi leaned forward to adjust.

Here, the water pressure was almost non-existent. Probably everyone showering for bed at once.

But it was just enough to… Remi propped her heels on either side of the tub. Scooting her hips all the way forward, she let the hot water sluice between the folds of her labia and thrum her clit.

She wiggled her hips to find a more comfortable way to hold her body.

With closed eyes, Remi let her head hang back. Sooo

good. This was what she needed—an orgasm to let go of her tension so she could get some sleep.

Tightening her muscles to gather energy, her mind was back on T-Rex. The size of his hands. The breadth of those shoulders, his pecs… Just. So. Good.

So. Good.

Remi let her jaw drop as she panted and groaned, building, building. And then a mild mini-orgasm. Hmph. She guessed it did its job of releasing her travel tension, but it did nothing to soothe her libido.

Her imagination of naked T-Rex was still there front and center in her mind.

With a discouraged sigh, Remi splashed water over her face and body, climbed out, slid her feet back into her bathroom flip flops, toweled off, and went to grab her backpack to find her toothbrush.

It was ten o'clock London time. But Remi's body was still on an Ethiopian time clock where it was midnight already. Remi's lifestyle wasn't conducive to a predictable bedtime, but she tried to be in bed by eleven. Since she was heading on to Lebanon in a day, there was no point in trying to acclimate to Greenwich Mean Time.

Remi moved through her nightly chores. "Set yourself up for success" was the mantra she used each night while organizing for the next day.

She opened her personal backpack and pulled out tomorrow's outfit. Same as today's.

A pair of cotton underwear and a sports bra since she was more likely to need to run than seduce a man.

A pair of socks were hidden below the edge of her shoes.

Black. Everything on this trip was black. It meant she didn't stand out. It also meant that everything matched.

The only source of color would be her scarf. Remi chose a beautiful peacock-colored scarf for tomorrow.

Wandering back to the bathroom to grab her shoes, she lined them up neatly under the table. They were comfortable European walking shoes. She could efficiently run, hike, and climb in them. They were quickly on and off when she wanted them to be, but they were also very secure. Once she'd found these shoes, she'd bought ten pairs. Then she'd taken them to a specialized East Indian cobbler who added steel toes.

Out on assignment, Remi had had enough toes broken to know to protect her feet—donkeys, falling rocks, aggressive stomping men. Yes, Remi had learned that if you can't walk, you can't chase a story.

With the new toes, the shoes were a little less comfortable. A little heavier.

You take the good with the bad.

Besides, they made "wicked good" weapons, as her Boston friend Calvin liked to say.

Remi didn't mind giving a quick kick to get herself out of a dangerous situation.

Next, she shook out a pair of black tactical tights. These, too, were reimagined on that trip to India. Now, they were long enough in the torso to tuck into her bra. This protected her from the utility bag rubbing and abrading her skin. It also helped her stay modest since her tunic slit went past her waist. The tights looked nice, Remi thought, under her tunics. The pockets were amazing and kept her functioning systematically.

With all of her organizational tools, everything had a spot, and she was meticulous that everything was in its correct place every time. Over the years of using a system, her hand would go to the right place and grab the correct item by muscle memory rather than taking up precious focus and time. This was a habit she'd learned from the special forces operators that she'd shadowed.

She moved her tactical pen, flashlight, and multi-tool to the new pants. They came in pretty darned handy this morning during the flock of birds incident.

Remi picked up her phone and sent out a quick text to Liu, "Did Jules keep his eye?" Man, it would be hard to be a photojournalist with only one eye.

A friend of hers was targeted by the American police during the protests earlier in the year. While filming on the West Coast, he'd taken a rubber bullet to the eye, and it had dislodged the retina. Two operations later, and surgeons couldn't get the retina to stay attached. There was still hope he'd keep his sight, but after this last surgery, that hope was dimming.

Remi looked at the ceiling as the sensation of disgust slid down her body.

Awful.

War reporting was inherently dangerous business. But domestic dangers weren't as typical.

Remi dragged her tunic out of the bag. That got a shake before she laid it neatly on the table to release the slight wrinkles.

Black, this too was a design that had evolved over time. And she had multiple iterations of them. Washed and stacked in her closet, all Remi had to do when she got the call to pack up and dash to the airport was to decide if this assignment required tan-colored clothing for camouflage or black for urban settings. She'd count off the number of days she'd be gone, lift that number from the pile, shove them in her bag with a like number of tactical tights, and she was basically ready.

In this design, the tunic sleeves had a good percentage of Lycra. The form-fitting sleeves kept people from grabbing the fabric and gaining control of her arm. It also gave her the most flexibility. The material used in the tunic construction was called CutPro and protected her against slashes. Outright stabbing? Probably not. But most attackers tried to slash you.

Bonus: it also protected against birds of prey.

Remi didn't have any injuries from the bird's talons, so that was a plus.

The tights, too, were made from CutPro and had saved her life. Once in Rome, some nut job tried to sever her femoral artery. Between the CutPro pants and the steel-toed shoes, she'd surprised the heck out of that guy. And he'd probably never be able to dig his balls out of his abdominal cavity after her adrenaline-fueled kick shoved them up there nice and high.

The tights had been designed with such a high waist band that Remi could tuck them under the band of her sports bra. The tunic slid over the top. The sides were slit all the way up to her bra line. The cut was purposefully made to allow easy access to her utility belt.

Remi had her survival gear packed into the belt. If she had to drop everything to fight and run, she would be running with gear. She kept practical things like hand sanitizer and tissues and life-saving things like a one-handed tourniquet and a packet of clotting cloth to press into bullet or stab wounds. Among other items, she included small mylar packages that held about a quarter cup of water in each. It was enough to clear her throat of smoke or help wash pepper spray from her eyes. And while she carried MREs in her pack, she was never sure if that would be with her, so she included a couple of meal replacement bars in her utility belt.

Adrenaline sucks calories.

And Remi couldn't run, leap, and climb to get the story if her limbs were shaking and weak.

Bonus, with the utility belt under her tunic, it thwarted pickpockets. And double bonus, it made her look like she might be pregnant, so men, in general, refrained from being too smarmy around her.

By having this uniform, Remi could whittle her luggage down to one personal backpack and one professional backpack with audio-visual recording equipment, a tactical computer, sat phone, and so forth. Remi chose cross-body backpacks because she could put them on, balance the weight, still access her utility belt, and keep her hands free.

Having your hands available at all times was a survival habit that Remi learned early on and took very seriously.

Her clothing and equipment choices were nothing like how she'd started life as a journalist. She'd honed her way down to these very specific items that were on her body.

She'd developed her habits. Some of them took longer to get used to than others. For example, she had her bedtime shoes.

Remi love being barefooted. *Loved it.* But bare feet were a luxury.

In the shower or bath—no matter where—she'd learned to wear her shoes. In the bathroom, she wore a pair of bright pink flip-flops. When she stepped out and dried herself off, she pulled on a pair of black cotton ankle socks and her bed shoes. These were a pair of lightweight tennis shoes that were given a bit of extra weight when she'd had that cobbler in India add the steel-toed reinforcement. Remi only wore these shoes at bedtime to keep the sheets clean.

Honestly, she hated them.

But the alternative was much worse.

Remi had been in too many situations where the alarm went up, and she was running for her life. She'd burned her feet. Cut her feet. Had her toes trampled by others.

Yup, comfort was for folks who lived serene lives.

Remi slept in her bed shoes. She also wore a cotton thigh-length night shirt. Over this, she strapped her survival utility belt—running for your life meant needing life-saving supplies. To do that, Remi had to learn to sleep on her back. Remi had read in an article it was best for keeping the face wrinkle-free. So you take the good with the bad.

Dressed for bed, morning outfit set out. The last thing she did was glance over her journalist backpack. For no precise reason, Remi pulled out her wrist braces and made sure they were secured into the side mesh pocket of the bag, ready for an easy grab and go.

They were her weapons of choice since journalists weren't allowed regular kinds of weapons.

Would she need them here in London?

Doubtful.

But then again, if anyone had asked her if she'd be attacked by massive birds of prey that would hospitalize her photojournalist, Remi wouldn't have considered that a viable threat either.

Live and learn: Always be prepared.

Who knew what tomorrow would bring?

Chapter 13

T-Rex

Thursday, London, England

As soon as they landed in London yesterday, the students and their chaperones went their own way. The robotics competitors had loaded onto buses at the airport. The London-based kids were back home and hosted the Iraqi girls' team for the two nights they'd be in London. During the day, the girls would be on bus tours of the city.

It occurred to T-Rex that it wouldn't be hard for one, some, or even all of the girls to ask for asylum or go underground.

Honestly, if it were T-Rex and he was a young woman anywhere near ISIS, he'd take the risk to have a chance at not just surviving but thriving in a country that allowed for women to have egalitarian footing. He'd seen up close and personal just how difficult survival was for the girls under ISIS.

It would be like the long list of Olympic athletes who grabbed the opportunity to escape their regimes as soon as they set foot in the host country.

It would make headlines. It could also make waves.

T-Rex was agnostic about that idea.

The teens were strategic thinkers; they knew their circumstances best.

If the girls reached for the brass ring, Remi would report that out, he had no doubt.

She had her job. T-Rex had his.

T-Rex had grabbed a couple of hours of shut-eye on the plane yesterday. And had a power nap last night before picking up guard duty in the early morning hours when he relieved Havoc outside of the senator's hotel room door.

Havoc got in what sleep he could but was in the gym now.

T-Rex lifted his watch. Another fifteen minutes and T-Rex could eat, take a quick shower, and dress in a suit. T-Rex hated suits. Hated them. But his tactical suit was better than most. At least it was cut for his athletic build.

Ty and Rory had already taken off in one of the cars, heading to Oxford, where Senator Blankenship was expected later this morning for her speech on global initiatives to get girls into STEM subjects and careers. Rory would search the venue to make sure there were no surprises. Rory was trained to find explosives. So guns, bullets, anything like that, Rory would sniff out in advance. He was a force multiplier when it came to protection with a small team.

Ty and Rory would guard the auditorium until T-Rex and Havoc escorted Blankenship on site.

Sitting around making plans last night, it was decided that once Blankenship was in the building, Ty and Rory would sit in the car. Protocol said that a car was always ready, engine running, outside of the exfil. In an event, they could just put their principal's head down and run them to the vehicle, load them up, and zip them out of the threat area.

The other armored cars supplied by the embassy would be parked behind Ty and Rory. The job of the other vehicles was to block while the principal's car got away.

T-Rex was glad to have had some time at the training loop before coming. Refresh the muscle memory for driving on the left-hand side of the road, even if it was just for this leisurely commute from London to Oxford and back.

Standing here in the empty hotel hallway while everyone slept, T-Rex had time to think.

A lot of that time, he was thinking about Remi.

On the plane, Blankenship, Diamond, and Remi talked about women's lives in the refugee camps.

"You've read Remi's articles, haven't you, T-Rex?" Blankenship had asked him.

T-Rex didn't want to get pulled into a conversation. Personal protection wasn't supposed to be "personal." They were supposed to follow along, ready to go kinetic should a need arise, not be distracted by conversation.

There was a truism that attraction equaled distraction. And Remi was proving to be problematic. He'd had trouble pulling his eyes away from her during his first assessment. Good thing this was a short gig. Six days and done.

Of course, that's what Ty had been told about his assignment with Kira. Less than a week, and Ty would be done, moving on to the next assignment. Ty had moved on to the next mission but definitely hadn't moved on from Kira.

Maybe after T-Rex was relieved of this assignment, he might reach out to Remi… *She* was rarely in the States. *He* was rarely in the States. He let the idea of seeing Remi outside of the scope of his work slip on by.

"The articles?" Blankenship repeated.

"We were given a packet of articles as part of our threat assessment."

"Threat assessment?" Remi raised her eyebrows. "Wow."

"That's not personal. We follow protocol."

Man, she was amazing in a crisis. Calm, thoughtful, pragmatic. She used what resources she had. She prioritized. No ego. No back-patting. No tears.

Badass.

Someone's morning alarm buzzed a couple of doors down, pulling T-Rex back from that memory.

Showers could be heard through the thin walls, despite this being a five-star hotel.

Remi would be getting up soon, showering. T-Rex's brain offered up some tantalizing images of that. He had a movie playing of her using the shower head to pleasure herself.

A door popped open to his right. T-Rex swung his head in that direction.

And there Remi was.

His heart pounded in his chest at the sight of her. He made sure that his eyes identified her, gave her a curt nod, and slipped away. He kept his body in the neutral stance he held while guarding doors.

Remi lifted a hand as she passed by. She wasn't heading for the elevator. She walked all the way to the window at the end of the corridor and all the way back, pacing the hall.

She wore the exact same thing she had on yesterday, only with a green scarf today. Same shoes, same everything. But clean. No bird feathers, rust, or filth. This must be her uniform, just like he wore the khakis and black polo for travel and guarding hotel doors.

This next time she passed by him—ignoring him completely—T-Rex saw that she had her phone in hand. A cord ran from the cell phone to a headset. The mic sat just in front of her lips, and she spoke in a low tone.

Stress slicked off her body. She tugged the scarf from around her neck, letting it dangle from her hand, dragging it along the floor behind her.

In the team's planning session, they had speculated that Remi had linked onto this trip with the senator so she could get to Beirut and see her friend Jean Baptiste who had been tortured by ISIS. Maybe she was getting information about her friends.

As he watched Remi pace, she seemed to be making her way through a list of call-backs. Call, talk, bye, and on to the next.

T-Rex wasn't trying to eavesdrop—and she spoke low enough that he couldn't even if he wanted to. The thing he was picking up now was how easily she shifted from language to language, dialect to dialect. The names Jean Baptiste, Marie-Claude, and Éloïse were mentioned in almost all of the conversations. Sometimes someone named Liu and a few times Jules.

T-Rex made a mental note to ask how the photographer was doing when they had downtime.

She kept moving up the corridor, her face strained. T-Rex would think that she was getting bad news, but in her line of work, it was all bad news, wasn't it?

As Remi passed him, she put her hand over her mic and tipped her chin up so she could catch his gaze. "Jules, the photographer, lost his eye. He's in surgery for his shoulder."

T-Rex nodded. "I'm sorry for your colleague."

But she had already moved along, heading down the length of the hallway.

She had a soft voice that had too much breath. It made her sound like she had just been through something and was winded by it—life. She was winded by life. She sounded completely different on camera. When he'd watched some of her videos on YouTube to get a feel for her, Remi's on-camera voice was much more like the personality she projected. Strong, straightforward, intelligent. Unafraid. And yet, when she talked in what T-Rex assumed was her everyday voice, she sounded like she'd just come in from a run.

His focus as she passed this time slid to her left hand. No gold ring on her finger, Winner had said no love relationships.

He couldn't imagine that was true. A woman like Remi? She could have her pick…

No, that wasn't right. She'd have to narrow her choices to men who weren't afraid of being shown up—outsmarted, outmaneuvered. Yeah, you'd have to have worked the kinks out of your ego to survive being in a relationship with someone like Remi. Her bulb burned bright, and it would illuminate a guy's flaws. If you dated Remi, you'd have to be okay with that.

He'd caught a look in her eyes a couple times when Remi thought he couldn't see her. Curiosity had been directed his way—interest, maybe even desire. He'd admit it, that had lit a burner on his own imagination. Remi hadn't exhibited a moment of unprofessionalism on her part. He just had to make sure that was true of his conduct as well.

Four years ago, he'd buried his wife. He'd loved her, fought with her, adored her, been vexed by her, planned with her, hoped, prayed, cried, and made love to her. No one else. Not since they first went out as high school sophomores.

T-Rex had always thought he was a one-woman man.

When Jess died, intimate connection and all that went with it died with her.

That Remi was sparking the kinds of thoughts and feelings that he thought were closed to him… It was throwing him off his game.

Job.

I'm here for the job.

Maybe I could connect with her after this mission was complete, he thought, again.

Yeah, that wasn't probable. Both Remi and he ran into the fray in the hairiest places on earth. When would they ever be on the same continent?

Let it go, man. Just let this roll on by.

Remi stopped in the middle of the hall, sliding her phone into her thigh pocket. She leaned her head back and tugged the elastic from her hair. Then she pulled the headset off to untangle the cord from the strands. She stuck the headset between her knees as she slicked her hair back into a ponytail, stuck the headset back on her head, and continued her pacing.

Senator Blankenship popped her door open. She startled when she looked at T-Rex. Standing there with her hand on her doorknob, looking a little lost, maybe a little frightened with her eyebrows up in her hairline. Her wiry gray hair rioted out in all directions. The senator stared up the hall at Remi with an empty gaze, almost like she were sleep walking.

"Senator?" T-Rex wasn't sure that she wasn't having some kind of medical event.

Blankenship spun and looked him in the eye, then went back into her room.

Remi arrived by his side. "Weird," she whispered. "Is everything okay?"

That, T-Rex didn't know.

Chapter 14

Remi

Friday, Oxford, England

"On the way back to our hotel this evening," Senator Blankenship said, "I'd like to drive by the new embassy." She changed the subject abruptly away from the details of today that Diamond was reading off to her. "I need to make some time to come and give it a tour. Not enough time this go-round."

"Uhm, yes, ma'am." Diamond was sitting in the front passenger seat next to T-Rex at Blankenship's insistence.

He'd wanted one of them, either Remi or Diamond, to ride in the car Havoc was driving in tandem. T-Rex explained that having someone sitting next to him created issues with tactical driving.

"Psh." Blankenship had waved a hand in the air. "Now, you know nothing bad's gonna happen here. The

British people have no feud with America—not since the seventeen-hundreds. Well, eighteen-hundreds. Well, okay, not since World War I. We're fine. Diamond's my right-hand gal, and I need her. And how is Remi gonna write about me if she's in a different car? You tell me that, T-Rex."

After conferring with Havoc, a plan must have been formed because here Remi sat beside Blankenship, and Havoc seemed to be doing some blocking and trailing maneuvers that Remi hadn't seen before.

"Did I ever tell you, T-Rex, about a close protection guy I had once when I was traveling over to Afghanistan? Delta Force guy named Buzz—you know him?"

"No, ma'am. I don't believe I know anyone that goes by Buzz."

"Probably before your time. The last I was in Afghanistan was way back when things were just getting ramped up over there. But Buzz, Buzz was one of the first in your special group back in the day. I mean way back to the time when y'all tried to save them folks in Iran under Jimmy Carter. Big ol' fireball of planes out in the desert. Anyway, this guy Buzz was a hoot and a half. I thought his name was from his haircut or maybe some crazy fly tactic. Turns out, naw, his friends gave him that name because he was worried about his gal back home. Granted, he wasn't much to look at, and I saw a picture of his gal. You see those two side by side, and a person's gonna wonder how that worked out. Anyhow, one night on leave, he got drunk and went out and bought her about a dozen different personal massage wands, if you know what I'm saying. He took 'em all back to his barracks, where he passed flat out. One of his buddies saw them there and decided to put in the batteries and turn them all on. There was such a buzzing and whirring that everyone headed to his room to find out where all that noise was coming from. He's been Buzz ever since. To this day, I wonder what came of that man."

"Yes, ma'am." T-Rex looked into the rearview mirror and his gaze caught on Remi's. Held. There was merriment twinkling and warming his brown eyes that Remi hadn't seen there before—or imagined as possible in such a gruff bear of a guy.

It was a moment. Something happened in that moment. Remi would be hard-pressed, even with her vast collection of words and phrases, to explain it. It was like…

Like they'd aligned. Hmm, no, not the right words. And now that the moment had passed, it was too ephemeral for her to latch on to and mull.

T-Rex pressed his fingers into his tie. "Echo Actual."

He paused. Remi assumed someone was in his ear, though she didn't see the normal tell-tale wire running down his neck into his suit jacket. Usually, to Remi's way of thinking, an athletic physique dressed in a suit was a strange look. But this tactical suit did amazing things for the man.

"We're pulling into the loading zone now," T-Rex informed whoever was in his ear.

"Loading zone? What?" Blankenship released her safety belt and wriggled to the edge of her seat. "I'm not scampering in the back door like a thief."

"This is part of our protocol, ma'am." He pulled in next to the cargo elevator. A security guard was standing to the side with a clipboard in his hand.

Havoc had pulled in alongside. The two operators stood outside of the car conferring, then Havoc opened the door for Blankenship and held out his hand.

Blankenship swatted his hand none too gently.

Anger ranged across her face, and Remi was paying close attention. Here was a new side of Blankenship. Remi pulled out her phone and pressed the video record button, sliding it into the breast pocket on her tunic that was precisely the right depth to hold just the aperture securely above the fabric. Remi checked that the video was functioning then lightly adjusted her scarf to obfuscate it. If she wanted to catch people acting naturally, they needed to forget her role. This video wasn't going to be the quality she'd need for a news feed, but it would provide her with research information and correct quotes.

"Ma'am," Havoc said, reaching out again. "We're tasked with your safety. Protocol includes—"

"Drive me around front where I can be seen entering the building like a lady. I'm not some tramp that you bring in and out the back door."

Diamond's eyebrows shot straight up in surprise.

So not a typical display.

"Ma'am," T-Rex's voice was soothing, "we don't have parking access on the street at the front door. It's quite a ways away. Because of the weather, we were offered these two parking spaces to bring you into the building in comfort. As soon as you're settled, our team needs to move the vehicles back outside onto the street, where they'll remain until your departure."

Blankenship—her face red, her lips drawn down in an obstinate frown—sat back in her seat, crossing her arms over her chest. "I don't like the idea of sneaking into a building like a common thief. I want to walk in and out of the front door where I can see folks, and they can get a picture with me. It's about diplomacy."

T-Rex didn't budge from his directives. "Protocol, ma'am."

"Four syllables," Remi muttered.

"It's too far to walk in the drizzling rain. We don't want your signature hat to be ruined on your way in," T-Rex said.

"My hat?" She reached up and adjusted the brim. "Well, now, that's something altogether different. It's drizzling?" She sent her gaze toward the exit.

Diamond exchanged a worried glance with Havoc as Blankenship shifted herself out of the car.

They'd driven with the windshield wipers on the whole way. How did Blankenship not notice the light rain?

"Alrighty then, mount up and let's ride on," Blankenship said, whirring a hand through the air and shooting a grin from Havoc to T-Rex.

It seemed to Remi that Blankenship had had a crack in her otherwise "Aw-shucks, let's be neighborly" demeanor, and maybe she'd just seen the true Blankenship peek out for a moment. But that moment had come and gone.

Havoc positioned in front of the senator, T-Rex slightly behind and to the side. They walked toward the guard at the elevator.

Remi had had her eye on that guard. He'd had his head down and was slyly watching them from under his lashes. And the thing that Remi observed was that he had an air about him of expectation. *Gleeful* expectation. He was a small man with a pronounced beer belly and weak-looking arms. Remi put these two things together—he was going to challenge the Delta operators, and he would win.

Wouldn't that just stroke the man's ego?

The elevator guard ducked his head and rolled his lips in, trying to hide a smile.

Havoc walked up to the elevator and reached out to press the button.

"This elevator isn't available to the public."

"Thank you. United States Senator Blankenship is a guest and was told to come in through this entry," Havoc said evenly.

The guard looked over his roster. He took an exaggerated amount of time. His countenance shifted slightly, now he was nervous. Whatever had been in his mind, he was about to play it out. *Here we go*, Remi thought, directing the camera in his direction. Her press credentials hung around her neck.

"Press isn't the senator." A smug wobble to his lips, almost a sneer.

"That's fine. I can find my way up from the front." Remi stepped back. By making this a non-issue, she stole some of the energy from his power play.

"She's not the senator." The guard pointed his chin at Diamond.

"She's my right-hand gal." Blankenship reached back and grabbed Diamond's arm, and dragged her forward. "No need for folderol. We'll just wing on up and give the lecture."

"You may use the elevator, Senator."

"The senator will go nowhere without her security team," T-Rex said evenly. "If there's a problem with that, I'll have the embassy reach out to Oxford's chancellor and have it cleared up. Your name, please?"

"The senator and her security may use the elevator."

Remi turned toward the bay door. "See you in a moment," she said, glad that she was wearing flats. This was going to be a hike.

Diamond, on the other hand, balanced on needly heels with pointy toes that squeezed Diamond's foot into the shape of a pizza slice.

Remi pulled out her phone, put her Google maps on "walking," swiped, and adjusted until she had a mental picture of where she was heading. With the phone back on video mode, Remi slid it back into her breast pocket.

"Petty. That is a man who feels powerless," Diamond said loudly enough that her words would easily carry through the echoing garage.

Though Remi had shortened and slowed her gait to accommodate the senator's aide, Diamond was already out of breath as they turned onto the sidewalk.

Walking together toward the end of the block, around the corner, they now started their trek toward a door. As they walked, Remi reviewed the exchange. Something about that trade of words hit her wrong.

A familiar feeling settled in her gut. *Heads up. Pay attention.* On autopilot, Remi reached to the side of her backpack and pulled out the hand braces made to support her wrists after long writing spells.

One of Remi's best and most used make-do weapons-at-the-ready were these wrist braces. They covered her hands from fingers to mid-arm, Velcroing shut, a metal bar helped hold Remi's wrists in a neutral position. If she needed to strike someone, she did it with the inside of her wrist, where the bar was solid and protective. She could also deliver a wicked palm strike that would easily break a nose or teeth. It wasn't much when faced with a bomb or a gun, but it gave her a little bit of comfort.

But something in her subconscious had dragged them from her pack.

Head on a swivel, it was a military caution, but she'd made it her own.

Remi picked up her pace a tad, hoping Diamond would do the same. Using the windows of the cars and the building to search the area, Remi tried to assess based on her many years around situations that were tinder looking for a spark.

How could that be true here in Oxford?

Was anything amiss?

Remi simply didn't have a good read on the area—what might be expected, what would be concerning.

A fair number of people loitered in the greenspaces without holding conversation, without really anything visibly giving them a reason to simply stand dotted around the mist-moistened sidewalks, the drizzle having stopped for the moment.

Everyone was about the same age, say mid-twenties. Remi might have chalked that up to this being a university. What made her question the scene was the uniformity of their male gender and their clothing choice of long sleeves that seemed too warm for the day.

Remi's clothing was certainly too hot for her, though it was in the mid-seventies.

Why hoodies in August? Was this paranoia?

Too little sleep for worry about Marie-Claude and Éloïse?

Something was making her body respond with adrenaline. Heat began as a point just below her ribs, radiating out until she felt engulfed.

Tugging at her scarf to loosen it around her neck as she climbed the marble steps, Remi reached for the handle at the front door. Dragging it open, she let Diamond walk through as Remi sent one last glance around. Her instincts told her to call T-Rex, and yet what would she say, "I'm hot. My lips are buzzing from adrenaline, no clue why"?

She'd been out with the military before when she'd heard soldiers over the radio sharing their gut impression. They'd communicate something like: "The little hairs on the back of my neck are saying something's off." It was an acceptable and important piece of information.

But Remi hadn't forged a relationship with T-Rex—the kind where they knew they had each other's backs.

When she thought that, Remi noticed a tiny voice from the back of her mind whispering, *"I'd really like that."* Trust between them. Support between them. Remembering back to last night's fantasy in her bath, Remi acknowledged, yeah, she'd like to take her acquaintance with T-Rex Landry a step further from fellow professionals to…what would she call it? Soothing her curiosity?

"Unfortunately, that's not what we have between us," Remi muttered. *I'll just have to navigate this scene on my own.*

Maybe once the team was together again, Remi could show T-Rex the video she'd recorded on her walk to the front.

T-Rex could draw his own conclusions.

When Remi passed through the double doors, she felt relief. Remi's prickles subsided.

She stopped at the map on the wall and found the elevator.

"Are you okay, Diamond?" Remi asked, watching Diamond yank at her skirt and smooth her jacket.

"Is there a ladies' room on the way?" she asked, peering at the map.

Remi pointed at the level of the lecture hall, traced her finger from the elevator halfway down the corridor, tapped, then traced further to show the entrance where they'd surely find the rest of their group.

"Good, just between us girls, something got me spooked out there. And now I have to go!"

Chapter 15

Remi

Thursday, Oxford, England

Remi stood another moment at the map. The guard down at the garage was still bugging her. Was it about power the way Remi and Diamond had read the interaction? Or was it something else?

Was the guy trying to split the team? Did that make sense? Not really. But Remi had learned to trust her instincts, and she was rattled.

Play it out, she thought. If the guard split the forces, the senator was still guarded by two Delta Force operators, and upstairs there was a third one with a K9, though what Rory was trained to do hadn't been spelled out for Remi. And wouldn't be, she well knew.

The best practices in a case where she felt vulnerable was to do the unexpected. Take the circuitous route.

But as she studied the building map, Remi realized that the only way to get to the lecture hall was via an elevator.

Yes, there were two sets of stairs, but it would be a long slog to get up to the sixth floor. While Remi could do it, she knew it would be hard to convince Diamond to hike the stairs in those high heels and pencil skirt unless she gave her a really good reason.

Remi wanted to make an alliance with Diamond in the hopes that with a little trust and friendly vibes, Diamond might give Remi better insight into the senator, like what was up with the Jekyll and Hyde show down in the garage?

Remi pointed in the right direction for the elevator bank.

A janitor stood behind a bucket with a mop, another man with a rag stood beside him. As the two women rounded the corner, the shorter one slid his phone into his pocket and punched the "Up" button.

Diamond focused on her tablet and her to-do list.

Remi stopped at a distance. She hoped that he'd called the elevator as a courtesy. Four people and a mop bucket in a small space… Remi thoroughly disliked elevators. Again, she just had to suck it up and move through the discomfort. This was part and parcel of being out in the world collecting stories.

The bell dinged. The door slid open. The men didn't move. *Good.*

Remi and Diamond stepped on.

Diamond pressed the sixth-floor button, and the doors were sliding shut when the janitor stuck his hand in, stopping them from closing. When he crowded in, his buddy followed.

The door slid closed.

Immediately, the janitor on the left thrust a flier into the women's hands. Diamond stepped back, focusing down on what he'd handed to her.

Without looking at it, Remi shoved her copy into a pocket of her bag. The smell of bleach filled the air and made her blink and cough.

"You're a journalist, yes?" the taller janitor asked from behind the bucket.

Remi reached out and pressed the button for the next floor. *Yup, getting off.*

"You have a press bag." He pointed to the cross strap on her backpack. "Press" was clearly written in block letter patches that ran up and down the strap as well as across the back, clearly demarcated as a non-combatant. Her press pass hung from a lanyard around her neck.

She was clearly the press.

The elevator slowed to stop on the next floor.

Thank goodness.

The guy who had handed out the flier reached over, thrusting a key into the control panel and turning it to the right where it was marked "Off."

The elevator car stopped between floors with a thud.

Shit.

Remi's claustrophobia wrapped around her like a heavy weight, making breathing a task. Or maybe it was the thick bleach solution.

"Journalism is a lot like what they do at the CIA, I think."

This was similar to Jean Baptiste. His captors accused him of being with the CIA.

She shook her head, trying to force herself to the cogent thoughts part of her brain because right now, all she had was mush and fear.

"Are you CIA?" The bucket man reached down and lifted a bottle of ammonia.

Bleach and ammonia, when combined, created chloramine gas. In small quantities, it was an irritant. High gas concentrations in confined areas with little air circulation—oh, like an elevator—could lead to coma or even death.

"I'm not CIA, I assure you." She mustered while lifting her credentials, making sure that the camera took in the men's faces. If she was going down, she wanted to make sure that the authorities knew how.

The guy raised a brow. "You're here with the oil drilling queen."

"What?" Remi asked.

"Blankenship is from Texas oil. Big oil money bought her place in the U.S. Senate, and oil will sustain her there as she helps destroy the world we live in."

"I'm here to report on the girls' robotic team from London. I have no connection to a story on oil."

The guy was unscrewing the cap on the ammonia.

Okay. Was that the plan? Gas the journo?

Remi was clawing through her memory, searching for a way out of this mess. Her gaze slid down their bodies, looking for weapons' bulges, but she saw none. Guns weren't easily accessed in the UK, but knife deaths were problematic. If he had a knife and Remi could get to it—

Talk. Just talk. As long as that cap stays on the bottle, you have time.

"Look, the CIA and others in the spy business have to behave ethically. They can't pose as medical workers, relief workers, or press. Why? It would endanger all of those helpers rushing in. The people setting up tents and supplying food and latrines, they'd be captured, tortured…"

"There were two CIA that were posing as journalists, and ISIS caught them."

Ah, see? If no other correlate existed in the two scenarios, this man had at least seen the news broadcast.

"Éloïse and Marie-Claude? Yes. They're colleagues of mine. They're journalists, that's it. Can you please turn the elevator back on and let us out? I'm glad to keep the conversation going outside in the hall." Her adrenaline was making her angry. Combative. But what she needed here was calm. And slow breathing to minimize the chemical irritants in her lungs.

Panic kills.

"Here is fine," the tall guy said.

"I'm a reporter. Is there something that you would like to say? If we get out, I'm glad to take notes and write up a report."

"You're a vulture, you know that?" the short guy snarled.

Was this a reference to the bird attack in Washington? No way they'd know about that here.

"You go in where people are suffering, and you take their pictures and exploit their pain. Blood money," the short guy snarled.

The bucket guy ran his tongue over his teeth and squinted his eyes at her.

"Look." Remi was having trouble breathing. The air was thick with the scent of bleach. Top that with her confined-space anxiety, she was battling through both to get out of this mess. "As a reporter, I think of myself as a first responder. Unlike your brave soldiers, I may not have a finger on the trigger, or an eye focused on a sight. I may not have the fire hose in my hands, but I am there with bullets whizzing over my head. I'm there with road rash from explosions, with other people's blood soaking into my shoes. I'm there as the real vultures are crouched in the sand, waiting for the death rattle to stop and the child to die."

"Snap a picture. Walk away. Exploit. That's how you make your money."

"Please, let's talk about this in the hallway." When neither janitor moved, Remi added, "I report what I see, so the aid workers know there's a crisis. We all have our roles to play. Mine is to be the eyes and ears for the world. To carry the information with me."

"What's it like to end up being part of the story yourself?" the tall janitor asked.

Remi looked up to catch his eye. "What does that mean?"

He pointed toward the fliers in Diamond's hands then started laughing.

"Calm down. Nothing's happening. We're just trying to get the senator's attention, is all." The short guy lifted the top off the ammonia bottle.

Was this a death wish? If they filled the elevator with gas, these men would be breathing it in, too.

Remi followed the shorter janitor's gaze down to the bucket, where she saw two sets of gas masks crammed between the bucket and the push handle.

This event had just turned that much more lethal.

Remi's mind whizzed through choices. She had a smoke hood in her belt. But no, it could be pulled away easily. They wouldn't allow her to keep it.

She could fight, but by the time she used any of her tools or tricks in this confined space—*confined space*—no, she couldn't take on these men in here. She had to get those doors open. It was the only way.

Emotions were like a daredevil's trick, revving the motors and powering up the ramp, flying out into the empty air, then came the descent. That's the point Remi was at now. She could either work the dynamic, or she would crash and burn.

Suddenly, fully formed, came the memory of the National Security Council meeting that she'd covered in Helsinki. A government official thought that a discussion with Russia was going off the rails. The woman told reporters that she had considered feigning a medical crisis by screaming toward the media to bring the event to a quick end.

While the woman had decided against following through, Remi was game.

"I have to get off. I think I'm having a heart attack." Her hand stretched almost to the panel where the key dangled from the insertion hole. But tall guy swatted her hand down.

Real-world, Remi's body was betraying her. She gasped and clutched at her chest. She leaned over, putting her hands on her knees, looking around wild-eyed and panting.

Her face slicked with an oily residue. The arm pits of her tunic and along her back were moist with sweat. She could feel dampness forming under her breasts and between her thighs. Heck, maybe she'd just peed herself.

Get control.

Diamond huddled soundlessly in the corner, watching.

The flier clutched in Diamond's hands said, "Oil is choking us to death."

A political statement with a deadly message. Yup, finding a journo and a senator's aide dead in a gas-filled elevator would do the trick, grabbing the world's attention.

But Remi would have to comply and die.

That wasn't going to happen.

"Air," Remi gasped. "Air." Banging into the wall to make a distracting noise, her hand shot out, quick like her childhood trick of snatching up flies. She failed to wrest the ammonia from the man's hands, but she did knock it to the ground.

The fumes comingling in the air might still be toxic, but they had to be less so than if the two fluids mixed, right?

The men both looked down at the puddle, and Remi took advantage by turning the elevator key back to the on position, dragging it from the hole, and tossing it into the bucket while simultaneously jamming her finger into the lit circle on the next floor's button.

Within seconds the door dinged. The men turned, exited the elevator, and bolted down the corridor.

Remi dragged her scarf over her nose and mouth even though she was holding her breath.

Reaching behind her, she hauled Diamond out into the fresh air. "Are you okay?"

Diamond opened her mouth and exhaled, then coughed. "Who knew I could hold my breath that long. That was crazy!" She stared after the men. "They're just plumb crazy."

Remi lugged Diamond along behind her as they made their way to the far staircase that Remi wished so hard she had just taken in the first place. When it came to cramped spaces, Remi couldn't distinguish between her intuition giving her good counsel and her phobia.

With her phone out, Remi dialed the UK emergency number 9-9-9 to let them know of the chemical spill.

Surely, it was toxic smelling enough that no one would dare get on the elevator.

But where did those men go?

Chapter 16

T-Rex

Thursday, Oxford, England

Remi finally arrived alongside T-Rex, where he stood in the wings of the stage.

There was a long pause in the senator's speech as the audience laughed at her latest punch line.

T-Rex sent Remi a scowl. She should be down in the audience, not here engaging him.

Remi was a big distraction on a personal level, and T-Rex hadn't gotten his head around his reactions to her. Both his mind and body had trouble turning away. For the first time in years, he was hungry to know a woman in all her dimensions. She was taking up brain space when he needed to be focused.

He didn't like it. Not here. Not now.

Maybe once things had wrapped up? That thought wriggled itself into his conscious, again, with a face bright with hope.

T-Rex pressed that possibility away. There was nothing for them. He was a Delta Force operator; she was a war correspondent. Not only would a relationship with Remi trigger a look at his security credentials—like Ty and D-Day had gone through. Beyond that, Remi and T-Rex's lifestyles and schedules weren't constructed to support an intimate relationship. Those thoughts came and disappeared in a flash. He'd been through them so many times since he first saw Remi that it had become a repeated riff.

Waggling her phone, T-Rex saw that Remi had a video queued up.

At first glance, he wanted to brush her off. She could show him her video later.

On second glance, the look on her face was similar to what he saw when she rounded into the hangar back in Washington after the bird attack. It was an expression that he'd seen on many a fellow soldier's face when they came in from a mission. A little bit shellshocked. A little exhaustion as the adrenaline left their systems. A little pale and clammy with eyes held too wide, searching for the next unknown.

He accepted one side of her earbuds she'd attached to her phone. She slid the other side into her own ear so they'd be hearing the video together.

Tapping the arrow to play the video, he quickly realized that this was a security breech. Diamond and Remi had been attacked.

Did this have wider ramifications to the senator's security, or was this a one-off?

He paused the video. "Are you okay?" His eyes scanned

over her front and back. She looked fine. Her skin color was paler than usual, but that was expected. She wasn't having difficulty breathing…

"Yeah, I think so."

Tapping the video, T-Rex watched Remi drag Diamond out of the elevator and get her into the stairwell, possibly saving Diamond's life.

Remi went up. Diamond went down.

"Where'd she go?" T-Rex asked.

"To sit in the car with Ty and Rory. That's what you told us, right? That when you guys got to the lecture hall, that he would go move the cars and stay there with Rory? She was too afraid to be in the building. She said she'll work on the senator's next speech there."

"I'm trying to get a read on what happened. How did they know to target you and Diamond?"

"Exactly," Remi said. "Security was with the senator. Diamond and I were alone. Was I targeted? I sincerely doubt it. They would have no idea that I'd be along. But certainly, the senator would travel with an aide."

Seemed like the clusterfuck of birds attacking the photojournalist that started them off on this assignment was going to color the whole mission. T-Rex wanted to stop that trajectory in its tracks. "Can I forward this to my team?"

"Sure." Remi took a breath and adjusted her shoulders.

Yeah, there was stress there. T-Rex bet Remi could use a drink and a massage. His mind sent him a picture of her tangled in the sheets, sweaty and sleepy with a contented smile—and he cut that thought off immediately.

"That was a close call," he whispered as he watched the scene unfurl a second time.

The video jostled as Remi jogged up the stairs toward the lecture hall. Along the way, she was dictating details and observations that wouldn't have been captured by the video in the elevator. The chemicals and their possible effects. The size of the containers. Descriptions of the men. All of that was important. Keen observation skills developed over her years in the field.

Standing behind the blue velvet curtain, T-Rex split his attention between the senator and the intelligence Remi was sharing. "What was the flier about?"

Reaching into her cross-body pack, Remi tugged a hot pink flier from the netting and handed it over.

He gave it a quick scan before he folded it and slid it into his suit pocket.

"After that incident in the elevator, I think we need to consider that the man down in the garage wasn't a security guard at all. He might have positioned himself there to split our forces and signal his colleagues." She shrugged. "A possibility."

T-Rex stood feet wide, arms crossed over his chest as he weighed her theory.

Remi scratched her thumb into her brow. "An aide, two aides, three? Didn't matter." She had gripped his bicep to balance herself on her toes as she whispered in his ear, brushing her breasts against him by proximity. The scent of floral shampoo filled his nostrils.

Focus, he had to admonish himself.

"The guy on the elevator basically spelled it out. Get the aide on the elevator, gas her. She's dead or close to it as they make their escape. Asphyxiation is the crucial point. Based on the flier, they wanted to make sure that someone died of the very thing they were blaming on the senator. But it feels like a red herring. I don't think that's what's going on here at all."

The video finished downloading to Echo's TOC. His fingers landed again on his tie as he pressed the button to open the communications. "Winner, you have incoming."

"It's downloading now," came through his earpiece.

"Oil is choking the world." He had read on the flier that Remi had handed him.

"A deadly political statement that was sure to be headlines across the world. 'If it bleeds, it leads' thought process," Remi explained.

T-Rex glowered. Diamond wasn't on his security list, but he certainly felt responsible for her. And for Remi. He needed to get the senator from the building, into the car, and back to the hotel without incident. "Diamond headed toward the cars?" he clarified.

Remi lowered her heels back to the ground as she nodded, then swiped her hands over his sleeve, relieving the wrinkles she'd created.

T-Rex depressed the comms button. "Echo two."

"Two. If you're looking for Diamond, she's jogging up the sidewalk toward the car, high heels and all."

"Copy. Put her in the back seat. Let her work. Don't let her talk and distract you. What are you seeing?"

"Nothing that's caught my eye."

"Out." T-Rex turned back to Remi. "Ty can see Diamond."

Remi scraped her teeth over her top lip.

"What are you thinking?" T-Rex noticed that she had stress splints on both her hands and wondered why.

"When we walked from the garage to the building, things felt off."

"Off." He repeated the word and let it dangle there so she'd fill in the blanks.

She took her phone back, queued up a video of her

walking out of the garage and to the front door. She played it on silent and at high speed.

T-Rex watched. "I can forward this?"

She nodded. Her eyes were on the senator, and T-Rex took a moment to do a scan before he focused on sending the video on. "Winner, we have a problem. Did intelligence say there was any chatter around the senator's speech?"

"Crickets."

T-Rex watched it again with a critical, assessing eye. Fighting-aged men dressed in brimmed hats that shadowed their faces and clothing styles that could conceal their identities. Clothing too warm for the day that could protect their skin from, say, chemical irritants. Too observant. Too fixed on looking in a single direction.

At this point, the problem was securing the senator and getting her to the cars. He could take Blankenship out a different door, but from the looks of this tape, the only exit that didn't have eyes and bodies was outside of the garage entrance.

"Winner. Do we have a real-time sky view of the building? Are the numbers still there?"

"I'm checking our satellite feed now. There's a group of, say, twenty who are gathering near the front door with placards. They've divided their groups, and it looks like they are covering all the exits."

The security guard this morning said the elevator to that exit wasn't available to the public. Ty said that direction was still clear. "The signs, are they environmental?" T-Rex asked. "Any chance you can see?"

"They tip them every once in a while—no, I can't really tell."

"They weren't about the environment," Remi said.

T-Rex caught her eye.

"The men on the elevator—I was dealing with some issues I have about confined spaces. I was focused on surviving the moment, so I didn't weigh all of the information. Reliving the situation through the videos, homing in on the accents, they sound Syrian."

"You sure? Hundred percent?"

"A hundred percent?" She shook her head. "But to my ear, yes."

T-Rex nodded. He'd kept his comms button pressed throughout this interview so TOC could hear what was going on, assess, and advise. "Winner?"

"On it."

T-Rex focused down on Remi. "Guesses on what's going on?"

"Uhm. Yeah. So the senator is heading to Lebanon to recommit to the United States' friendship with Beirut. While prepping for this assignment, I spoke to my contacts in the area to get their take on the senator's visit. In some pockets, there's a great deal of relief. However, the opposition doesn't want the senator to go to Lebanon to deliver the U.S.'s declaration of alliance."

"This is England."

"If they were to take out the senator or the senator's aide in London under the guise of 'big oil killing the planet,' then no one in the Middle East would deal with the ensuing ramifications, England would." She paused with a tip of her head. Her mind obviously whirring. "Do you remember that story out of Slovakia recently? There were all of those environmental scientists that were kidnapped. They were blaming it on that poor man with schizophrenia who thought the trees were talking to him. He needed to have been put in a hospital long before he was exploited. At least now he's getting the help he needs."

While he listened to Remi, T-Rex's gaze scanned for trouble. "What has that kidnapping to do with our present situation?"

"The Norwegian oil executive—the company's president—planned the kidnapping and set it up with a fall guy. The president—I can't remember his name right now, sorry—Ah! Got it. It's Edvin Odegaard. Odegaard was supposed to go in and 'save' the kidnapped victims from the bad 'eco-terrorists.'" She put save and eco-terrorists in air quotes. "To be the hero. That would bring good publicity to him and his company. But instead, he was arrested by the Slovakians and tossed in jail. He's awaiting his trial."

"Okay, I remember that story on the news. I'm not following why you're bringing it up here." T-Rex furrowed his brow. With every word out of Remi's mouth, this mission was ramping up the danger quotient.

"I'm speculating that this might be yet another copycat. It's imaginable that a group wants to preempt the senator from going to Lebanon by causing a major crisis here in England. They blame it on environmentalists. An easy target. Just like last summer when fires were set in America. *That* was blamed on certain groups. But it turned out that all of the people who were identified and arrested for the fires were agitators looking to spark unrest. Many of them were linked to the Taylor Knapp video games and books—the ones that were psychologically engineered to foment anger and distrust in America."

T-Rex shot her a look, then turned back to his principal. Russia? That was who was behind the psyops with the video games. They were also behind an attack within Fort Bragg on his very own Echo team. Deadly dangerous. And yes, they liked to play mind games. That could very well be correct. It didn't have to be Russia, though they had a stake in the Middle East. Like Remi said, some group could just use their tactics as a blueprint.

"It's kabuki theater. The guy who split us at the elevator wasn't British. Nor were the guys in the elevator. And the men outside just don't look like tree huggers, if you know what I mean."

"Echo Six?" T-Rex called Havoc.

"Six." Havoc stood at the foot of the steps that would allow audience members up on the stage.

"When the clapping begins, we'll be following protocol Mongoose."

"Mongoose, copy."

"Out."

The speech was lasting an uncomfortably long time. The senator strayed from her prepared remarks to deliver her folksy stories that had the audience doubled over laughing. The senator was obviously thrilled by her reception. But every minute allowed the bad guys to get organized and in place.

T-Rex stared at Blankenship until she turned toward him. He made a lasso movement with his finger to tell her it was time to wrap it up.

She seemed taken aback, scowling at him.

Turning back to her audience, Blankenship closed with the remarks on the teleprompter.

The audience applauded, rising to their feet with appreciation. Havoc was up the steps, gathering Blankenship's things in one arm, putting his other hand under the senator's elbow, and guiding her off the stage to where Remi and T-Rex waited.

"Where's Diamond?" Blankenship asked, swinging her head around.

"She wasn't feeling well, ma'am," T-Rex told her as he set off in front of her.

Havoc continued to maneuver the senator along. "She went to the car to sit with Ty and Rory."

"Oh, okay. But what's the rush? Is it bad? Does she need to go to the hospital? You could have just sent her along. You don't need to be herding me in this little stampede of yours."

Neither man responded. They were in go-mode. Every sense focused on the task at hand.

"Echo Actual. Ty, we're coming your way."

While Ty sat behind the steering wheel of the lead car, the other two vehicles were left with the doors locked, engines running. In an emergency, seconds could make the difference between life and death. That was a lesson drummed into Echo team during their training with the Secret Service when they showed the tapes of their man racing toward Kennedy as shots rang out. Two seconds more, and the agent could have been in the car on top of the president.

Two seconds between life or death.

So they didn't mess around with things like starting engines. When they were close enough, they'd throw Blankenship into the back seat of Ty's car with her aide and Rory, fob the other two cars open, and jump in to assist with whatever evasive maneuvers were needed.

"Ty, you got anything going on in your direction?"

"My status hasn't changed. The cars are half a block to the north of the garage door. I parked on the far side of the street to make the passenger side accessible. The weather is clear. No other movement."

"We're working plan Mongoose."

"Mongoose. Copy."

"I'll be putting the senator in the back seat. Move

Rory if he's not up front with you. Clip him into his safety belt in case we need to make evasive maneuvers."

The senator sent him a startled glance and quickened her gait.

Yeah, she was getting it now. *This* was the dangerous part.

Chapter 17

Remi

Thursday, Oxford, England

They took the stairs rather than risk the elevator.

That made sense to Remi. If anything looked worrisome, they could push through any of these doors and race down the corridor. Possibly take refuge in an office space.

Yeah, Remi could understand this choice. It was what she liked to do, take an alternate route. What she should have done on her way up to the speech. Remi had an issue with following her gut at times. Her sense of safety was obscured behind her childhood traumas and the inevitable PTSD that came with the job—the reason why so many of her fellow journos self-medicated.

At first, she was confused why the team didn't call

for the building security to come and help them make their way safely.

But, on second thought—as she clattered down the stairs, last in line—they didn't know who was involved in the attack earlier. Perhaps their contact would act like a friend but actually, be luring them into danger.

They had a plan—even named it. *Mongoose.*

The senator was really moving. Remi hadn't thought this level of aerobic exercise was something she could do. But Blankenship was keeping up with her security force. Maybe she sensed that something was seriously up. The men were professional through and through. Their posture had taken on a lethality. The shift in comportment was vivid.

Remi rounded another landing, angling her body to keep from falling as she scuttled down the next flight. They were silent except for the clatter of shoes.

"Echo Actual. Echo Two, we're three minutes out."

She couldn't hear what Ty said in return.

Four more flights of steps, then they'd pop out of the stairwell door, cross the garage, out into the open. Three minutes, and they'd be powering up the road toward London and into the high-security hotel. Safe.

Three minutes.

Remi had been on enough dashes to safety. She might feel like a moron afterward, but she'd prep just the same. She checked that the Velcro was well secured on her wrist braces. If someone were slashing, her clothes would keep her safe, but if they were stabbing, she'd need to block the thrust.

Her scarf was whipped from around her neck. Remi didn't need anyone grabbing hold of it and using it to capture or choke her. That got balled up and stuffed behind her utility belt under her tunic. Another layer, lest she be stabbed. While she was there, she snatched her flashlight and her tactical pen, holding one in each hand.

Ground floor.

She took a deep breath.

Havoc slowly opened the door with his hand held up, indicating they should stop.

He looked through the crack. Taking his time, being thorough. With a nod, Havoc went through the door. T-Rex's boot stopped it from shutting.

Unstrapping her pack, she turned the senator toward her. "This is for your protection," she said, sliding the strap over the senator's shoulder, letting the pack cover the senator's chest, and belting it around her middle.

"It's heavy," the senator complained.

T-Rex sent Remi a quick quizzical glance, then continued to assess the stretch of space across the garage and out to their convoy.

Remi was watching the team's tactics with a keen eye. She never knew when something she picked up along the way would become a lifesaving technique in her repertoire.

Havoc made it to the center of the garage and looked around. He wandered to the bay door and scanned the streets. His hand went up, signaling to Ty that they were coming. Then he turned and gave T-Rex a hand signal to come on.

"Ma'am, we are going to move quickly but calmly through the garage, out to the sidewalk. We will be turning North. That's to the right." When he said right, he tapped the senator's right shoulder. "Right," he repeated.

He sent Remi a look. Checking in.

She gave him a nod. She'd heard. She'd keep up.

An overabundance of caution, that's all this was. A bad incident warranted this level of vigilance. The team was doing a thorough job. Into the cars, off they'd go.

T-Rex pressed his tie. "Echo Actual. Moving."

"Echo Actual" sounded so badass. No time for the libido to kick in, Remi told herself. Then she consoled herself with having about an hour's drive ahead of them where she could fantasize about T-Rex to her heart's content.

First, let's get into the car.

They were three steps into the garage when the elevator door opened. Crammed full of men, they raced to block the American's exit. One blew a whistle in three distinct blasts.

A signal. *Crap.*

T-Rex turned on a dime directing the senator back toward the stairwell.

As they did, the two box trucks parked side by side popped their back doors open, and groups of "protestors" leaped to the ground.

She'd seen those trucks earlier when they came in the garage to use the elevator this morning. Had they been packed full of men this whole time?

T-Rex pivoted, bent, scooping the senator over his shoulder. Lowering himself like a linebacker desperate to get a football over the endzone and win the game, T-Rex powered forward. He grabbed at people who came within his range and pushed or tossed them into their fellow goons.

Dangling like a rag doll, the senator clutched at her red cowboy hat.

T-Rex's head bobbed amongst the assailants as he forced his way through the crowd, rounding toward Havoc.

Remi was surrounded. On her own. The one thing she had going for her was that the men were focused on getting through Havoc to T-Rex and the senator.

Sliding a hand back under her tunic, Remi pulled out her range glasses to protect her eyes from chemical irritants or flying projectiles. She didn't want to find herself in Jules's state, blinded while reporting out a story.

As Blankenship might say, this would be a humdinger of a story.

She'd write it up later for Liu, but first, she had to get safe.

Briefly, she checked to make sure her video was recording from her breast pocket.

Getting herself out of this was all on her.

The men were fighting with Havoc, whose exertions gave T-Rex space to get free.

But now, some of the men were noticing her as she tried to sidle silently along the wall.

There was zero thought in her next actions. She was acting on instinct and fear. Her strobe flashed in their eyes. Her pen jabbed into thighs. Punches to throats. Knees to groins.

Hands came at her, grabbing, trying to get hold.

This was one of the genius design elements of her clothes. What could be grabbed was slick to the hands and stretchy with Lycra. Spinning, she'd found, was the best way to force someone to lose their grip. Her shoes were doing their job delivering kicks that put men on the ground.

Engines gunned out on the streets. They were racing off.

Had the team left her behind again?

Wow!

Remi redoubled her efforts. Her goal was to get out

on the street, in public view, and perhaps get caught under some security camera.

Her flashlight was knocked from her hand. She pulled her elbow back and thrust an open palm at the guy. The metal in her arm band slammed into his eye. He shrieked and peeled off.

"Remi! Now!" The growl came from her right.

Now! Okay…

She slid through the door up into the planting box that ran the length of the building. Filled with holly bushes, she snaked along the wall as she saw T-Rex in the last car. His head was bent looking back at the garage, driving forward just fast enough to keep the men's hands off the car.

She put her hands up over the bush.

He spotted her.

He gunned forward toward the crossroads.

Glad to be shielded by her work uniform and protective eyeglasses, Remi crashed along the line of prickle bushes to the end. Running as fast as she could, she wanted to be at the end of the planter by the time T-Rex turned.

As he wheeled forward, Remi realized she was a good five feet off the ground as the slope had given way.

With a massive leap, she fell to the sidewalk where she tried to land the way she'd been taught, like a drunk frog. She kept her ankles together, pressed her knees wide with impact, then toppled over and rolled a couple of times.

The commotion caused the elderly people sitting at the bus stop to look up with alarm.

T-Rex slammed his car to a stop just as Remi was popping up.

When he slowed, she grabbed the handle to the passenger's side.

The crowd was giving chase to the car. They, too, were trying to open the doors and crawl in. T-Rex's long arm shot out and grabbed Remi's wrist. He hauled her into the vehicle as his foot came down on the pedal.

The tires shrilled as their tread worked to grip the roadway. Remi faceplanted in T-Rex's lap, her legs dangled out the door.

She pedaled her feet, contracting her abs, pulling her legs in. She gripped at T-Rex's fancy pants. The Lycra in the fabric made it difficult to get a solid grip. Remi kept snatching at him, realizing that she was pinching up his skin as she did.

T-Rex reached to find something to hold on her. He met the same clothing issues as Remi had had grabbing him. After failing three times, he simply clapped his hand between her legs and jerked her inside.

A passing car hit the open door, effectively closing it as the driver blared his horn.

Just a second earlier, her legs had dangled out that door. That would have been a devastating blow.

T-Rex pushed her upright. "Seatbelt."

He was steaming ahead, catching up with the other two cars in their convoy. Ty was straight ahead of them. Havoc was in front.

After securing her seatbelt, Remi dragged her glasses from her face and tucked them into the utility belt under her tunic. Grabbing the assistance handle with both hands, she squeezed her eyelids tight. If she tried hard, she could just imagine this wasn't T-Rex and the Echo team trying to outmaneuver whatever strangeness was happening at the Oxford lecture hall today. No, she was at a theme park on some kind of wild ride. Fast. Stop.

Right. Left. *Just hang on. Don't scream, or your friends will think you're chicken. The ride will be over soon.* She tried to get her mind to go along with this storyline.

She jerked when she felt a warm squeeze on her thigh.

"You okay? Did they hurt you?"

She blinked her eyes open. T-Rex's gaze was sliding over her body head to toe then up again. "Do you need to go to the hospital?" He refocused on the highway.

Remi knew from experience not to just say, "Nope, all's good." Adrenaline can mask some pretty heinous wounds.

"Checking." The last thing she wanted to do was be a distraction. She started a visual scan as she compressed and tested her joints and limbs. She was tender all over. She had taken her share of blows back there. But they were to her limbs, not her head or torso, that would have made her more concerned.

T-Rex pressed his tie. "Echo Actual. Copy, Winner. Route C. Out."

After a moment, he glanced her way. "Hospital?"

"No. I'm okay."

"Protocol stipulates that we protect our prin—"

"You were doing your job. I get it. All of it. I'm fine. Just another day of being a journalist."

"Are you serious? That's what it's like?"

"Pretty much." Remi slid down in her seat. *Man, am I tired.* Events like that, especially moving through hostile crowds, always wore her out. If they'd just let her sneak her little press-credentialled ass out of the garage, it would have been fine. But it felt like she was targeted every bit as much as they had targeted the senator.

Remi had to assume the janitors let their friends know they'd failed. And Diamond wasn't to be found. So the focus was on her.

Remi thought the only thing that saved her was that people think they can do violence until they're confronted with the moment. Some of those men were fine beating a woman. Others, she'd realized during her escape, were trying to make a show of it. And she was grateful for those men. Not only did they not hurt her, but they'd tried to swarm to look like they were giving it their all. And in so doing, they'd blocked the really dangerous guys from getting her.

Dumb f-ing luck that I survived.

Chapter 18

T-Rex

Thursday, London, England

T-Rex stood outside of Remi's door, feeling uncharacteristically nervous. Fist lifted, he hesitated, listening to make sure he wouldn't interrupt a phone call, then tapped a knuckle lightly on the door jam.

Footsteps moved across the room. Remi stalled at the door; he assumed to check through the peephole.

"T-Rex," he said.

The bolt slid back, and the door swung wide. Remi, dressed in a nightshirt and bright pink flip-flops, swished her hand through the air to invite him in. He turned to shut the door softly behind him and to surreptitiously adjust his dick so it wasn't leading the way as he went to talk with her.

Yeah, she had nothing on under that nightshirt. Her

nipples were readily visible. The soft mound of pubic hair was a tantalizing suggestion. "I brought back the pack that you gave to the senator."

"Oh good, thanks." Remi was stretched out on her bed, her back propped against her pillows, her laptop settled back on her thighs.

"It weighs more than I'd expected." He walked farther into the room and laid it on the lowboy. "What've you got in there? Why did you give it to the senator?"

She hadn't offered him a seat. He felt awkward looming there above her like that. He leaned a shoulder into the wall. His dick throbbed uncomfortably under his suit jacket. He looked down to check that the button kept everything neatly out of sight.

"I pack typical journo equipment: netbook, camera, comms. Most of the weight comes from my press ballistic vest. I carry it with me whenever I'm out on assignment. I've had too many brushes with the unexpected to not show up prepared."

He nodded. He didn't like the idea of Remi in danger. Remi had proven time and again now that she was tactically smart, resilient, prepared, and capable. Still…

"Sometimes, I don't have time to get the vest in place, so I carry it lined up with the back of the pack. That way, in a situation that goes bad fast, I can pull the pack in front of me—head or torso—to give myself a little protection."

"But you gave it to the senator. Why?"

"I didn't realize that you were going to throw her over your shoulder. I thought she was going to be walking through the crowd. She was, I presumed, the target. I figured you'd help her navigate the rabble, and if anyone were to try to stab or shoot her, whatever…it could possibly help her get out of the situation unscathed." Remi stopped and swallowed.

"But you..."

"For me, working alone, the bag could create problems. With the straps, it's something that could be grabbed and held on to. If I had you helping to block, that wouldn't have been an issue. When I'm on my own, I've found the sleeker I am, the less they can grab and hold me and the easier it is for me to snake away."

He laid a hand over his heart. "I'm sorry."

"About what? Leaving me behind in the middle of a rabid horde?" She laughed. "Don't be."

"I wanted to talk to you about my conduct today." He felt his ears pink at the tips.

"I've been at this job for well over a decade. I'm going to let you off whatever hook you might think you're hung up on. You were doing your job, exactly what you were supposed to be doing."

T-Rex shook his head. He felt sick about what had transpired. True, he had one job, protect the senator. True, he'd been warned at the outset that he was not responsible for anyone else, and he wasn't to be distracted. He had one principal. He followed orders, even when he hated them because he believed in the chain of command.

"I liken it to the medical workers," Remi said. "Could I lend a hand and help the doctors and nurses working in the aid stations? Yes. Do they desperately need an extra set of hands? Yes. But then, I wouldn't be doing my job, which is to observe with sangfroid. To assess. To interpret what data I've gathered so others can better understand the circumstances. If I'm embroiled in the middle, it hurts my objectivity. Even if I want to, I can't involve myself. Other than, I suppose, doing something like shielding a child with a metal chair or offer the senator the protection of my ballistic vest."

T-Rex didn't know what to say to that. T-Rex's mom would call this little speech 'gracious.'

"We each serve a purpose, and I never expected security to be extended to me."

He nodded as he gathered his thoughts. "When you were getting in the vehicle, I grabbed you by… It was unfortunate."

"I'm not writing an article about you grabbing me between my legs. There was no other way you could have hauled me into the SUV. And right after that, the passing car slammed that door shut. So, if anything, I would like to thank you for not leaving me behind and then protecting my legs. I can't do my job if I can't walk."

"Or run away."

"Exactly."

"But you *are* writing an article about the incident?"

She canted her head, focusing curious eyes on him. *Was he going to ask her not to?* "I already wrote the story and submitted it to the Washington desk."

"So fast?"

"It was an hour's drive from Oxford to London. I composed it in my head on the trip back to the hotel. I dictated it into the computer, cleaned up the grammar, and sent it with the videos along to Liu, my editor."

T-Rex stilled. His heart pounded in his chest. They hadn't had a talk yet about making sure that she didn't take any photographs of the team. He'd never seen a camera in her hand before the Oxford incident, and with the photojournalist left behind, he hadn't anticipated it being an issue. "The faces of the team—"

She held up a hand. "I doctored the tapes, removing

the team from any frame. I'm not putting you in danger for zero reasons."

"Remi…can I sit and talk to you for a minute?"

She pointed toward a chair at her table. "Pull it over, so I don't have to yell. These walls are as thin as paper."

T-Rex brought the chair along the bed. He was sitting about where her ankles crossed; her naked legs stretched out long and shapely on the bed.

"First, I thought you'd like to know about the girl that you protected at the airport."

"Is she okay?"

"She needed stitches and antibiotics. She'll be fine."

"Good." She nodded. "Thanks."

"There's already been arrests from today's incident."

Remi reached for a notepad. With a pen poised, ready to take notes, she lifted her chin.

"They've arrested the three men you encountered at the elevators, the one down in the garage, and the two who were making the gas. Scotland Yard was able to put your video through their systems and pop up their names. Syrian refugees."

She nodded and scribbled. "Can I get those names and the charges?"

"I'll get that information to you as soon as it comes through."

Remi lifted her gaze to meet his.

"The guy in the security office was knocked unconscious. The interior video feed was cut off. The only way that anyone will be caught and punished will be through your videos. Thank you for that."

She smiled a flat-lipped smile. Obviously, she didn't need to be congratulated or stroked.

"They would like to interview you."

"They…?"

"Scotland Yard. They'll be involved in security now until we leave England. They're interviewing Diamond as we speak."

"Yeah, no thanks. If you get me an email, I'll send them a copy of my article and notes. Other than that, I'm not getting tangled in that."

At first, T-Rex was surprised by her refusal, but that had to be something that journalists did, maybe. If they were testifying in every event they reported out, there would be no time for them to report on other stories. Possibly. He'd never given it much thought.

"I have a question for you." She laid her pad and pen down. "Why didn't the garage mob follow us out? I might have been wrong, but there were so many people. Forty?"

"There were a lot. You might not be far off with that count. My team analyzed the video you captured. Some of the men were slow to get out of the trucks. It looked to us like there were only a handful of men who were really invested, and they had been on the elevator. They concentrated on Havoc and me."

"Yep, that was my impression. Not to say I was unscathed. Maybe I was just surprised that they didn't kill me." She offered a nervous laugh. "On the planning board, people think they'll be able to follow through. I've found planning and doing are two very different things. I think of it as 'talking a big game.' It takes training to go from concept to fruition."

T-Rex couldn't fault what she was saying.

"Maybe they picked the men that would be first on scene. The guys in the elevator seemed the most trained or most aggressive. Perhaps they thought that by showing a good example, the others would follow suit?"

"Could be."

"Not really sure what dynamic was at work," Remi said. "I'll be interested to know what Scotland Yard learns. But do you know why they didn't leave the garage? I'm guessing that there were street security cameras out there that the mob couldn't access to turn off."

"That was Scotland Yard's conclusion. The assailants didn't want their faces on camera." He paused, and they just looked at each other for a long moment. T-Rex felt emotion streaming between them like a ribbon, tying them together in this moment. That impression was awkward for him; he didn't know what to do with these feelings, so he brushed them away. "You handled yourself beautifully. All day. That was a lot. But you seem okay." He stopped and leaned forward. "Is that a bruise forming across the bridge of your nose?"

She lifted her index finger and rubbed the spot, then tipped her ear toward her nightstand.

There, T-Rex saw her tactical glasses. Surprisingly, a crack snaked from the bridge toward the outer edges of the lenses.

He stood and went to pick them up. "These are the same kind I use. They shouldn't be damaged." He examined them closely, trying to imagine what level of impact was required to break the lenses.

"Some guy had a metal baton. It hurt like hell, but the glasses did their job."

T-Rex let the fear swim through his veins. That could have killed her. She could have died. He had been *right* there. He opened his mouth to exhale.

He put the glasses in his lapel pocket then withdrew his own pair from the inside pocket of his jacket.

He caught her eye for permission, then slid them onto her face, observing how the earpieces fit. He gently lifted them back off and bent his head to adjust them to fit her properly.

"If you're planning on giving me those, I can't accept a gift."

"Not a gift. An equal exchange."

"But you—"

"I have backup pairs."

"That's right, the whole 'One is none, and two is one' philosophy."

Having finished his adjustments, he reached out to set the pair onto her table. As he lifted his hand away, his gaze settled on her vibrator lying next to the phone.

He stalled.

When he turned toward Remi, a little smile played across her lips. There was a question in her eyes; did he want to do anything about that?

Damned straight, he did.

"Remi..." *Man! This was torture.* "I have to be downstairs in ten minutes." It sounded moronic to his ears. The tension in his voice was him restraining himself. It was taking all of his willpower.

She lifted her brow seductively, moving the computer off her lap, leaving her stretched out and inviting. "Ten, huh?" Her voice was welcoming.

He'd had his engines cranked up since Washington. Ten minutes was enough to get *his* rocks off. But it wouldn't be much fun for Remi.

Remi obviously took care of her own needs. He got that. That's how he handled the hormonal part of his sex drive. What he'd been missing since he became a widower was the intimacy of making love. The deep satisfaction of making his lover come. Hard.

For him, it was the best part of sex. And that took time. Patience. Focus.

A quicky? No. It's not the kind of guy he'd ever been. He liked sex to be savored. And he liked sex in a committed relationship.

His body twitched to attention like a bull in the china shop kind of way.

Remi was watching him. Unabashed. And that was all the more arousing.

For the first time, he was looking at another woman and feeling desire. Desire to know her and spend time with her. To hold her and listen to her thoughts. He wanted her to sleep in his arms.

Would she be okay with that?

If they did find a way to be together on this trip, and then they parted to go on about their lives, was T-Rex okay with that?

Chapter 19

Remi

Thursday, London, England

If Remi could read T-Rex's body language, Remi thought there was a moment of shock and confusion when his eyes landed on her vibrator, replaced by curiosity. And lust. She wasn't quite sure what that was about, but he was obviously thinking hard.

She'd reported out on the exploits of the Secret Service and the special forces operators and how sex got them in trouble. Was he running through the ethics of his acting on that hard-on his trousers did little to conceal? No. That didn't ring right. And yes, while he was on a protection detail, that didn't mean he worked 24 hours a day. The three-man and one K9 team were round-robining the work.

Sex wasn't inebriation. Inebriation was problematic

because if there were an emergency, they'd be a man down. But sex was just sex.

Though, honestly, Remi knew she wouldn't be satisfied with just sex. She wanted to know him. All of him. And that would take a long time. Maybe…their whole lives?

What a novel idea that was for Remi. Brand spanking new. Never before contemplated with any man.

Should she make a move?

Was he worried she'd put this in an article? She didn't write articles about herself.

Nope. No article, no ethics issues—not even for Remi since the close protection team wasn't the topic of her being here. They were simply fellow travelers on the same journey.

It sure would be nice to assuage her curiosity. She'd wondered what T-Rex would be like in bed ever since he looked her up and down at the airport in D.C.

His rare smiles lit her heart. His beautiful straight white teeth. His soft, full mouth. When he smiled, the emotion warmed his hazel eyes and took her breath away.

Deciding to dip a toe in the water to see how an overture might be received, Remi smiled with a tip of her head. A question and an invitation.

She was wet, and her nether regions were humming. Remi parted her lips as she became breathless and tingly.

With one more glance her way, T-Rex turned on his heels and headed toward the door. His hand landed on the knob. Another long hesitation, then in a voice, low and lusty, he said, "You have my cell phone number should there be an emergency." And he left.

Remi picked up her little red mouse. "Don't take this the wrong way," she told her toy, "but I'd rather have fucked the Delta."

* * *

After T-Rex left her room to go babysit the senator in the bar downstairs, Remi decided to dress and go down, too. She needed to see if she could make inroads on any of the stories she'd queued up with Liu.

Maybe Remi could pick up on some advance information about the stop in Iraq so she could get some research in place, a few skeleton words on the page, lighten her load, so she'd have more time at the hospital with Jean Baptiste.

That's what she told herself.

The truth was, she wanted to be where T-Rex was. That in itself was a revelation. Remi hadn't felt this goofy around a guy since Benny Woolstencroft in freshman biology class back at Yale.

Years later, here she was, giddy with discovery. And, thoroughly disappointed that when the sexual electricity was arcing between them in her room, that T-Rex hadn't made a move.

He was right to walk away. There were too many reasons why Remi's crushing hard on this guy wasn't just wrong but improbable. The hormones she could take care of herself.

And the emotional connection?

It would probably sever quick enough when it became evident that their lives went in opposite directions.

Still, Remi was bummed.

"No. No. No. I hate everything about this speech." Senator Blankenship was sitting at the end of the bar in an otherwise empty hotel pub. There was a major scowl on her face and a visible tic under her eye. "Look, I'm taking the girls home to Iraq. I'm getting off the plane, saying fifteen minutes of uplifting crap, and getting back on the flight to Lebanon. If I regurgitate the speech I gave at Oxford, no one will cover it, not even Remi." She lifted her tumbler in a trembling hand, extending her index finger to point at Remi. "Already this has gone cattywampus because of the damned 'Save the Earth' folks railing against Texas. *Texas* of all places. Texas is the closest thing you can get to God this side of Heaven."

"Yes, ma'am." Diamond was obviously having her patience tested. Today had been hard on everyone. And they were dealing with jet lag on top of everything else. "I need another angle," Diamond said.

Remi wondered why the senator thought that the attack in London had to do with the Climate Crisis. Maybe that's what Diamond had told the senator.

Diamond hadn't been in the stage wings while Remi had offered other possibilities.

Scotland Yard had confirmed that at least three of the assailants were Syrian. Were they Syrian forces, radical extremists? Remi would have to ask when more information had been gathered.

Blankenship snapped her fingers in Remi's face.

Remi jerked her head back away from the noise and the personal space violation.

"Give me something," Blankenship demanded.

"An angle for a speech?" Remi asked. She was here to gather a story, not write speeches. But sometimes, reporters needed the rails greased. If she helped, she could make an ask in return. It was a simple psychological ploy. People don't like to be beholden.

"Well, duh." Blankenship gave her an overly dramatic look as if she were a child making faces in the schoolyard. This conduct wasn't anything Remi had seen from the senator in the past. Maybe this was what she was like when the cameras weren't rolling. It seemed…odd. Remi wasn't sure what to make of this or how she could portray this in a piece. Maybe it was fatigue. Or stress from the event. Or perhaps the sardines on the senator's finger sandwich at high tea were bad.

Diamond was looking at Blankenship with concern and a little surprise. Maybe she'd never seen the senator in this state before, either.

Remi let her gaze crawl up the wall until it reached the ceiling. She wanted to help Diamond out. "Okay. Let's see. You're trying to support women in the region."

"In the world," Blankenship emphasized.

"Right. World. But do you want to make this a global speech or one that focuses on Iraqi women?"

"Iraqi, if you have something." Diamond's voice floated softly across the bar.

"Iraq…okay, how about the Iraq Women's Chamber of Commerce?"

"The Chamber is one of my biggest benefactors." Blankenship licked her lips.

"This isn't associated with anything going on in America," Remi clarified.

"Still, just getting that name into the speech. Folks at home won't parse this," Blankenship said. "They'll think local Chamber of Commerce. It's good. This is good. Run with this. What about the Iraqi Women's Chamber? I've never heard of it."

"The purpose of their organization is to energize women-owned businesses."

"Do you have any stats on that?" Diamond asked.

Remi scratched her forefinger along the part of her hair. Then reached into her bag for her netbook. Powering up, she dug through her research files. "There are over 50,000 female-run informal businesses. Think of that as piano lessons in the women's homes. Tutoring. Eldercare. That kind of thing."

"And formal?" Diamond asked.

"Mmmm, around three-thousand. 'Formal' would be shops. I know an American woman from Texas who went to Iraq to teach English and decided to open a tattoo parlor. She would be one of the three thousand. These numbers are associated with the chamber. Surely, the numbers of women in both formal and informal business will be larger around all of Iraq."

"Is that safe?" Diamond asked.

"Is anyone giving that Texas gal a problem?" Blankenship interrupted. "Bet she'd show them a thing or two."

Remi focused on Diamond, giving a slight shrug. "Is anywhere safe?" Remi turned to the senator. "The Texan hasn't had an issue yet. She keeps a baseball bat next to her in the shop. Last I heard, she hadn't needed to use it. Anyway, these businesses that I'm telling you about are new. Last five years or so."

"Supported by the United States?" the senator asked.

"Mmm, not as much. Mostly the world community. When our troops withdrew, we told the Iraqi people that we were committed to increasing job opportunities. Unfortunately, especially given the numbers of widows in the country, those opportunities tend to go to bigger businesses and—"

"Men." Blankenship scowled.

"Yes. Exactly," Remi replied. "So the U.S. involvement is a harder message to pull off in a speech. But the resourcefulness and resilience of women, many of whom are now head of households, is inspiring. Particularly given the lack of education for many women."

Diamond cleared her throat. "Not an 'America did this for you' twist. I agree. That's a bad look and inaccurate. Maybe something else?"

Blankenship stabbed a finger into the air. "We're not political fluffers."

A fluffer was someone who prepared a porn actor for his scene by getting the guy hard. 'Fluffer' wasn't a word that Remi had ever heard when talking to a politician. And it didn't sync with the senator's folksy reputation. *Was this who she was behind the scenes?*

This all felt *off* to Remi. She tried to adjust herself. She'd seen it enough times: The grandfatherly caring man on camera. Round belly, pink cheeks, white hair—a Santa stand-in. Then, one of Remi's colleagues gets the goods on him. It turns out his computer is chock full of pedo-porn. Off to prison he goes, where the other prisoners extra punish the guy for preying on kids. As *should* happen in Remi's mind.

Her phone pinged, and she looked down at the screen.

Jing-Wu: Remi, did you hear about Tariq?

Jing-Wu had added a URL. When Remi tapped it, the headline read: Tariq Sulfia, Pulitzer Prize-winning photojournalist from the World Press Association, was killed last night reporting on a battle between the opposition and the Afghan security forces.

Shit, Tariq!

She pulled a hand through her hair. The world around her oscillated fuzzily. Her breath was loud in her ears. She held on, waiting for the sensation to pass. She felt T-Rex's eyes hard on her. Curiosity, but not in the titillating kind of way. He was in operator mode. He'd wonder if her reaction somehow upped the danger on this already nutso assignment.

Catching T-Rex's gaze, Remi decided to let his threat level drop back down. "An associate was killed photographing a skirmish in Afghanistan last night."

The look in his eye changed instantly. A shot of pain. A moment of compassion. Then back to stoic. "I'm sorry for your loss."

Remi turned her attention back to the senator and her assistant. She'd wait until she was back with her tribe, and they could mourn together. Lift a glass. Tell war stories. Solidify their memories since that's all they'd have of Tariq now.

The senator tipped the rest of her scotch back. And Remi winced at the thought of the burning sensation, but Blankenship acted like it was water. "You got all that, Diamond?"

"Yes, ma'am. I'm taking notes and recording. Oh, Remi, I'm recording. But it's just so I can go back and check the details. I promise to erase it when I have the speech written."

"Okay." Remi paused while the senator swirled a finger over her empty highball, indicating to the bartender that she wanted another.

"So this is women helping women." Remi shook her head with her hand over her glass when the bartender lifted the bottle her way. "It's good for Iraqi women. It gives women connections to the greater world. When they're connected, there's the potential to build relationships."

"Which is good for..." Diamond prompted.

"Stability. Survival, really. These women are housing, clothing, feeding their families. Safe, stable homes and an opportunity for education are ways forward for Middle Eastern women."

"Emphasize that, Diamond." The senator had lifted her glass and was peering through the amber liquid. "'A Path to Survival.' No. 'A Path to the Future'…work on it to set the right tone."

Diamond paused her pen. "What tone are you looking for?"

"Celebration and optimism. Yet—"

"Got it."

"About the 'yet,'" Remi said. "There's been an escalation in violence over the last five or six months. Not as much in city centers, which are easier places for women to run their businesses, but out in the rural areas. It's the magnetic bombs that are causing so much trouble."

"IEDs?" Diamond asked.

"IEDs are not the same as magnetic bombs. They're also called 'sticky bombs.'"

The senator frowned. "Never heard of such a beast."

"It's been what, two-three days ago, a government official in Kabul Province had his SUV blown up. He died, along with his secretary. Two of his bodyguards survived but were badly hurt."

"Kabul, Afghanistan, not Iraq," Blankenship pointed out.

"No, ma'am, that example didn't take place in Iraq. The magnetic bombs are in Iraq, too. Just… I was trying to give you an example to explain the damage that this new type of bomb could do."

"Sticky bombs. Sounds like something I'd order at an upscale D.C. restaurant," the senator said.

"You wouldn't want this, ma'am. And I'm sure your security detail is well aware of the risks." Remi shot a glance toward T-Rex, who was listening intently even if he wasn't looking their way. "It's probably why your security team doesn't want you on the ground in Iraq for more than forty minutes."

"Can you tell me what happens? I don't think it's going to make its way into the speech," Diamond said. "I've never heard of them before, is all."

"Right—" Remi began.

"Now, you hold on right there." The senator had drained her whisky again. This time she hugged the empty glass to her chest. "These are attacks in Kabul? That *shouldn't* be. I sit on the committee. I reviewed the agreement the U.S. made with the various players. There should be no mass-casualty attacks. No truck bombings."

Remi shrugged. "When has the opposition ever followed the rules?"

"I still don't understand what we're talking about here," Diamond whispered.

"A magnetic bomb is constructed of plastic explosives and powerful magnets. They work efficiently in urban settings. You have someone like the deputy governor, who basically lives in a protective cocoon. Lots of security measures. It would be too difficult to get to him or his car at home. But you get choked up in the street, pinned in a traffic jam. The attackers are on mopeds or the like. Or even pedestrians. Though, the bikes are easier to get where you need to get. They simply drive up alongside, usually next to the gas tank, and they hold out the bomb. It's then magnetized to the car, and the bomber scoots off to safety."

Blankenship's hand came up to her throat. "Terrible."

Diamond noisily sucked in a lungful of air. "Wait!" she gasped out. "Is that why Ty was driving like that?

Is that what was happening? They were trying to evade motorcycles and their magnet bombs?"

Magnetic bombs—but who cared what words she chose? "Your security is trained to prevent that from happening," Remi said dispassionately.

Nothing bad had happened. It was all just *potential.* Remi had had so many brushes with violence that she'd learned that it was always a good day when you got home and could count all ten toes and fingers and no stitches to hold you together. No oxygen bag or stretcher.

Even Jean Baptiste, beaten and dumped. Better to be Jean Baptiste than Éloïse and Marie-Claude.

Remi had enough. She wasn't getting a story out of this. The senator was slurring.

And if she stayed here, Remi would start drinking for all of the wrong reasons—something she worked hard never to do. Remi looked across the bar at the row of alcohol bottles. Those bottles had the power to make her numb. To take away grief and fear. Pain. She wanted another drink. Bad. To feel the thick cool glass in her hand. To lift it to her nose and slowly pull the fragrance through her olfactory senses. To have the heat burn the back of her throat, making her cough up today's thought pollution. The pessimism that crept in and wanted to lodge in her chest, she'd like to cough that all away and have the alcohol spread through her veins.

She didn't feel a lot of willpower at that moment. And she knew the siren call of alcohol was every bit as destructive to war correspondents as those mermaids of lore were to the sailors who steered toward the mermaid's song. Better to leave than to fall under the influence.

Sending a smile from Diamond to Senator Blankenship, Remi said, "Maybe I should head up for the night." She looked at T-Rex. "We're meeting down here to drive to the airport at zero five hundred?"

"Yes, ma'am."

Their eyes caught and held.

Remi hoped that when he was off duty, he'd come and tap at her door.

Chapter 20

Remi

Thursday, London, England

It was lonely in her room. She looked at the king-sized bed, much too big for one person. Her thoughts traveled back to T-Rex standing there looking at her vibrator, thinking his lascivious thoughts. Yeah, she'd seen his body react. He was wearing a suit coat, and he probably thought he'd hidden his hard-on, but while he was standing, it was pretty obvious to her.

This is messed up, she thought with a shake of her head.

On to a new subject, Remi picked up the television control wand and zapped on the news to see what was up in the world. See what her friends were reporting on.

Right now, some talking head, sitting in a comfy

newsroom, reading a teleprompter, was going on about a drone attack in the Persian Gulf.

Listening, Remi went to brush her teeth and get ready for bed. After the Oxford debacle, Remi had showered, washed her hair, and changed her clothes. A ritual for removing the garbage—physical and mental—from her day. Now, there was minimal to do to distract her from her T-Rex thoughts.

Lay out her clothes. Do some stretches. Rub arnica into her bruises and aching muscles, boom, she'd be done.

Her phone pinged.

Remi spat the toothpaste into the sink, then tapped the screen.

Liu: Your article will be page one above the fold in tomorrow's paper.

Nice. Remi smiled. Well, at least today's kerfuffle wasn't for nothing.

She rinsed her mouth. She was tugging her tunic off when she heard. "The World Press Association is reporting tonight that Polish crime reporter Eryk Biela is fighting for his life in a Warsaw hospital. Biela is known for his aggressive reporting on crime families in former USSR countries, including the formidable Zorić and Prokhorov families. He was shot in the street in front of the capitol earlier today."

Remi clutched at her chest. Man, but this had been a bad week for journalists. It was getting worse. Each week more and more of her colleagues around the world were suffering for their journalism.

"Three suspects were detained by police. One is thought to have been the shooter. No further details are available as the investigators are keeping their cards close to the chest."

When Remi's phone rang, she answered it on autopilot, eyes still glued to the television screen.

"Hey there."

Remi had to pull the phone from her ear and look down at the name on display. Karen. "Hey."

"Where are you in the world?"

"Oxford, England. You?"

"Me? South Africa for the next four months. England's not your usual beat—is there a coup in play?" Karen asked with a chuckle. There was clattering in the background, and Remi assumed Karen had called while she did her dishes or maybe was cooking. "Not that I'm aware of. What's up?"

"I heard about the FR-13 folks. I was just wondering if you knew—"

"I'm on an assignment that gets me to Lebanon at least long enough to check on Jean Baptiste. He's at St. George Hospital in Beirut. I promise to give you a call once I know something firsthand."

"Anything on Marie-Claude or Éloïse?"

"Darn." Remi frowned. "I was hoping you were calling me with an update. I have nothing."

"I have next to nothing. I was talking to a friend of mine over at the FR-13 office. A ransom demand arrived this morning. It's in negotiations."

A glimmer of hope. "At least France will comply if possible. If it's money, they should get that. If it's another attempt to get those folks out of prison after the Paris terror attacks, that's not happening."

"Agreed. There's hope. Hey, have you talked to Sima in the last few days?"

"Sima Noori? Not in…months. Why?"

"Let me read this to you. Hang on." Remi listened while Karen walked across the room. There was a rustle of paper. "This is a release from the U.S. Department of Justice. Ready?"

"No. Not really. I'm getting overwhelmed with bad news about my friends. FR-13, obviously. Yesterday, Jules lost his eye while videoing—"

"What?"

"Yeah, a crazy bizarro scene out of a Hitchcock movie. Then I was down at the bar tonight and heard about Tariq."

"Utter crap. Yeah. Tariq was covering a fight between the Afghan troops and the opposing forces. He was due to fly home today. They were inducing his wife. I need to check and see if the baby's been born. I'll send flowers and put both our names on the card."

The line fell silent. That baby… Remi had forgotten that Tariq's wife was expecting. Remi felt her body heat with anxiety and sorrow.

In a small voice, Karen said, "I interrupted you. You were ticking off bad news."

"Eryk was shot and is fighting for his life."

"Where is he?"

"Home," Remi said. "So you'd think he was safe."

"Not really, which is why I'm calling."

"Okay," Remi said after a moment. "I'm braced for it. Was Sima hurt?"

"No. But she's the story instead of the reporter. The DOJ said that they indicted four men. Intelligence Officers on…reading now, 'charges of conspiring to kidnap Manhattan-based journalist Sima Noori. They wanted to return Noori to her homeland, where they planned to criminally charge her for shifting public opinion and affect regime change'."

"But she's fine? They didn't get to her?"

"Shaken for sure. I talked to Sima over Zoom, and she's got huge hive welts all over her. She's heading to the doctor to see if they can't give her a shot or something to calm them down."

"I'm…trying to wrap my mind around that. They were caught, though. That's going to heat things up between the U.S. and regional opposition." Remi made a mental note to tell T-Rex about this. Remi was sure that he was plugged into the intelligence community, and they were monitoring the temperature in the Middle East. But this might be worrisome about the senator landing in Iraq. And there were always anti-west supporters to worry about.

"More importantly," Karen said. "The reason I called to tell you about this is that you need to watch your back. You've written some pretty damning articles about the regime."

"I travel too much for them to find me and act." Though today in Oxford… Huh. Maybe she needed to think this through.

"It doesn't take much to stick a bomb on your car." Karen raised her voice over the running water.

Remi was up and pacing. "I don't have a car."

"Slap a magnetic bomb on the side of whatever vehicle you're riding in, then."

"Huh. Weird."

"Weird in what way?" Karen asked with a bang and a clatter. The sound of water cutting on then off again.

"I was down in the bar, and the chick traveling with the senator was just asking me what a magnetic bomb was."

"In London? That's a stretch."

"Read tomorrow's paper. I got above the fold."

"Wow. Kudos to you! Will you be in England for long?"

"We're heading to a secret stop tomorrow, then Lebanon. I attached on to go see Jean Baptiste in the hospital. With Marie-Claude and Éloïse held prisoner, I'm having trouble keeping up with all the crap happening."

"It's a wide world with a lot of good in it. It's our circle of friends who are wading into harm's way. It's expected that bad things happen in dangerous spaces."

Remi exhaled. Yeah. She knew. She'd grappled with it since the start of her career. It wasn't like she had a death wish. But she felt compelled to be there, to see it firsthand, and to tell the world, so they could step forward and make things right.

Karen filled the empty space. "Ah, well…as the bad boys of the United States military like to say, 'Watch your six.' We don't want you going kaboom!"

Chapter 21

T-Rex

Thursday, London, England

He had a small window to grab a power nap, but his mind was racing. Over the decades of military life, T-Rex had trained himself to close his eyes, order up a snooze and a specific wakeup time, and let his brain do the rest.

But here he was, lying on his back. He'd crossed his arms behind his head while his ankles dangled off of the too-short bed. Awake.

Remi filled his thoughts. He wanted her in his life. Wanted a last call before he went out on assignment. He missed worrying and caring about someone. He was ready. But was she interested in something like that? Because it would take a heck of a lot to make it a go.

Special Forces relationships were tricky. He knew

it from his own experience with Jess and watching his teammates navigate the issues with their wives.

But their wives lived on base. They weren't out traipsing the earth with a go-bag and a videorecorder, looking for a story. Honey Honig sprang to mind. A fellow Delta now retired. He was with Iniquus, working jobs all over the world. His specialty was saving kidnapped victims. Honey met his now-wife Meg in Africa, where she worked as an animal migration specialist. They'd adopted a son, Ahbou. Two different continents. They made it work. How? Honey said he, Meg, and Ahbou video chatted every day. So far, it looked like a successful marriage was possible despite their being so far apart. Sometimes life got in the way. For Honey, it was assignments that took as long as they took to resolve and get the kidnapping victims home again. For Meg, she might be out in the bush. They sent pictures, texts, kept things going…could it work for him? For them?

Honey talked for a living. He was the voice on the radio or phone when they made contact with the kidnappers. He could read between the lines. He could pick the right words out of nowhere.

Words weren't T-Rex's forte.

But if you want something badly enough…

He turned his head toward the door, where a light tap sounded.

Swinging his legs off the bed, he made his way over, bent to look through the viewer to see Remi standing there, looking nervous.

He swung the door wide, brushing a hand through the air to invite her in.

From the tightness of her muscles and the frown on her face, this wasn't a booty call.

"I'm so sorry," was her opener.

"Are you okay?"

"I just got off the phone with a friend of mine, Karen from the Montreal Gazette."

"Where is she now?"

She put her hand on her head. "Uhm, she's in South Africa, but it's not about that."

"Do you want to sit?"

She moved to the chair at the table and plopped down, then sprang back up.

Okay, nerves. The least T-Rex could do was not loom. He moved back to his bed and positioned himself much like she had been when he'd visited her in her room earlier.

"Did you hear about the DOJ arresting four men in New York over the kidnapping plot of Sima Noori?"

"I just got off the phone with my TOC about that."

She exhaled deeply. T-Rex had watched Remi's pattern breathing enough now to know it was a coping mechanism for anxiety. "I'm concerned about the Iraq layover," she said, "retribution…"

"A plan has already been formed. I was going to text you when I got up."

"You were sleeping. I'm so sorry. You don't get to do that a lot on assignment." She started toward the door. "We can talk—"

"Remi, you're always welcome. Please stay." He waited for her to turn. "We're going to fly straight into Lebanon. Once we get there, the plane will go on to the Jordan-Iraq border with the girls. Diamond will go and deliver the senator's remarks."

"Diamond's okay with that? She was pretty freaked out by the elevator incident. The car chase, I'm sure that didn't sit well."

"I think she wants to keep her job."

Remi leaned an ear toward her shoulder. "I guess you've got to do what you have to do, but if she felt unsafe—none of you three is going with them?"

"We're here to protect the senator."

Remi's gaze settled on the carpet. T-Rex could see her mind whirring. "Okay, well, Diamond's an adult. I guess she can make those choices for herself." Her hand rested on his ankle. "Are you on duty soon?"

He looked at his watch. "Cat nap, then I'm on door duty."

She held his eye.

So she'd come down with an invitation, not just information swap and plan coordination. A glimmer of hope sparked for him when he read disappointment there. He reached for her hand, tugging lightly so she'd sit down closer to him. "Not tonight," he said as she turned her hand and laced her fingers into his. "We'll figure it out, okay?"

"Yeah, I'd like that." She leaned forward for a kiss.

When their lips met, it was soft and sweet. T-Rex closed his eyes to savor it. Just a taste on his tongue. A ripple of warmth flooded through his body.

As he blinked his eyes open, she sat, then stood, waved, and walked away.

He wanted more.

The door clicked lightly shut behind her.

Nope, that wasn't a fuck-me kiss. That wasn't lust. That was...the kiss from someone who wanted to explore a possibility.

That kiss sealed the deal for him.

Now, he just needed to find a way to make this work before they went their separate ways and anything else became regrets in his rearview mirror.

Chapter 22

Remi

Friday, London, England

Remi finished her sorting and packing, placing everything neatly in its correct spot for easy access.

The morning news played on the TV. They reported out the unusual occurrences in Oxford and the involvement of Scotland Yard, lauding the agency's quick and professional actions to both secure the senator and bring justice.

Frames from Remi's videos were shown, the newsroom accredited Remi's newspaper as the source. Remi would check with Liu later to make sure that had been agreed upon.

She stopped as the perps traipsed across the screen with their T-shirts pulled up over their noses, trying to hide their faces from the cameras.

Yup, there was Tall, and Short, and the smarmy one who dressed like a security guard down in the garage.

"Arrested in London, in their shared flat, these men are undergoing questioning for their involvement with the rabble who swarmed the senator on her way out of the lecture."

So they traveled in for that event. Who was paying them? What was the get?

And they were cooperating with investigators. Good, more perp walks to come.

Pulling the zipper closed on her bag, Remi heard a commotion next door in the senator's room.

Last night, Remi had gotten little sleep. The senator was up and puking most of the night—well, puking that turned into dry heaves.

Senator Blankenship had been complaining of a headache since Washington. Was she ill, or was that the alcohol?

Remi wasn't the only one with questions.

Early this morning, Havoc must have taken over guard duty at the senator's door. Remi had heard a clear knock at Blankenship's door. "Ma'am? It's Havoc. Can I help? Do you need a doctor?"

Blankenship answered with a sailor's string of expletives that had Remi not heard herself, she never could have imagined coming from the senator's mouth.

It still felt off to Remi. Something just wasn't right about the situation. She wondered if the senator was dealing with some medical issue that she wasn't willing to share even with her security.

The Delta team was clearly in the dark.

"Echo Six. Hey, T-Rex, I'm not sure what to do here, man."

Remi could just imagine T-Rex's answer: "She's a

grown woman. She'll ask for help if she needs it. We're here to monitor outside threats." Something like that. Or maybe. "Try again. See if she needs a suggestion. Work the problem."

"Work the problem" was one of those phrases Remi had picked up from reporting on special forces men over the years. She liked it. It gave her a sense of personal calm. Anxiety would bubble up, and she refused to give in. She'd just try to define the problem, describe what an acceptable outcome looked like, then try to connect the dots. How could she move from problem to solution?

It was the base for many of the habits she'd developed. Her personal kit. Her way of moving through experiences like at the airport, the elevator, and then the garage.

When she couldn't wish it away, when she couldn't delegate it away, when she was forced to square off with a challenge, she took a breath and told herself sternly, "Work the problem."

"Senator Blankenship? Ma'am, it's Havoc. Would crackers or ginger ale help? Is there anything I can do?"

"Go away and leave me alone."

So while Remi was tired from her sleepless night, Blankenship must be absolutely exhausted.

Remi walked her bags to the door and propped them against the wall there. Then unabashedly, she crawled up on her bed and put her ear to the wall to listen.

"I don't *want* to come off as chicken shit for not going," the senator protested.

"Ma'am, few people know you were heading to Iraq. We can keep it on the down-low." That was T-Rex. Steady. Pragmatic. It was probably killing him to speak whole sentences to Blankenship. He much preferred to point at things and have his men comply or stick to his four syllables.

Was that fair? He wasn't talkative. Definitely not a storyteller. But he communicated clearly, succinctly, honestly, and many of their interactions were heartfelt.

Remi thought back to his hand on his heart, pain in his eyes, and his apology for leaving her behind, though, honestly, he didn't have much choice. He didn't roar off after the others, which had definitely happened to Remi in other circumstances.

She actually kind of liked the way he communicated.

Liked his innate physical and mental strength.

Liked *him*. More than liked him, in fact.

The strong silent type, she smiled with pleasure. Yeah, maybe soldier-boy *was* her type after all.

That thought felt scary because she couldn't imagine that there was growing room for those feelings. They had a couple of days. Then they'd be off running into hot spots. Each with their own missions and agendas.

"This call isn't coming from us," T-Rex continued, unruffled by the senator berating them. "It's up the chain. It's ultimately up to you, ma'am. We can't assure your safety. And if I might add a twist if we were to go and have to secure you with our lives, that will be reported out, and it will be wall to wall on the news. It might be viewed poorly that you were counseled but refused."

He didn't mention Remi like she was the bad-guy tattletale.

He was right, though.

Blankenship stopped yelling. That last argument made a difference.

In his same even tone, he continued, "The plane will land first in Lebanon for your comfort. Then the pilot will fly to Jordan with the robotics team. The camp is sending a bus to pick the girls up at the Jordanian-Iraqi border."

"Can you imagine Diamond giving that address and the journalists asking, 'Why doesn't the senator want to be here?' The senator most certainly does want to go there. If I walked up to the line but didn't stick my pointy-toed boot over, it just looks like I'm chicken shit."

Remi couldn't make out what the senator said next, but T-Rex responded, "Our logistics professional, Winner, is figuring that out, putting a plan in place."

"Winner? 'Winner, winner chicken dinner.'" Blankenship's tone completely changed. A complete 180. She was back to affable Senator Blankenship.

Remi thought she might get whiplash from the senator's sudden change of tone.

"Do they say that from where y'all are from? 'Winner, winner chicken dinner'? You know that phrase came out of Las Vegas way back when. It just has a ring, doesn't it? Just look at the time. Let's get the show on the road."

Remi got off the bed. She pulled her bags into place over her shoulders and opened the door to find Diamond standing in the hall, staring at the senator's hotel room door, looking flummoxed.

The door opened. Havoc stuck his head out, reviewed the corridor, and opened it wide to allow the senator to exit.

The senator caught Diamond's eye. "I've had a splitting headache since those birds attacked the girls' lunches. It's like to kill me." She put a fist over her left eye. "A hot poker run through me."

"Would you like to see a doctor, ma'am?" Diamond asked.

T-Rex and Remi's gaze caught for a brief moment, a check-in. He was laden with suitcases.

"Me?" Blankenship reached out and patted Diamond's arm as they walked side by side. "Naw. It'll be fine. 'Winner, winner chicken dinner.' I was saying that to the boys. Now, I'm hungry."

"You just ate breakfast, didn't you? The hotel brought a continental tray to my room when I set my wakeup call," Diamond pointed out.

"Yeah? Did I? Huh. Okay, maybe I'm just thirsty. Diamond, would you pour me a cup of joe? Black."

Diamond looked back at the senator's door now closed.

"It's time for us to get to the airport, ma'am. I'll put that in a to-go cup for you." Havoc swiped a card to go back into her room.

T-Rex dropped the bags, Remi supposed, so that his arms were free in case there was a sudden hazard in the otherwise empty corridor.

Empty except for more men in suits, one at each exit, two at the elevator. They must be the reinforcements from Scotland Yard.

Remi wondered if British security would follow their group all the way to the airport for takeoff.

Would they leave England without any more mishaps?

Remi sat in the back seat of the lead car with Ty and Rory.

It was interesting to Remi that Ty and Rory never stood at the senator's door. It seemed Ty was there to handle and care for Rory.

Rory's job seemed to be going ahead of the group to sniff out the situation. Rory was a powerful, high-energy dog. Ty ran him ten miles a day and threw a ball with him until Ty was exhausted. Rory didn't seem like he could ever tire. Such an amazing dog.

It was a pity Remi wasn't allowed to snuggle with him.

Rory had his head draped over the seat and was sniffing her. He stretched out his tongue, trying to give Remi a lick. When he couldn't reach, Rory tried to climb over the seat.

Ty put out a hand and commanded Rory to "leave it." Then, "Rory likes you, ma'am."

"Just Remi, not ma'am, thanks. I'm sorry if that's problematic. I don't want to interfere with Rory's job."

"I've got it handled. I always trust my dog. If he likes you, I like you." Their eyes met in the rearview mirror.

"That's heartwarming. Thank you."

And that was the last Ty said until they reached the airport. Ty's head was on a swivel. Remi noticed he made sure that when a motorcycle showed up, it got nowhere near the senator's car.

They pulled into the private hangar where the jet waited. There was a crowd of reporters held back behind a cordon. Officers in uniform were on site this time.

Remi waited by the car while Blankenship slid out of her vehicle, hat in hand. When she saw the crowd, she turned and used the reflection from the car window to rake her fingers through her hair and tug her red cowboy hat into place.

Senator Blankenship looked like shit.

Remi put a hand to her own forehead for a quick check. No fever. Honestly, Remi had been nauseous and achy since the bird fiasco. It was hard to tell what was nerves and what might be a bug that she'd picked up along the way. She desperately hoped she wasn't getting ill with whatever was going on with Blankenship.

When Remi went to see Jean Baptiste, she didn't want to carry any germs into the hospital room with her. Remi needed to hug Jean Baptiste and tell him how glad she was that he'd survived.

Remi wasn't the only one who noticed that the senator didn't look well. When they reached the press pool, the very first question from the British tabloid was if she was all right.

"Senator Blankenship, did yesterday rattle you?"

"Shoot, little thing like that? Now, if you ever want to know about a frightening commotion, y'all just come on out to my ranch, and I'll show you what happens when the cattle stampede."

A ripple of laughter moved through the press.

"Are you happy to be back in Oxford, senator?"

"I loved my time here as a Rhodes scholar." She held out a finger to point at the sun. "Though I don't miss the rain, so I packed up some sunshine as a hostess gift."

Another reporter stepped forward. Uh-oh, Remi thought. There were daggers in that man's eyes. "Senator Blankenship, why didn't the United States act with integrity concerning your diplomats like Belgium did just yesterday?"

Blankenship leaned toward Diamond. "What the heck is he talking about?"

Diamond shook her head.

The senator turned toward Remi. "Do you know?"

Remi moved up and whispered in Blankenship's ear. "Yesterday, Belgium recalled their ambassador from Seoul because his wife smacked a shopkeeper for the second time."

"The woman just hauled off and smacked someone?"

Blankenship's brows disappeared under her hat's brim. "Why?"

"Uhm, a cleaner let his brush accidentally touch her."

"That woman is plumb crazy. Of course, they couldn't allow that kind of conduct from a diplomat's family. But what has that got to do with the United States?"

"Belgium waived diplomatic immunity for the ambassador's wife. She's being prosecuted by South Korea. When they caught an American diplomat's wife shoplifting at the jewelers in London last year, she didn't face the consequences of her actions. I believe the reporter is asking about the policy differences. In Great Britain, there's been anger and frustration about how that incident was handled. How friends treat friends..."

Blankenship looked the man in the eye. "Good question." She gave him a nod then walked toward the plane.

With Havoc and T-Rex encasing her, Blankenship put her foot on the step. Her whole body swayed like she was drunk.

T-Rex caught her arm. "Ma'am?"

She turned to look to her right where nobody was standing. From behind, Remi watched her grin broadly. "Isn't this a hoot and a holler?" she said to no one. Without any context, she added, "I think I need to use my Aqua Net Super Hold if we're going to continue to have days like the ones on this trip."

As she climbed up the stairs behind the senator, Remi tapped her video camera off.

Chapter 23

Remi

Friday, Private jet, Beirut Bound

"Remi. Come sit next to me. I want to pick your brain."

Remi had been looking forward to finding a more open space to sit now that half the girls were home. Maybe leg room would make her phobia a little less aggressive. But, with the senator's invitation, Remi was glad to sit next to Blankenship.

Something extraordinary was going on, and Remi smelled a story. Blankenship's behavior was beyond eccentric. There was something truly odd going on here. Senator Blankenship wielded an enormous amount of power, making life and death decisions in her committee meetings. If she was not of sound mind, her constituents should know.

Still, it was important that Blankenship not think of Remi in anything but professional terms. "Ma'am, I'm here as a journalist."

"Psh. Come." She patted the same seat where Remi had sat on their flight from Washington.

T-Rex gallantly took Remi's packs as she pulled them off, tucking them up in the bin. Remi wasn't sure she should let him, given that they were both on work duty now.

"You're Lebanese, Remi?" the senator asked as Remi buckled her belt.

"My mother is Lebanese. My father was born in France, Lyon. I was born in New York."

"And where are they now?"

"Mom lives in Paris. My father's deceased." Remi was uncomfortable; she didn't want to talk about her family.

"Now, Remi, I know you need a story but, I'm more interested in you. In reporters' lives in general. I can tell you're not the kind of person who likes to talk about themselves."

"No, ma'am, I do not."

"Fine then, we'll speak more globally. In America, we're having quite the conversation about the press. I've been reading up on your articles. Had to. Needed to know what battle ax you might wield against me." She smiled to take the sting out of her remark.

"My job, ma'am, is to find the facts, not to wield axes."

"Yes, I see that in your reporting. Tell me the state of your people."

"By people, you mean?" Remi pulled her safety belt in place and tugged it tight across her hips.

"War reporters… Foreign correspondents." Blankenship barreled forward with her conversation despite the flight assistant standing at the front of the plane, playing a voice recording of the safety instructions in Kurdish. At the same time, she demonstrated how to access oxygen.

"We give so much praise to the bravery of our soldiers." Blankenship looked past Remi to T-Rex. "Deserved. But others are doing their jobs in harm's way. For example, my committee has taken up the issue of interpreters and others who risked their lives and continue to risk their lives in the Middle East, working for the United States. As things draw down, I think we owe them what they were promised, a safe harbor in America. They've earned it. That aside, it's another job that puts the worker in harm's way every time they go out."

"For interpreters," Remi added, "it's not just when they go out. It's when they go home. It's their wives and children. Their families. It's dangerous for all of them. *Extremely* dangerous."

"And for you."

"I have no children. No one to torture to get to me."

"No husband? Sorry. I should be more careful. You may well like women. Wife? No wife?"

Remi could feel T-Rex's attention brighten. *Crap, now he thinks I might prefer women.* She forced herself not to turn toward him and say, *"Nope, I like sex with men, and I'm really hoping you'll bed me before this trip is over."* Instead, Remi kept her focus on the senator and said softly, "I… Please don't make this personal for me. I'm here as a reporter."

"Okay. Let's talk about something that's been on my mind of late. Ethics."

"May I record?" Remi asked.

"Fine." Blankenship petted a hand over her head.

Whenever the senator removed her hat, it always left the top of her wiry hair crushed, and the sides were wild. It gave her a mad scientist vibe.

As Remi reached under her tunic for her recorder, Blankenship said, "Ethics certainly are changing. Technology makes us have to rock back on our heels and think a spell. Have you ever heard of the Great Law of the Iroquois?" Without waiting for Remi to reply, Blankenship pressed on. "They say that the decision-makers, like me, should think about how our policies will affect our people seven generations ahead. I counted that out. That's a hundred and forty years. Long way. That might have been possible at one point in time. I'm not sure how we can make that stick nowadays. The computing and the Internet. Trolls and bots. Saboteurs, spies. The Earth's climate is changing just as fast as fast can be. We have no idea what next year will look like, let alone a hundred and forty years from now."

Remi held the recorder in her hand and just let the senator ramble.

"When I started in public life, that's what I vowed to do, follow the Iroquois. But the technology swings too fast. I swear I feel like I get my aerobics in just chasing after the bad effects that technology has on the world. I have no idea how to rein it in. Granted, technology is doing a lot of good, too. It's like any relationship. You have to balance the good with the bad. Try to improve. But. But… Huh, lost that thread of thought." Senator Blankenship looked around, disoriented.

"Yes, ma'am." Remi knew the senator wasn't feeling well and had little sleep. Time zone changes, jet lag. She was in her late sixties, and things had been going haywire their whole trip. Maybe all that was adding up for Blankenship. Remi quietly realigned the senator with their subject. "You quoted an Iroquois proverb, and you were saying that you wanted to apply that to your government position. Technology makes it impossible to predict seven generations ahead."

"I did? Huh..." She blinked vacantly.

Remi shot a glance toward T-Rex.

T-Rex's face was stoic, but Remi was learning to read his eyes. He was worried.

The engine noise rose as the pilot taxied out onto the runway.

Remi tightened her belt and leaned her head back, pressing it into the headrest as she gripped the armrests and closed her eyes.

The plane had barely leveled off when Blankenship tapped Remi's hand. "How's our reputation?"

Remi felt a bit whiplashed by this newest non sequitur. In all the videos Remi had studied of the senator in preparation for the trip, Blankenship was cogent, knowledgeable, deft at using her words like a sword. Folksy stories and humor disarmed her opponents. This though... "I'm sorry, what are you asking me?"

"What's our reputation amongst foreign journalists coming to the United States?" Blankenship clarified. "It's important that they have a good experience in the U.S. We know that shades their word choices. We have a reputation to uphold worldwide."

"Ah. Yes. That's true. After last summer, our reputation isn't great, to be honest."

"Last summer is a specific timeframe. Tell me more."

"Journalism is a tight-knit group. We're all aware of what is happening on the ground. Stats about journalists being injured circulate widely in our profession. The perception is that last summer, foreign journalists were targeted by police. Of course, the police can't tell if they're foreign correspondents or local."

"When you use the term 'targeted,' that sounds authoritarian."

"You asked me what the foreign press is saying. With our current laws and the number of gun-related deaths… Look, being a foreign correspondent in the United States is considered by my colleagues to be a risky assignment, much like I perceive my assignments to more turbulent countries."

Blankenship scowled fiercely, swiveling in her seat. "They think of America as a war zone?"

"That's probably pushing it too far. But, yes, my foreign colleagues consider the assignment to come here to be dangerous."

"Well, that's not good. I'm sorry to hear that. But it's not true. People should report the facts unless they're opinion pieces in the editorials. America is a peaceful country. We're not a war zone, even if we have our kerfuffles."

"Journalism is dangerous," Remi countered. "In the last decade, over a thousand journalists were killed. War zones aren't the only hazardous assignments." Remi thought of Jules. Taking pictures at a Washington D.C. airport and now, blinded in one eye.

"In the war zone." Blankenship stabbed her pointy red fingernail into Remi's thigh.

"Take 2015 as an example. Over a hundred journalists were killed. Eleven in Syria. Another dozen in Iraq. All the rest were targeted with violence in what would be considered peaceful areas. The U.N. says that journalism is one of the most dangerous professions in the world. More journalists die than say, SEALs." Remi turned to T-Rex and gave him a grimace. She turned back to Blankenship. "With social media, it's getting worse. Harassment. Personal threats..."

"Elsewhere. Good thing that journalism is safe in the United States. Why, it's in our Constitution. That's how important the work is."

Remi wrinkled her nose. "I mentioned last summer and the reputation that we developed worldwide? There was an international advocacy group that looked at a single three-day period. There were over three hundred examples of journalists in America being physically attacked in that short time frame. Britain, Germany, Australia...about fifty were arrested—"

"For breaking the law."

"No charges. Booked. Held. Then released. No. They were simply arrested. Another fifty-ish incidents were documented where equipment was destroyed. Professional-grade equipment is not cheap. Almost two hundred journalists were assaulted, almost all of those were by police, tear-gassed, pepper-sprayed—which is no fun, let me tell you—rubber bullets. Yup, almost a hundred reporters were shot with rubber bullets. I mentioned Australia. They're conducting an investigation over one of their news crews being attacked by police. That incident has created some major diplomatic issues."

"They're our allies."

"Even if they weren't, reporters shouldn't be targeted. We show up to do a job. That's to observe and share our observations. But I don't report in America. I'm sharing the conversations I've had with my friends from around the world. This is about their perceptions. That's what you were asking me."

Blankenship cocked her head to the side. "Are you ever afraid?"

"Yes, ma'am." Remi pressed her hands into her thighs then smoothed them to her knees. "Almost always. I've learned to live with that feeling."

"But you choose to be there in the middle of the war, bombings and such."

"That's the difference between my fear and the fear of the people I'm reporting about. I'm there by choice and can easily leave at any point. They? They're stuck in that situation. Petrified for themselves and their children. From the time they get up in the morning, and all through the terror-filled nights, they are just trying to survive one day to the next." She put her hand on her heart. "I am so fortunate."

"You're a woman writing about places like where those girls back there making all that noise are from." Blankenship stuck a finger over the chair to point at the robotics team that sounded like they were having a blast. "It's not a great environment for women."

"That's right. And I've been injured out reporting. To be honest, that's something I handle okay. I report, I retreat to a safer place, rest, and recoup. But what's frightening are the online attacks. Threats of being killed, tortured, raped…" Remi stopped to swallow. "Misogyny seems to try to push women's perspectives and women's voices out of the newsroom. It's really become quite bad."

T-Rex turned his head. "Excuse me, Remi. About those threats. Have you received any?"

"Yes, of course. All the time."

His scowl deepened. "All the time. Recently?"

"Today. Is that recent enough?" Remi pulled out her phone and showed him an email she'd received, taking her step by step through the man's fantasy about her sexual enslavement. "The guy's an idiot. I tracked him down in less than ten minutes. He's in Oklahoma. Based on his job, family, living circumstances, he may have these thoughts, but it would be financially challenging to act on them."

"But there are others. Have you tracked them all down and cleared them?" T-Rex handed her phone back.

"It's like a hobby. Has to be. I watch TV at night, and instead of knitting, I search for the people making the threats."

"How do you think your threats impact the safety of this mission?" he asked.

"Look, if you're traveling with a known reporter, you're traveling with a threat vector. Period."

Chapter 24

Remi

Friday, Beirut, Lebanon

After the plane landed in Beirut to let Senator Blankenship, Remi, and Echo off, they made their way through customs. Senator Blankenship asked to be taken straight to the hotel for check-in. She was tired from traveling over the last couple of days and wanted to rest in her room.

"Diamond's dropping the girls off," Blankenship grumped, "and giving *my* speech without Remi covering it." She caught Remi's gaze. "Remi, I think you should have gone on with Diamond."

"I have a personal matter to attend to this evening," Remi said. It wasn't like she could jump back on the plane; it was gone. Besides, Remi had a copy of the speech in her inbox. No reason for her to stand there and watch Diamond deliver it.

Remi had already written a feel-good piece about the robotics team on the plane ride into London when she'd gone back and interviewed the girls. That box checked; she also got the above-the-fold story from Oxford. As far as her duty to the paper to pay for this trip to Lebanon, Remi was covered.

"When Diamond gets in," the senator said, "she can update me on what all went on out there on the border. Other than that, I'll see everyone bright and early in the morning."

Standing there, checking her Google maps app, Remi was thrilled to see that they were just a couple of blocks from the hospital. Remi could easily walk it. A little exercise would do her good. She was less thrilled to find out her room was positioned right next to the senator's again. She hoped the walls would be thicker than those in London.

Here was an interesting detail Remi discovered that she would *not* share publicly. T-Rex always had the room to one side of the senator. And then, one guy stayed in the room directly above hers, and one guy was in the room directly below hers.

So it made a bit of sense to Remi why she had the room she did. She helped to create a cocoon of safety for Senator Blankenship. They'd have to get through one of the team to get to the senator in any direction.

Diamond, on the other hand, in both hotels, was on a different floor.

Remi thought that too was by design since Diamond probably arranged for the room assignments. If Remi was traveling with a demanding boss, she too would want at least a little separation for the times when she was off duty.

The room was lovely, Remi thought as she pulled off her packs. She walked over to the little Juliette balcony, opening the doors to the beautiful weather and salt air. She looked out to the harbor and the boats, drawing in a deep breath.

It was getting late, what with the added two-hour time change.

Remi needed to get a hustle on if she were to be able to see Jean Baptiste today.

Taking a moment to drag a comb quickly through her hair, then wash her face and hands to rid herself of travel germs, Remi tucked her key card into her utility belt and headed toward the hospital.

Standing in the hallway at St. George's Hospital, Remi's nostrils were assailed by the smell of disinfectant. The phenol smell like that of insulin. Peeking into the window of Jean Baptiste's room, where the curtain hadn't been pulled fully closed, Remi saw her dear friend lying with his head propped up by the angle of the bed and a plethora of pillows. His hospital gown was askew.

It was a strange sensation, horror. Like a camera app that could make the background blur and pop the focus onto some small detail. Right now, Remi couldn't drag her focus away from Jean Baptiste's arm. The splint and bandages, the IV line. It was a storyboard. The welts and bruising. She didn't want to guess what had left marks that looked like that. But she knew from interviewing past torture victims that those were most probably electrical burns.

Her stomach sloshed.

Jean Baptiste turned his head and caught her eye. He attempted a weak smile and a come-hither curl of his finger.

Remi smiled back and lifted her hand in a wave, then turned to push through the door.

"You're awake," she said softly. She didn't want to be bright. Or fake. They'd known each other too long. She also didn't want Jean Baptiste to read disgust on her face at man's inhumanity to man. She tried to bubble up the essence of T-Rex. Calm and steady.

That image helped, and Remi leaned into it.

Pulling a chair to his bedside, Remi slid her hand under his. Remi wanted him to feel her compassion and concern but not do anything that would cause him more pain.

She licked her lips and then sat silently.

That moment held for a long stretch. Both of their faces were wet from tears that dripped without being tended to by the swipe of a finger.

Finally, Jean Baptiste said, "Don't expect to see them again unless they show up in a propaganda video." His voice, barely a whisper, pushed out through cracked lips.

Remi's face crumpled. She swallowed.

"And then, for your sanity's sake, don't watch."

Remi shook her head.

"I was there. I went through it. I watched Marie-Claude and Éloïse go through it. I know how tough you are with strangers. I promise you, it will eat your soul if you watch it happen to your friends. You'll be done with this business."

Remi blinked hard to clear her vision. "Are you serious right now? Are you done?"

"Done. I talked to American University, accepting

their offer of a professorship. I'll be teaching over there. If ISIS starts pushing over the border, I'll jump into the Mediterranean and swim to Europe if that's the only way I can get out. I was with them for hours, and I'm headed to a life of nightmares. Don't. Make. This. You."

"I'd be an observer, not a participant. This is a horrible consideration. Look, I talked to Karen. She said that FR-13 got a ransom."

"Promise me you won't watch."

Pressing her lips together, Remi stared out the window for a long moment while Jean Baptiste squeezed her wrist.

"Remi?" He pressed her for the promise.

"Don't you think it's important that their friends watch should it come down to that? Isn't it craven to simply say, 'You suffered, and I'm going to turn away and pretend it didn't happen'?"

"For others? Yes. They should watch and know the dangers. And know what happens when governments fall to terror. Let others carry that."

Remi shook her head, eyes still focused out the window.

"Remi, we need you. The world needs you."

Remi started laughing. She laughed so hard she snorted. With her wrist covering her mouth, she focused back on Jean Baptiste. "Sorry. Nerves, apparently."

"I'm serious."

Remi sobered.

"We're a unique brand of nuts," Jean Baptiste said. "It takes an insanely sane person to do this job. Very few can. It's *important*. I didn't burn out. I was burned out of the profession by becoming the story. Experiencing it for myself."

"And you don't think that personal experience would help you better explain to the public?" Remi asked.

"I think that it will open old wounds. Retraumatize. My mental health was always kind of rocky. It has to be. Who but someone with Swiss cheese brains could walk through a mire of dead women and children, searching out the best image to explain the story?" He tapped his finger on her wrist. "Granted, photojournalism is my job, not yours. And there's a big difference." He paused. "The point is the same. It's a unique personality that can be both sensitive and insensitive. Willing to face humanity's worst and stay with courage, looking for glimmers of hope. And still have self-preservation somewhere in the mix. Some of the people with those characteristics become military. Some aid workers. We," he tapped an index finger to his nose, then pointed it at Remi, "we're the storytellers. Not many can hack this line of work. Don't watch any videos of Éloïse and Marie-Claude. Guard your ability to do the job for as long as you can. It's *important* work. You never know what tomorrow brings."

Remi looked over her shoulder as a nurse pushed through the door. "I'm sorry, visitor hours are over for today. It's time that I get Monsieur Roujean fed and cleaned up for the night."

Standing, Remi leaned in carefully to kiss Jean Baptiste's cheek. "I'll be back tomorrow. Have the nurse text me what I can bring you besides flowers and flan."

Taking the stairs to the lobby, Remi answered her phone.

"Remi? It's Puck." It was a reporter friend covering the Department of Justice, Washington D.C. "I read your story in the paper today. Kudos."

Remi didn't like the tone in his voice; this was a preamble. "Thanks."

"Listen, today, the DOJ seized thirty web domains that are associated with regional propaganda and disinformation."

"Okay."

"Some state-owned TV channels were taken down as well. The DOJ was targeting allied rebel groups in Yemen. One of them was based out of Beirut."

"Oh, interesting. Did they give a reason other than Yemen?" Remi's voice echoed in the stairwell as she clattered down the steps.

"Disinformation campaigns aimed at U.S. voters. The web domains were owned by U.S. companies."

"That would mean webpages that aren't on American domains are still functioning. They're just not able to reach U.S. citizens. Is that right?"

"That's right. I thought that you might want a heads-up. You're in Beirut, traveling with Senator Blankenship, who has a lot of sway on these kinds of issues. I've been watching the chatter amongst the stakeholders. I need to warn you, being in close proximity to the senator right now might not be healthy."

Chapter 25

Remi

Friday, Beirut, Lebanon

Remi walked out of the hospital into a twilight sky.

While she was visiting with Jean Baptiste, the streets filled with the masses protesting the government's lack of action in providing for basic needs. Chants were going up now about the fuel shortages.

Remi had recently done an article on how bad it was for the Lebanese citizens. The quantities of fuel smugglers took over the border into Syria, turned the already difficult situation dire.

Before wading into the crowd, Remi took a moment to put her wrist supports in place. Since she was off duty, she pulled her bag off her shoulder and tugged at the embroidered press patches that were Velcroed in place. Without backup, she certainly didn't want to be a target. She'd just blend in as she made her way back to the hotel.

When Remi moved through dense crowds like this, it was her practice to grab her own wrists, holding her bent arms up at chest height. Not only was she ready to throw a block or a punch, but her sharp elbows discouraged people from crushing her from the right and left. The space she created in front of her chest protected her from being pressed so tightly that she couldn't inhale enough air and possibly pass out.

Remi had been in Paris at an S.O.S. Racism concert at the Bastille for le quatorze juillet celebration. The stage held a string of famous artists. The area was a beehive of humanity. Remi was only there because she was reporting on the celebration and the influx of francophone refugees. Pressed so tightly together that she was lifted off her feet, the undulations of the crowd moved her about like she was fighting a riptide. Remi had been terrified both by her claustrophobia, the feeling of zero control, and the genuine chance of being crushed or trampled.

As people passed out, they were lifted overhead, and their unconscious bodies were passed, person to person, like a stage diver into a mosh pit. Eventually, the person in crisis made it to the other side, where a line of ambulances waited for the next victim to be handed out of the crowd.

At one point that night, Remi saw a guy she knew. Big, like T-Rex, Remi had screamed his name. His long arm had shot out into the crowd. He grabbed her hand and hauled her back to him. He was so big that he had become a pillar of refuge. He had five other women clinging to him. Remi was the sixth. They all just hung on for dear life as he pressed the masses away.

Christian, yeah, that was his name. She could use that kind of help now if only T-Rex were here.

When Remi had finally left the Parisian concert, she made it to the last Metro of the night. Everyone was so anxious to get on those cars and get home that there was another press and swell of humanity. As the train approached, bodies heaved forward. Remi had climbed a metal ladder attached to the wall for her safety. She decided that once the station cleared out, she'd try to find a taxi, or rest on a bench until the trains started up in the morning.

Clinging to the rungs, head and shoulders above the swarm, Remi watched as a woman lost her balance and fell onto the track. She was killed by the train.

Remi's camera had the right angle for the pictures. Her story made the front page top fold. It was the story that launched her reputation as a significant journalist. But Remi would have been just fine if she'd written her little article about racism in France and gone home to sleep in her bed, and that woman was still alive.

Crowds could be lethal.

Remi had to get herself out of this bruhaha.

After a few minutes of struggle, Remi made it to the other side of the throng, where she saw him. T-Rex stood there scanning the crowd.

At first, Remi thought he was trying to assess the dangers of the rally in proximity to the senator's hotel. But when she caught his eye, and saw the flood of relief on his face, Remi knew he was there to find her.

She raised her hand to wave, then jostled through the last of the human knot and out into a pocket of air.

They walked across the street together, away from the others.

"Are you okay?" were the first words out of his mouth.

"Good." She needed to catch her breath before she said more.

T-Rex had an interesting way of splitting his focus. He seemed to both look at her and assess their surroundings. She could well imagine him in the streets of Kabul or wherever, looking over a map while maintaining awareness of the comings and goings of possible threats.

It was a skill born of requirement.

T-Rex slid a hand down her arm to her wrist then lifted it to see better. "What's this about? Are your wrists hurt? You had them on yesterday in Oxford."

Remi didn't want to tell the truth because there might be accountability. She simply turned them over. "Braces," Remi added. "Journalists are forbidden from carrying a weapon."

He ran his finger up the metal support. "Unless it's a weapon of opportunity."

She smiled. "In countries like London, where even as a civilian I can't carry things like pepper spray, I often wear these when walking alone."

"You don't think it makes you seem like a target?"

"Because I look wounded?" She adjusted her pack to keep herself from reaching out to touch T-Rex. "Hopefully, my bearing shows them that I'm not a victim. My eye contact. My voice when I need it. But yes," she held out her arm and twisted it this way and that, "this makes an excellent close protection tool." She held it out to him. "I had it lined with an anti-stab material, so I can fend off knife attacks, which are prevalent in some parts of Europe."

"Like London." He released her wrist and focused on her eyes. "Clever." He tipped his head and started to walk away.

That was that.

Man, Remi knew they called these guys the silent professionals, but T-Rex seemed to take that to extremes.

She jogged a couple of steps and fell in beside him. "Hey, I had a heads-up from a friend about a DOJ Beirut connection that may or may not show up in your intelligence reports. Connecting the dots, it might lead to Senator Blankenship."

He stopped her at a bench under a date tree. Scanned the area for any ears. "Give me a minute, please." As she sat there, watching him, T-Rex pressed his sternum. "Echo Actual."

And just like every time he did that, hormones shot through her and left her panties damp with need.

T-Rex moved to stand far enough away that she couldn't hear him. Remi took advantage of the opportunity to stare at him, taking in his muscular thighs, the length of his legs, his huge feet. Remi reached up to run a finger along the corners of her mouth to make sure she wasn't visibly drooling.

Luckily her phone pinged with a text distraction.

Liu: Since you're hanging out with special forces beasts (lucky girl), I thought you might like to see this.

She tapped on the link. Scanning down the article, reading about the unnamed female sailor who had completed a thirty-seven-week training course to become the first-ever special warfare combatant-craft crewman. Remi stopped and mouthed that title. It sounded daunting. Thirty-five percent of those who begin that course succeed in graduating, she read. *Wow.* Remi would *love* to interview her. Maybe one of her contacts could find her a way in.

This gal was going to head one of the three Navy Special Warfare's boat teams. Good for her.

"You look happier," T-Rex said as he came over.

"Five syllables," Remi said.

"What?"

"Nothing. About my look, I was excited about the potential for a story." She handed her phone over to T-Rex, and he scanned down.

It was a test; Remi would admit it. What would his reaction be, having come up through SEALs to his present position? Would he be upset that some estrogen had made its way into the all-boys club?

She was not disappointed when a big old grin crossed over his face, handing the phone back, he said, "Good news."

God, she loved his smiles.

"Two syllables." Remi accepted her phone and swiped the screen closed.

"Are you playing a game?" he asked.

"Of sorts, I guess." She slid the phone into the thigh pocket on her tactical tights. She was tired and wanted to go in. But it might mean that she couldn't be with T-Rex, so she didn't move from the bench.

"When I found you coming out of the crowd, you looked like… Did you get to see Jean Baptiste? Did he have news about Marie-Claude and Éloïse?"

"Your team keeps you well informed. Yes. I saw Jean Baptiste for just a moment. He seemed to believe that our friends Éloïse and Marie-Claude will, in all likelihood, never come home. Knowing what I know, having followed so many stories, I'm afraid that if they do come home, they will most likely have had their souls crushed into a billion sparkling pieces, each one sharp enough to draw blood." She found stability and support in T-Rex's gaze. "I don't know what to pray for. A quick death? No one is going to save them—no one's going into Syria." She looked out over the harbor. "I want to turn back time. To beg them not to go."

"Turn that around," T-Rex said, "if you had a story you were following, would your friends be able to keep you back?"

She stared at the water for a long time. Too long. She should say something, and yet no words would come to her. She was a blank. Finally, she sniffed and opened her mouth to say no—but instead, she pulled out her pinging cell phone. Boxing up her angst for Marie-Claude and Éloïse and putting it on the shelf with her worries about all her other friends in harm's way, Remi swiped the screen.

Diamond: I can't get the senator on the phone. Plane issues. Spending the night in Jordan. Should be there by noon and her speech at American U. Thanks for passing on the message.

"She should get a better night's sleep wherever she is," Remi said, handing the phone off to T-Rex, again, so he could read it, too.

Remi stood and adjusted her pack over her shoulder.

T-Rex fell in step with her. "What are you doing now?"

"I thought I'd go up to my room and call room service for some dinner."

"Are you hungry?" he asked.

Remi stopped and sent him a lust-filled look that she hoped he'd read as an invitation. "Starved."

Chapter 26

T-Rex

Friday, Beirut, Lebanon

"Starved," Remi said with those gorgeous eyes of hers.

She took his breath away. Blood thrumming through his body, his dick stood at attention. He definitely wanted to follow through with the invitation he read in her eyes. *Work the problem,* he told himself.

After Winner had called with information about the protest down the street, passing by the hospital where Remi had gone to see Jean Baptiste, T-Rex had swapped his schedule with Havoc's, then went after Remi to make sure she made it back to the hotel safe and sound.

She'd been fine.

Physically.

Bad-freaking-ass.

But he'd been worried about her mentally. Not about the things that had happened on their trip. She seemed fine about that. But from overheard conversations, T-Rex had learned during their short time together that Remi's friends were family, just like his Echo brothers were family to T-Rex.

The FR-13 team was facing brutal circumstances.

Remi seemed to be able to compartmentalize like he and his brothers in special forces were trained to do. T-Rex was beginning to see the parallels in some aspects of their careers.

Even with that training, T-Rex was having trouble with compartmentalization. Remi was a distraction. She wasn't trying to be.

"Starved." Yeah, so was he.

He couldn't hold her hand, put his hand on her back, or heck, even walk too close as they moved into the hotel. Winner could be at her computer watching them cross the street now with eyes in the sky. Not that spending personal time with Remi was against the rules. He simply thought that Remi would appreciate the privacy.

T-Rex took a breath and counseled himself, *go for it. Make a move*. "I was heading to my room to order dinner. I'm not on duty until zero two hundred."

Remi looked up at him expectantly. It was the look he'd been hoping for.

"Would you like to join me?"

She rolled her lips in. A moment of hesitation. "Yeah, I'd really like that."

Keeping his hands to himself, maintaining proper social distancing between them, was killer. Waiting until they reached the fifteenth floor to touch her, to taste her lips? Agony.

They climbed onto the elevator, and it filled behind them with people in costly designer clothes.

Remi didn't do well in confined spaces. He'd watched her psych herself up on the planes and in elevators the whole trip and was at a loss for how to help her navigate that. It wasn't his place, still…

But right now, she seemed fine. Nervous, but so was T-Rex.

Shit. He hadn't been with a woman in almost five years. He deployed, and then his wife died. Five years, he hoped he didn't embarrass himself with too much enthusiasm or too little self-control.

The door slid open, two people got off.

Remi moved a little closer to him. Her breast brushed against his arm.

His dick stood at attention, saluting her amazing body. His heart pounded.

The doors open and the family got off. Now they were alone.

As the door slid closed, Remi bubbled with laughter. "Nerves," she said.

Man, he wanted to scoop her into his arms, crush her into him. He wanted his mouth on her. His hands.

He licked his lips.

The light flickered.

The elevator was thrust into sudden pitch black. Then came a sudden, stomach-dropping thunk as they came to an abrupt stop.

Remi cussed under her breath. There was a pop and then sudden illumination as Remi held up a pink chemical light.

"Blankenship was right. You're like Mary Poppins."

"What's that?" She looked up at him, confused. Those long eyelashes. Those sweet lips.

"Did you grow up in the U.S.?"

"Yes." She tipped her head.

"There's a movie called Mary Poppins."

"I'm… Yes, I just don't understand what you're talking about."

"You keep reaching into various pockets and pulling out random things." He waved a hand toward the glowing pink stick. "Chem-lights."

"Live and learn," she said.

"This happens frequently here?"

"Very unfortunately, yes. They have trouble with the electricity. It won't take but a second. They just need to power up their generator. It's a good thing all those people got off first. Normally, getting stopped is its own kind of torture. I'm not great when I feel trapped."

Brushing his fingers down her sleeve, T-Rex reached for her hand, but she rolled into his embrace instead, wrapping her arms tightly around him and cuddling her head into his chest.

T-Rex held her tight, painting a hand over her head, tugging her hairband from her ponytail, running the strands through his fingers like silken water.

They held.

Honestly, T-Rex was fine being just here, doing just this.

But the moment lasted longer than he'd expected. Seconds turned into minutes. Remi's body banded against him. Her stress levels rising. "Are you okay?" he whispered.

"This…we should be out of here by now."

Without letting her go, T-Rex pressed his sternal communicator. "Echo Actual."

"Havoc. The senator's asleep. I checked on her. She won't even know we had the power outage."

"Did you call the desk and get a timeframe?"

"Negative."

"Remi and I are in the elevator between the fifth and sixth floors."

"That's crap. Is Remi okay? She's claustrophobic."

T-Rex dropped a kiss into her hair. "I've got her. Can you find out what the holdup is?"

"Wilco. Out."

"Havoc is going to get us some more information," T-Rex told Remi.

"I think I'm going to sit down. I'm…it's not awful, but because this didn't resolve. Yeah, I should warn you, I'm starting to freak out a bit."

"Does it help to talk?"

"Ha! Yes. So I'm in an elevator with a guy who prefers five syllables or less."

"Oh, that's what you've been doing?" He sat first so Remi wouldn't lower herself and have his bulk hovering above her. "Counting my syllables?" For whatever reason, he was charmed by that. By her.

She sat down between his legs and leaned against him.

"What should we talk about? You pick a topic," he suggested.

"Okay. T-Rex," Remi said. "When did they start calling you that? Why not Godzilla?"

"I got the name my first day of kindergarten when I was learning what recess meant." He kissed her hair again, and she twisted to offer her lips. It was one brief kiss. But it tasted so sweet. "I went out with the rest of my class after lunch, and we were playing dinosaurs."

She chuckled. "As one does as a five-year-old." She absentmindedly played with his fingers. "My favorite dinosaur is the stegosaurus. It seems after you reach a certain age, say seven, people stop caring what your favorite dinosaur is. But for some reason, they continue to care about your favorite color. Or horoscope sign—but that's based on birth dates, not preference."

"Favorite color?" he asked.

"Indigo. You?"

"*Navy* blue."

"Of course it is." She held the pink light straight up, her eyes searching around the elevator car.

He didn't want her thinking "trapped" thoughts.

"Scorpio. October 25th."

"Passionate. Yep."

"You?"

"Gemini, June first."

Remi pulled her phone from her thigh pocket. Opened it and scrolled. "Let's see," she murmured. The anxiety in her voice ticked up. When she settled back against him again, that strain in her muscles released. He felt like a giant of a man. He felt like a protective force.

She didn't need that from him. But he liked the sensation all the same.

"Gemini. It says that you are great at staying calm in stressful situations." She laughed. "Focused on what needs to be done. Geminis don't find fear and panic to be helpful. Hmm, who does find that helpful? Uhm, Geminis don't like escalating a crisis… Geminis can talk someone out of their fears. Lot in here about fear… Geminis are solution-based. Well." She turned her phone off and slid it back in her pocket. "There you have it. I'd say that was just about perfect." She peeked up at him. "You're keeping me sane. Thank you."

At some point, T-Rex wanted to know what caused her phobia, but this was absolutely the wrong time to ask about that.

T-Rex sat there perfectly contented.

"Playground," Remi whispered as she angled her chin up. "Go back to that. There's a story there."

"Mom and Dad were both college athletes."

"Where was this?"

"Maryland. Mom was a six-foot-three basketball player. My dad played college football."

"Big genes."

"From the get-go. I was out on the playground at my very first recess. We were stomping around being dinosaurs. I wanted to be a triceratops. That's my favorite dinosaur."

"To this day?" Remi asked.

"Yup. I still love triceratops," he laughed, "but the other boys insisted I be T-Rex."

"It's your bizarrely short arms, isn't it?" His skin warmed as she rubbed her hand up and down his arm. She pulled his hands tighter around her. Inching back a little more. "I bet that made all those pushups in boot camp easier, less distance to travel." She turned and planted a kiss on his bicep. It felt playful like she wanted to make extra sure he knew he was being teased. Like she was protecting his feelings.

And that sensation of Remi protecting him, caring, turned on a switch. Suddenly there was light and warmth where he'd been in the dark for so long.

I'm ready. That thought was a revelation. He'd crossed "relationship" off his life plan. Or pushed it out into the future. And here he was, for the first time since Jess, wanting to understand what made a woman tick. All of her. Intellectual. Emotional. And yeah, definitely sexual.

"They kept calling you that after your first day of school?"

"From that point, I took on the playground security job. My pals called in 'The T-Rex of Doom.'"

She laughed, and T-Rex's spirit soared.

"What would you do?" Remi asked. "You can't beat people up at school."

"They'd call, and I'd do my best dinosaur roars as I stomped my way over to stand between the bully and my friends. No one in Mrs. Pennyworth's kindergarten class was bullied or harassed."

Remi shook against him as she laughed. His whole body was waking up.

"That was where I met Jess."

"Your wife? That's amazing."

What was amazing was he'd blurted that out. It was inexplicable, but T-Rex felt compelled to tell Remi about this. "Yup. She was a scrappy little thing. I remember the first time she put me in my place. She was in a boxing stance, fists up, yelling, 'Try it. Come on, just try.' The boy was circling. Taunting. That kid was like a third-grader and almost as big as I was."

"Wow. Did it turn into a fistfight?"

"He ran away. Instead of gratitude, Jess turned to me. 'Why'd you get in my way?'"

"Ha!"

T-Rex pitched his voice like a little girl. "'I was going to whoop his butt.' I protested. I said she was so little, and the guy was too big for her to fight. And, man, I remember this like it was yesterday. She said, 'My daddy says it's technique. The bigger they are, the harder they fall, mommy says.' I stopped her. 'Your mommy wants you to fight?' His voice rose again to imitate five-year-old Jess. 'My mommy says if anyone gives you trouble, you know how to protect yourself. We'll stand behind you. My mommy's a soldier, and I'm going to be a soldier, too'."

Remi squeezed his thigh. "And you fell in love with her smart tongue?"

"Oh, I knew right then and there I wanted to marry her. She rejected me outright. And kept rejecting me all through middle school. Then came the miracle of high school. When her body started to change, she added a little makeup to her routine. I joined the rugby team. She started showing up to the games. Finally, sophomore year, she said yes, she'd be my girlfriend. It took me almost a decade of patience. But we got there."

"When were you married?"

"Right out of high school. Spring, senior year, we found out Jess was pregnant. I joined the Navy to support us. We kept our marriage and the baby secret until after graduation. We were afraid our parents wouldn't be on board with our decisions. I headed off to boot camp. Jess had a miscarriage."

"I'm sorry."

"Bad timing for all of that. In hindsight, it was best. We would have loved that baby and done our best, but we had already decided that we didn't want kids."

"Did that ever change for you? Do you have children?"

"No kids. And no. I'm just not that guy. I think it's best if I'm godfather to my friend's kids." He realized he was testing the waters. It would be unfair for him to want a relationship with someone who wanted something he wasn't willing to give.

Her saying, "Same," blew through him like a sigh of relief.

"I'm curious," T-Rex began. "How do you handle the mental part of your job? You've been to some of the most dangerous places on earth. You've interviewed some of the most lethal people."

"Oh, I'm terrified most of the time. No, that's not right. I am terrified, just never at the time when I should be—always after. Except for claustrophobia—that's an immediate sensation—I think it's kind of funny that I feel fear—the adrenaline dumping, sweaty, hot, gross fear all the time. And it's almost as if I have to find a life-or-death event because, in that, I have clarity. I have peace—no, that's a poor choice of words. I have *respite* from the fear during an event to stay alive in that place and time. Some of my friends suggest that I'm addicted to adrenaline when it's really the opposite. I *despise* the feeling of adrenaline and seek ways to dissipate it. It just so happens that I feel relief from terror in the very places where I should feel it most acutely when I have my head in the lion's mouth. That's true, except for confined spaces that I can't leave. Fear of being trapped is a whole other beast."

"I get what you're saying. I do. When I'm on a mission, my senses expand. I'm right there in the moment, dealing with the events. No time to ponder. No time to focus on emotions. There's a Zen quality to it. Pure presence."

"Yes, that's it."

They fell into silence.

T-Rex let his memories float him back to his teen years. He'd signed on the dotted line to join the Navy. Jess started college in criminal justice to become a police officer…

They'd decided it was the safe place for her to be, a sleepy town cop.

His job with the SEALs moved them to California.

Back to the East Coast to Virginia for a short stint with DEVGRU—SEAL Team Six.

Then on to North Carolina when he joined The Unit.

And in North Carolina, things weren't quite as sleepy.

Jess was killed saving a family from a husband who was out of his mind on drugs.

Dead. Four years. T-Rex would never recover from it. It was a constant bubble of pain in his chest. It was like losing one of your senses and spending your days realizing it was gone, not coming back, and now he'd have to learn to navigate the world anew. Diminished.

On missions, T-Rex packed those emotions into his case and carried them around with him. They waited on his empty cot for him to get back to base from his assignment.

Missions required him to be laser-focused. And T-Rex knew exactly what Remi was saying earlier about being in the middle of chaos. If you wanted to survive, it took up every available cell and electrical impulse. The senses expanded, the mind sharpened. If he wallowed in emotion, he'd be dead a hundred times over. He didn't feel grief amid the chaos. And she was right; he experienced respite when he stuck his head into the lion's mouth.

A revelation.

It was in the downtime when the grief was a fog that blurred his view of the world.

And he didn't even hope for sunshine to disperse the mist.

T-Rex was startled when he realized he was sharing this aloud. "Listen to me talking to you about this shit."

Remi had spun around to face him, kneeling between his legs, her hands resting on his thighs. "I'm glad to hear what you're thinking."

"Part of the job."

"I'm not on the job. I have personal time."

"Not what I meant," T-Rex clarified. "Part of your success at your job must be an innate ability to be a good listener."

She blinked up at him…so beautiful in the glow of the pink light. "Yeah. I guess you're right. That's been my lifelong gift. I sit down, and people just spill out their stories."

"Echo Six." T-Rex heard in his earpiece. He put a finger in the air to pause their conversation.

T-Rex pressed his comms button. "Echo Actual."

"I'm down in the lobby. Someone stole the fuel for the generator. The staff is scrambling to find some, even if it's just enough to get the elevators to a floor and the doors open. You two aren't the only ones trapped. They're hoping ten-fifteen minutes to get the elevators cleared out. It will probably be a lot longer until they can get the lights to stay on. Blankenship is still asleep. Ty's outside of her room."

"Copy. Over." He looked down at Remi with her trusting eyes. "Ten, maybe fifteen minutes."

"We were talking about fear. How do you deal with it?"

"I've been asked that a lot. And the truth is, I feel like I'm where I'm supposed to be. I feel like there's a divine shield over me," T-Rex said.

"Does it extend to those around you? Because if that's the case, I think your shield might have a crack in it."

"Bad things happen. No reason in this world that the bad things should happen to other people and not me."

"Yeah. I get that sentiment. I really do. Why should my life be magically comfortable and easy when children are getting blown up, standing in line at the spigot to get some water for their family?"

"Man, this is dark."

"Yep. How about you ask me something you wonder about me?" Remi suggested.

"Were you ever married?" Not what he'd meant to say. But fine, he kicked that door open, might as well walk in.

"No."

"Close to it?"

"No."

"How about love?" He held his breath. His heart pounded.

"What about it?"

"Have you ever fallen in love before?"

"Oh, so many times. I've fallen in love with sunsets over preserves where giraffes and elephants roam free. I've fallen in love with the gentle lapping of water against the side of our little boat as we made our way through Vietnamese rivers past rice patties. I have fallen in love with the wide eyes of newborns who look so wise with their toothless milk smiles. Like they still remember all of the secrets of the universe, and what a shame it is that by the time they can speak, they've forgotten. I have fallen in love with peace amongst the chaos."

The silence fell gently, blanketing them.

"I want to go to your room for that dinner when we get out of here," she said. "But the dining room won't be working until the lights come on."

"I have MREs in my pack—and that actually might be a good thing."

"Oh?"

"My room is right next to the senator's. Havoc will be back on guard duty."

"And he'll see me going in. Is that a problem?"

"Not when I'm feeding you an MRE."

And with that, there was a whir and a chunk. And the elevator moved.

Chapter 27

Remi

Friday, Beirut, Lebanon

The lights blinked on.

The elevator shook.

T-Rex reached up and pressed the button, and they came to an immediate stop on the sixth floor.

"I think it's prudent to take the stairs," Remi whispered as she emerged from the elevator into the lighted hallway, chem-light still clutched in her hand.

"Copy that."

They didn't hold hands, didn't walk too closely. They were professionals on a work assignment, not giddy kids returning from a frat party to their dorm. Decorum was important to Remi. Though, she hoped the magic she'd experienced trapped on the elevator with T-Rex wasn't a mirage.

When they shoved through the stair door, the lights went out again. "Huh," was T-Rex's only reaction.

They crept up the stairs, casting pink monster shadows on the cream-painted walls.

Pushing through the door on the sixteenth floor, Havoc watched Remi and T-Rex make their way down the hall.

"All's quiet?" T-Rex asked Havoc when they reached his room.

"The senator's snoring," Havoc said. Havoc had his own light stick in his hand. There were more laid at intervals down the hall. Havoc would know if anyone were trying to sneak up on him to get to the senator.

Tipping her ear closer to Blankenship's door and concentrating, Remi could make out Blankenship's snores drifting from between the cracks.

"We're starved," T-Rex said. "I'm making MREs. Can I fix you one? I'll take over your post while you eat."

"Thanks, man, but I ate while Ty was at the door. It's all good."

T-Rex lifted a hand, then pulled a key card from his pocket.

"No electricity. Can we get in?" Remi asked.

"Batteries." T-Rex turned to her. "Three syllables."

She sent him a self-conscious grin.

Swiping the card, T-Rex pushed the door wide, allowing Remi to go in first. As the door shut behind him, she whispered, "I could hear the senator snoring. The walls must be thin like in London."

"Not as bad as in London, the senator snores loudly."

Remi nodded. She stepped forward and pressed herself against T-Rex. "I want to be with you. Would you be okay with that?"

T-Rex's slow smile did magical things to her libido. "Are you asking for my consent?"

"Checking boundaries." She rose on her toes to whisper, "And to see if you have condoms handy."

T-Rex frowned his disappointment. "I don't have a need to carry them. No."

Remi reached under her tunic and unclasped her utility belt, laying it on the lowboy. Her fingers tugged a foil packet out from the center-left pouch. She twiddled it in her fingers for him to see, then laid it next to her belt.

And lest he thought she was promiscuous and always ready to bang one out, she added, "They're a handy tool in a dirty situation."

"Yeah?" He cocked his head to the side. "Is this what you call a dirty situation?"

"I meant like explosion debris in the air, I can put my phone or my recorder in it to keep them safe."

He picked it up. "Then this can't be lubricated."

"Not an issue," Remi said.

When she turned toward him, T-Rex brushed her hair out of her eyes. "You are somewhere between Mary Poppins." He kissed her. "A Boy Scout." He kissed her. "And Mata Hari." He pressed her against the wall, dragging her hands over her head. Holding her there as their kisses grew more demanding.

He leaned his hips into her, his knee pressing between her thighs. She moaned.

With a chuckle and a glance toward the door, T-Rex locked his lips on hers then lifted Remi off her feet, moving them farther into the room, away from Havoc's hearing.

When T-Rex set her down, she whispered, "Music,

so we don't have to be so conscious of noise, maybe?" She lifted her brows.

Taking advantage of T-Rex's scrolling an app for music, she slid off her shoes and socks. Classic rock filtered through his speakers with its heart-thumping beat, mimicking the thrum of her blood.

When he lifted his gaze to hers, checking that this was acceptable, Remi nodded.

T-Rex placed the phone on the nightstand and leaned his shoulder against the wall.

Remi unwound her scarf and dropped it to the floor. "I want to watch you undress." Had she imagined him correctly during last night's attempted stress relief with her vibrator?

The electrical outage and pink light added a sense of romance and maybe a little danger. Remi was bright with anticipation. She smiled, feeling deliciously taboo.

T-Rex gamely moved toward the lowboy where she could see him head to foot. He lifted his shirt and tugged off his conceal carry holster. Opening a drawer, he slid his service weapons inside. Every move was smooth and graceful. No ego. No posturing.

They seemed to sync, the two of them.

This level of comfort wasn't something that Remi had anticipated. It baffled her; it made her nervous that he didn't make her nervous. She sat on the bed, and he let her just look at him. Drink him in. She wanted to know every inch of this man's body.

Bending, he simultaneously untied both his boots. He toed them off, kicking them out of the way.

Grabbing his shirt, dragging it over his head.

Remi's fingers itched to explore the ridges of his abs, the breadth of his massive shoulders. Remi had only seen muscles like this in sports magazines, romance novel covers, and in her fantasies.

As she made her way over to him, T-Rex flexed his pecs, making them bulge rhythmically to the beat of the music.

A delicious lusty laugh bubbled up, filling the room with Remi's joy.

He was glorious.

This wasn't how she'd anticipated their first time together. She'd imagined him tossing her around like a rag doll, all testosterone, and need. She'd been with someone who'd acted like that before. It wasn't like it looked in the movies. It was actually pretty unnerving, and she never slept with that guy again. He'd frightened her too badly. She'd felt too vulnerable in the face of the guy's strength. She hadn't trusted him to exercise self-control.

T-Rex was nothing if not sublimely in control of himself.

Remi couldn't imagine him trying to hurt her. He just didn't need that to bolster his sense of self.

On her part, Remi wasn't quite sure what to do. Awkwardness—new was always a bit fumbley. And yet, she'd never felt excitement like this before. Her libido had never roared this loudly.

This felt...*inevitable.*

Her eyes drifted down, watching T-Rex's fingers, unbuckling his belt. His cock tented his zipper. "Good?" He was checking in.

"More." The anticipation sent a wave through her body, making her weak in the knees. She put her hand on the wall. Her bottom lip dropped open as she panted.

Slowly, slowly he tugged down the zipper. His thumbs slipped into his waistband, and he slid his trousers and boxers off at the same time, catching the tops of his socks. One graceful flourish, and he stood free and proud. His heavy dick pulsing in his palm.

"Now you." Sitting on the slipper chair where his towel had been draped to dry, T-Rex stroked his cock as he watched her.

Remi closed her eyes, feeling the rhythm of the driving beats in the music. Letting the thrum sync with her heartbeat, Remi swayed. Her head fell back as she let the experience of this moment take hold of her. Let her body bask in the sensations of desire, the hot neediness of it.

Slowly she slid her tights off, grateful that this morning, when she was dressing, she eschewed her normal gym-styled undergarments and had chosen, instead, a lingerie set that made her feel wanton with its satin and ribbons.

As she stood, she let her fingers slide along her legs, showing off their length, their smooth curves. Yeah, when she was trying to low-key seduce him the other day in her room—lying there with her legs stretched out before her—T-Rex had had a hard time dragging his attention away. He'd followed their lines up to the hem of her shirt, his tongue slicking a quick lick over his lips. Remi had wished he'd focused that swipe of tongue on her skin.

The thought of his mouth on her made Remi's body convulse with need. And no, that wasn't lost on T-Rex either. He leaned forward and stretched a hand toward her. Reeling her gently in. He laid his forehead against her stomach, petting his hands up and down her legs. When he looked up, she cupped his cheeks in her palms and leaned over to kiss him. Pressing her lips hard against his, then opening them to him.

His hands explored under her tunic as their tongues tangled. Hooking into the sides of her panties, he drew them down her legs, the rasp of the elastic…now, he'd know just how wet she was for him.

One foot then the other, he slid Remi's panties off.

Remi was in no mood to wait. Slow just wasn't going to cut it here. She'd been lusting for this man's body since she walked across the empty bay at the airport in Washington.

Remi reached for the foil packet, biting and tugging to open it and release the condom.

With his hands under her tunic cupping her ass, Remi leaned over and painted the condom onto his cock. "I can't wait," she said as she stepped a foot out to either side of him.

He held the base of his cock steady as she slid herself down the length of his shaft, feeling the delicious sensation of fullness.

Hands resting on his shoulders, eyes shut, head dipping back, she let T-Rex take over her senses.

He groaned as he gripped at her hips.

"Sh-sh-sh." She giggled. Nodding toward the door where Havoc was feet away.

Reaching for the hem of her tunic, Remi tugged it over her head and cast it to the side.

T-Rex kissed her neck. His breath was hot on her skin. He licked at the sensitive spot behind her ear then caught her lobe between his teeth.

As his thumbs traced rings around her nipples through the satin of her bra, Remi balanced herself with her hands on his shoulders, riding him into oblivion.

His giving her control when he was Echo Actual, the alpha amongst alphas, was intoxicating.

Remi dropped the straps of her bra.

T-Rex's lips found her pebbled nipples. He squeezed her bra hooks to release the closure. Casting the garment to the side, giving his mouth full access to her breasts, swollen with lust, a shiver ran the length of her body.

Nipping and licking, sucking and kneading, her breasts were adored.

Remi rolled her hips.

Kissing his way back up to her mouth, T-Rex's hands gripped into her ass, squeezing and releasing.

The room grew hot, their skin slick with sweat.

T-Rex drew her hand between her legs, pressing her fingers onto her clit. Their foreheads rested against each other as they both looked down, watching the erotic act.

Lost in the sensations, Remi masturbated, undulating her hips.

Her body tensed.

Her toes curled into the carpeting.

She gasped.

As an orgasmic cry rose up her throat, T-Rex caught it in a kiss.

Her muscles pulsed around his dick.

Pressing her arms around his neck, T-Rex reached under her thighs, stood, and walked them to the bed. There, cradling her head, he put a knee into the mattress and laid them down.

Remi lifted her hips and wrapped her legs around his back, crossing her ankles with pointed toes, feeling herself elongating and tightening around him.

One hand pressed into the mattress to hold his weight, the other fisting her hair, tugging it just enough to give her a bite of pain, T-Rex slid in and out, building, building, building toward an orgasm.

Waves rippled through his abdomen. Heat bloomed from his chest.

"Please," she whispered, unwilling to come a second time without him.

"Please what, Remi. Tell me."

"Come. Please come," she gasped.

His head tipped back, his eyes squeezed shut, his mouth rounded and tensed as the orgasm thundered through his system.

T-Rex lowered his forehead to hers.

They gulped at the air.

"Oh, man," T-Rex finally said as Remi's legs fell heavy and quivering to the mattress.

"Yeah," Remi replied, closing her eyes. There weren't really any words to describe just how mind-blowing fucking T-Rex had been.

Chapter 28

Remi

Friday, Beirut, Lebanon

Remi laced her fingers with T-Rex's in a post-coital haze.

They'd had sex without discussing what it meant to be together.

Was it a one-and-done?

Had he satisfied his curiosity?

Did he want more?

She did. *Most definitely.* She was contented by her orgasms, but Remi couldn't imagine being satiated. The longer she touched T-Rex, the more she craved him.

But since they hadn't said anything about a tomorrow, she felt self-protective, realizing her heart was vulnerable to T-Rex and these new sensations. So she rambled, "Sex is an escape vehicle. Almost meditation."

She lifted their hands, contemplating their laced fingers. "That being in the here and nowness…."

T-Rex watched her through heavy lids.

She dipped her head to kiss his chest. Remi could feel herself falling for T-Rex. She'd never experienced love before. These thoughts, these sensations, they were overwhelming her sense of control. The phrase "head over heels" was making sense to her now. Remi went fishing. "This was probably not even a thought for you."

"Because…"

"Of the number of women in your rearview."

"One was my number."

Her eyelids held without blinking.

"Jess."

"Four years ago…"

"Exactly."

Remi loosened her grip on him. "That makes me feel weird. Oddly like I've stepped on someone's toes."

He rolled over on his stomach, posting his chin on his stacked fists. He looked at her for a long moment. Reaching up to twist a piece of her hair between his fingers, he said tentatively, "I wasn't trying to break the ice with you and launch into a new phase of my life. I'm not a one-night stand guy."

"No. Obviously." A sucky answer, but her nerves were ripe. She had no idea where this was heading. None.

"Sex for you, is it what you just said? Stress relief?"

Honesty, Remi, she counseled herself. "It can be."

"With me? Is that what this was for you, stress relief?"

She swallowed.

"Seriously, if that's what this was, it is what it is."

She rubbed her lips together.

"Okay, I'm asking you to walk out on a ledge by yourself. I apologize. Let me go first." He paused to take a breath. "I think you're amazing. I'm attracted to you, intrigued by you, drawn to you. I want to share more with you. All of you—your mind, your body, your spirit. And I have no idea how to make this work, zero, but I want us to take a stab at a relationship."

"That's a very violent way to go about a relationship." She smiled.

His brow drew together.

"Stabbing… I'm nervous. I've got a lot of big feelings for you that I've never experienced before. This kind of conversation doesn't happen in my life because I'm always heading out the door to the next assignment."

"The next mission. Go. Go. Go. But two people who want to badly enough could be creative and committed. It's possible the effort would take them somewhere good. Us. Take us to something that works for us. We don't have to fit into a neat box. We could be unconventional."

She breathed out through pursed lips.

"Am I scaring you off?"

"No. I'm actually feeling better. Relieved. I thought that saying goodbye to you would be a very painful end to this—what do you call it? FUBAR mission."

"It's not FUBAR. Messed up beyond all repair? Nah. It's had its challenges. The senator is safe. You're in my arms. It's actually going great right now."

"Yeah, well, when I get home, my fellow wombats will find this whole adventure highly entertaining. Sans sex. I'll leave this part out."

"Fellow wombats? What's that exactly?" T-Rex reached out. As he turned to his back, he tugged Remi's hand until she crawled on top of him, her knees bent on either side of his hips. Her head resting on his chest.

"Oh, it's what a group of my friends call ourselves."

"Why wombats?" He stroked her hair sleepily.

"A group of wombats is called a wisdom."

"Ah. Wisdom is so much better than a wake of vultures and a shiver of sharks."

"Hugely better. Wombats are spectacular." She sat up, and his dick hardened beneath her. Sadly, she only had that one condom. "Did you know that wombats poop square-shaped poops?" She laughed. "I can't believe I just said that." Sliding her hip to the mattress, Remi stretched out, propping her head up with her bent arm. She let her other hand paint over the satin smoothness of his shaft. Lazily playing with him.

"Poops?" His eyes were laughing.

Remi smiled at him, no longer needing to hide her affection. "They poop about a hundred blocks out each day."

"Why?"

"You think they have a choice?"

"Evolutionarily speaking, sure."

"They stack them."

"Like a poop barricade?"

"Ha, well, they stack them to mark their territory. And that also helps wombats attract a mate."

"If only it were that easy."

She giggled at his tone. She could tell he liked her giggles from the gentle smile that tweaked the corners of his mouth.

"Wombats," he said.

"Are my favorites. I love them."

"Are they dangerous?"

"Depends. They do have killer asses. How did this even come up? Why are we talking about this?"

"It started out as you had a 'wisdom of friends' and seems to have degenerated quickly from there."

"Yeah, that happens to me after sex. When I'm relaxed and buzzing, my brain shuffles around like a guy who needs a midnight snack. Just rooting around in the cupboard, pulling out random things to look over and reject before reaching for the next."

"You have an image of this guy?"

"Boxers and T-shirt, oversized raggedy robe, slippers. Sometimes a cigarette dangling from his lips. Balding."

"That's your alter ego?"

"Meh, just a guy in search of a snack. I call him Uncle Joe. I think he would have a Brooklyn accent if he ever talked."

T-Rex laughed. "Good, well, I look forward to the many snacks that Uncle Joe will lay on the counter along the way."

"Do you have your own Uncle Joe? Some personification that shows up in your imagination?"

"Sadly," he stopped to drop a kiss on her forehead, "I don't." His hand rounded over her butt cheek, squeezing and kneading. "The wombat butts that make the poop cubes? Do they shoot death lasers, too?"

"We're back to wombats? Mmmm no, no lasers. So they don't have a lot of nerve endings in their bottoms. What they do have is bony plates with fat and fur."

"So they face the enemy butt first?"

"They go in their burrow and block the entrance with their butts."

"Uh-huh."

"But they leave a little gap." She demonstrated with

her hands. "And when the predator tries to squirm into that gap, the wombat thrusts upward with its armored butt and crushes the enemy."

T-Rex barked out a laugh. When he tried to rein it in, his whole body shook with stifled amusement. "Wait. They do what?" he finally managed.

Remi turned over on all fours. "Say this is the entrance to my burrow." She dropped her chest to the mattress with her butt up in the air. The whole time she was watching herself do this in the mirror, thinking, *my god, you're a moron*, but said, "Then the predator tries to crawl into the space I've left and get in to eat me." She looked over her shoulder at him.

A slow smile crawled across T-Rex's mouth. "Eat you?" he asked. His hand wrapped her ankle, and he tugged her to the mattress, rolling her onto her back, bringing his mouth down to her thighs.

Chapter 29

Remi

Saturday, Beirut, Lebanon

Remi slept hard.

Slept like the dead.

Slept better than she had at any other point in this lifetime.

Peace had wriggled into place in her mind, nestling in, getting comfortable. It felt like she didn't have to stand vigilant at that moment.

Of course, she thought, peeking at the clock next to her bed, T-Rex was outside her room, securing the senator, and she, by proximity, was safe.

But what had dragged her from her sleep?

Why was she waking up? She squinted at the clock, again. This time trying to process the information.

It was just past four a.m.

Remi flung over in her king-sized bed, stretching her arms wide, wishing that T-Rex was there, and she could cuddle into him and go back to sleep.

He'd invited her to stay in his bed. And while that had its appeal, he would be standing guard, and she liked her nightly rituals in her own space. They made her feel ready for whatever headed her way.

She lay with her memories of making love with T-Rex, how it felt to be in his arms. Remi hoped imagination would fill the void, and she'd drift off again. It was such a good sleep. It had felt so wonderful to be that restful.

Her eyes popped open. Nope. She was awake now.

Maybe her body was so used to nightmares and discomfort that sleeping here under T-Rex's watch had been like a turbo charge cord on her phone. She'd just had her fill.

A scraping, animal noise came from her balcony.

Remi froze.

All of the admonishments from her fellow wombats filtered through her mind—you're at risk from the DOJ's blocking the websites; you're at risk because you write articles about things that others dispute; you're at risk because you expose… All of it was true.

But this was the sixteenth floor.

And *something* big was scratching around her balcony.

Her mind spun—call the desk? Call T-Rex? Investigate it yourself?

Yeah, that one. Go look and see if two seagulls were making a nest up here. No reason to freak out and drag T-Rex in here to find birds laying eggs.

She threw back her covers and put her shoe-clad feet onto the carpet, pulling down her night shirt and adjusting her utility belt. She was set to run if needs be. Like always.

Remi stood and paced slowly forward at the edge of the room so she could sidle up to the window and peek around the edge of the curtain.

Keeping her body from any place where an assailant would point a gun was second nature now.

Such a deranged thought. How would an assailant possibly get to her balcony? There were another ten stories above her. They'd have to play Ninja or think of her as a mark in a Mission Impossible film.

No one would do that. They'd wait until she was out in public and unprotected, then a sharpshooter would simply line up his sights and ventilate her brain.

As Remi grabbed the pulley to open the drapes, there came a pronounced rapping on the glass door.

Remi jumped, then dragged the curtains wide.

There stood Senator Barb Blankenship, her bedsheet wrapped toga-style around her loose-skinned body, one naked breast drooping out, exposed.

Unlocking the door with trembling fingers, Remi shoved the sliding glass to the side, reached for the senator's hand, and dragged the senator into the hotel room.

"What the..." Remi leaned out to check her little Juliette balcony, scanning for a means, a way, a method that Senator Blankenship would have been out there.

Someone had propped the dinette chairs from in the room's dining area across the three-foot space separating their balconies. They rested on the slick aluminum balustrades.

The chairs, both of them, had barely an inch of overhang on this side. And both of them showed signs that the joints were pulling free.

Shock washed over Remi.

She stepped onto the balcony and looked down to where the cars looked like matchbox toys. Remi turned. "Senator, did you just crawl onto my balcony?" While it seemed evident, how else would she have gotten there? Still, it was so bizarre that Remi couldn't wrap her head around this scene.

"They're coming for me," Blankenship said from the corner of the room where she'd plastered herself.

"Who? Who's coming for you?" Remi came back into the room and over to the wall to click on the overhead light.

Blankenship's eyes grew wide. She clutched at the curtains, trembling.

Though a good distance from Blankenship, Remi held up her hand. "You're safe with me. I'll protect you. But who's after you? Let me get them locked out." Remi was afraid that the senator might launch herself back out onto the balcony and be endangered. She closed the door, locked it, then pulled a chair over, tipping it down, effectively blocking it from sliding.

"T-Rex," Remi lifted her voice. "Get in here!"

"Why did you do that?" Blankenship hissed, bending in two, gripping the curtain with one hand, swiping out with the other. Spittle flying, her hair wild, her breast slinging out.

"T-Rex!" Remi yelled. "Help!"

This time, Blankenship sprang at Remi. Remi dodged, leaping onto her bed like a child playing keep-away.

"Remi?" T-Rex was at her door.

"Help!" Remi called out.

Blankenship scrambled toward Remi. "Don't call him in! Don't let him know I'm here. Evil! Evil!"

T-Rex must have picked the lock to her door because

it flew open, catching on the safety arm and holding. "Remi?"

Remi sidled to the side, trying to get to him.

"Evil!" Blankenship hissed, her spittle flecking Remi's arm, saliva pooling at the sides of Blankenship's mouth.

"Who's in there with you? Come get the door," T-Rex said.

Remi took a sidestep to the edge of the bed, then leaped and dashed past the senator. As Remi lunged for the door, Blankenship jumped on her back. "Die minion of the darkness."

Remi did not want to fight the senator.

But she had no choice.

"Echo Actual. We have a situation. Status report." She heard.

The team would accumulate in the hall, of no use to Remi. Unless they had some det cord, they weren't getting in until Remi moved that security arm. She'd already inspected the lock for its solidity. T-Rex wouldn't be able to push kick his way in here like he had at the airport, saving the child.

Remi was flat on her stomach, the rug scraping her cheek.

Blankenship had grabbed Remi's hair in both her fists like it was reins, dragging Remi's head back. "Whoa there, Lightning. Whoa."

Yeah, Remi was done. Congresswoman or not, this wasn't going to continue.

Remi put her hands together the way Jean Baptiste had taught her. Pulling her knees into her chest as far as she could get them, Remi curled her toes under her, then thrust forward, shooting out like she was diving into a pool. As she slid from under the senator, Remi twisted, flipping over just enough that she could get her hand under her shoulder and lift her torso. At the same time, she brought her elbow back hard into the senator's face.

Blankenship toppled.

Remi scrambled for the door. Shutting it just long enough to peel the safety bar from the hook, she flung it wide again.

There lay Blankenship spread eagle in her sheet. Each pendulous boob drooping over her sides and catching under her arms. A trickle of blood sliding from her nostril down the crease of her cheek and pooling at her lips.

T-Rex was as taken aback by the scene as Remi had been.

It was mind-boggling.

"Senator?" he said. His voice was calm and smooth. "I'm T-Rex. I'm your security. I'm here to protect you."

Blankenship sprang to her feet, twisting the sheet between her hands. "Stay away, Evil." She flicked the sheet out like a locker room towel fight.

"Yes, ma'am."

He turned to Remi. "Are you hurt?"

"I don't know." Remi stood back out of his way. She had no idea what to do here. "Are the others coming?"

"Are. You. Hurt? Check yourself."

Fine. Remi patted over her body. Yeah, some rug burns, maybe a couple of bruises. Nothing that she couldn't attend to later. "I'm okay."

"Now, how did she get in here?"

"She crawled from her balcony to mine."

His eyebrows drew together. "What now?" Sliding along the bed, hands up where Blankenship could see them, T-Rex went to investigate for himself.

Blankenship retreated into a corner, pulling a chair

protectively in front of her, then crouching low. T-Rex lifted the curtain and looked out. He pressed his comms button. "Echo Actual. Winner, we need a doctor sent to the senator's room. ASAP. Check with the embassy. See whom they trust for circumspect medical interventions."

He paused.

"Let's get a confidential assessment of the situation. Out." As he said that, Blankenship screamed, "No one is coming near me. Do you understand?" She lifted the chair and threw it at him. There was little strength behind the move, so the chair fell ineffectually to the ground.

Psychotic break was all Remi could think.

Was it a stroke? She'd been having those headaches. This was like nothing that Remi had ever experienced before in person or on paper. This was nuts.

Whatever was happening, T-Rex probably had some training. Knew some way to manage this.

Blankenship bolted for the door.

T-Rex reached out a hand, then Remi guessed he realized the woman was stark naked (and stark raving mad). He hesitated then went after her.

Remi was on his heels to see if she could help.

In the hall, T-Rex lifted Blankenship off her feet, tipping her over his shoulder, like he had at the Oxford garage when he was playing linebacker breaking through the violent crowd. He spun and locked eyes with Remi.

"Her key card is in my front right pocket."

Remi reached for it, but Blankenship grabbed hold of Remi's hair, trying to rip it from her head.

Hiding behind T-Rex's legs, Remi snaked her hand into his pocket, thinking it was a good thing she'd had familiarity with his body parts earlier, or this would be really embarrassing. Remi drew out the card, got the senator's door open, the lights on, and then she scuttled out of T-Rex's way.

And Liu thought that the ambush in Oxford made a good above-the-fold story?

Wait until he got a load of this.

Chapter 30

T-Rex

Saturday, Beirut, Lebanon

He'd seen a lot of crazy in his day. But this, this was extra special sauce kind of crazy.

T-Rex got the senator back in her room and wasn't sure what to do with her now. Her clothing and other things were strewn about the room like it had been through a cyclone. He spun in place as Blankenship beat her fists into his back and kicked her legs in the air, but he was afraid to put her down.

Remi shut the hall door and threw the security arm. If the senator were to try to escape, T-Rex would have an extra few seconds to restrain Blankenship. Then Remi went over to the balcony, shut, locked, and barricaded that exit before disappearing into the senator's bathroom. "I'm going to look for prescription bottles," she called out. "Maybe she took something wrong. Mixed something up?" Remi was cool and steady. T-Rex appreciated that right now.

He cast his gaze around again, searching for a solution to the problem. His focus settled on the bed. He remembered a story that Jess had told him about the guy who was psychotic and thought there were dragons on the ceiling flying around his house. He was trying to chop them out of the air with his ax. And so was chopping his house up while his kids hid upstairs.

The ETA on the ambulance that night had been forty-five minutes. It was icy with several car crashes. Jess and a backup officer were on their own, so they used a sheet to "burrito wrap" the guy. A technique Jess's partner had learned to help calm his autistic son.

T-Rex formulated a plan.

"Nothing," Remi said, coming out of the bathroom. "Some pain killer, and it's a full bottle."

"Okay, look, I need a sheet. The one the senator had in your room. Can you get that for me?"

Remi dashed out of the door to get it. "Get your key card and lock your door," he called after her.

T-Rex was jostling the senator higher on his shoulder as she beat and kicked at him. When Remi plowed through the door, he said, "Now take that sheet, fold it in half and lay it back down."

Remi complied, looking up for his next instructions.

"Have you ever swaddled a baby?" T-Rex called past the senator's hysterics. He was worried about her being upside down for this long with blood rushing to her already messed up brain. "That's how Jess described this. 'Burrito,' she called it."

"Yes, yes. A friend of mine burritos her son when he gets overwhelmed. He's on the autism spectrum."

Remi prepped the sheet. "Put her here and get her arms up over her head."

T-Rex tried to talk to Blankenship, but she seemed to have lost contact with reality. She was blabbering to people who weren't in the room.

Laying the senator down as gently as he could, it took a well-placed knee on her hip bone and more strength than he anticipated to get Blankenship configured the way Remi was instructing. The right arm came down, and that was tucked into the sheet. They dragged the sheet across Blankenship's left arm, then rolled her.

T-Rex checked to make sure that they weren't compressing her lungs.

"Deep pressure is helpful," Remi said as they worked together to get Blankenship's head up on a pillow. "I'm glad you thought of this. My suggestion was going to be to put her in a hot bath."

T-Rex caught her eye.

"In the Netherlands, in the olden days, they had bathtubs for people who were psychotic. They'd put them in, and a human, it seems, simply can't stay agitated in hot water."

"I'd try it now, but I'm afraid she'd drown."

"Yeah. Those tubs had canvas covers that fitted over the rim. In the canvas coverings, they had a hole for the patient's head. The hole was laced up behind their head, so the patient couldn't slip under the water."

"Psychosis. Do you think that's what's happening here?"

"I'm not a doctor. It could be psychosis. But it could also be rabies."

They looked down at Senator Blankenship with the white phlegm and spittle that foamed at the corners of her mouth. Her gaze caught on something she was following across the ceiling.

"There's a doctor en route?" Remi panted from the exertion, her hand smoothing over Blankenship's head as if to calm her. "Don't you think she needs to be in a hospital?"

"I think she needs help. And I think that these symptoms are a lot more complicated than calling an ambulance to take her in."

"Diplomacy-wise?"

"Diplomacy as well as her public reputation. If someone loads up a video of the senator with this level of reality break, things will be rough for her. And undressed this way?"

"We could maybe get her dressed," Remi said.

"Are you sure?"

"No. Now that I said that out loud, I think it's a terrible idea. I'm not willing to fight the senator into a pair of panties." She caught T-Rex's eye. "The doctor's coming?"

"Winner is communicating with the embassy."

"Where are the others? Havoc and Ty?"

"They're out doing prep work for the senator's speech."

Remi looked toward the clock. "This early?"

"Ty is running Rory, then they're going to the university to sniff out the auditorium and guard it. Havoc was driving the various routes that are in our plans."

"How many contingency plans did you have in place for today?"

"Four. We're not going to need any of them. Havoc should be heading this way. Ty and Rory are seven miles out on foot. They've turned around."

He pressed his comms. "Echo Actual." He reached for Remi's hand and brought the back of it to his lips as he listened.

"Echo Six. I'm going to have trouble getting back to you. I'm caught in a traffic jam. Something's up heading northeast. It doesn't seem like a morning commute issue. I'm not sure what's going on. Seems that the interest is directed toward the water. Have you heard anything?"

"Remi, is anything going on out the window?"

Remi scooted over to the balcony. After checking to make sure the senator was secured, Remi dragged her phone from the utility belt she had around her waist.

"There's a fire," she called over to him.

Remi quick dialed. She was speaking in rapid French. T-Rex thought of himself as reasonably fluent in the African pronunciations of French. This sounded different. He only caught words here and there. Nothing that was making a lot of sense to him. But she was obviously working the phones, probably calling her fellow wombats—that brought a smile to his lips.

Hopefully, Remi's connections would give them the answers they might need to ensure this was a safe location to wait for medical help.

Remi slid her phone away as she came back over to him. She was dressed in her nightshirt with nothing underneath, her tennis shoes, and the utility belt. T-Rex made a mental note to ask her how she got that and her shoes on when the senator had woken Remi up.

"What did you see?" he asked, his hand planted on the senator's shoulder so she wouldn't be able to move.

"There's a massive fire by the wharf. Over in that section, there is a trove of warehouses. No one seems to know what's in the warehouse that's on fire or how it started. I can't tell you about toxicity or flashpoints. The emergency crews are heading out now. So if we need an ambulance, we won't get one now. They'll divert what resources they have over to the fire."

The phone rang, and she answered. She started mixing languages together. Franglais. He'd listened to her seamlessly shift between Arabic, French, and English during their short time together. From the Arabic and English side, he could say she never missed a beat, and the translations were clean. She was nervous. Something had cracked her Teflon professionalism.

He didn't understand the situation. But from the uptick in Remi's voice, it was bad.

"Echo Actual. Winner, we have a compounded problem. Can you see a fire in the warehouse down by the water?"

"I've got it on my screen now. We're trying to figure out what's in the warehouse and if the fumes are toxic. My best advice right now is to stay put and wait for the embassy doctor to get—"

From over at the window, Remi's scream filled the air.

He was instantly on his feet to get to her.

T-Rex was airborne, flying through space, with no sense of up or down. The ringing in his ears blocked all sound. He crashed into something solid, and the world faded to black.

Chapter 31

Remi

Saturday, Beirut, Lebanon

Remi's ears filled with a high pitch whistle. She blinked her lashes, heavy with plaster dust. A bomb, her brain screamed at her.

It felt like a bomb. Could that be right?

Remi had been through them a few times. She'd developed a system.

Panic will kill you. Work the system.

It was an internal fight to grab hold of logic.

She stilled and started her assessment. First, where was she? Beirut. She'd come to see Jean Baptiste. She was in the hotel, in Senator Blankenship's room. Blankenship had gone nuts, and Remi had helped T-Rex restrain her.

T-Rex!

She flung a piece of the ceiling from her shoulder and saw blood on her hand.

Stop. Don't be an idiot. This calls for being methodical.

A bomb. No. There was a fire at the warehouse; Remi had seen the explosion. She knew what came after; it wasn't the bomb at this distance that could kill her; it was the concussion that followed seconds afterward. As soon as she'd seen the explosion, she'd tried to warn the others. She'd opened her mouth, and all that came out was a high-pitched scream as she threw herself to the ground, hoping the wave would wash over her.

Hoping that the only impact might be to the window.

Luck wasn't with her.

It was bad.

Remi slid her hand under the debris that covered her, checking to ensure she was wearing her utility belt. Her fingers tapped over her tourniquet and blood clotting bandages.

She couldn't feel her body. Pushing off panic, Remi reminded herself that she was probably in shock. *Give it a minute.*

As Remi filled her lungs with dust and particles, she tried to cough and clear her throat. But her chest couldn't rise.

Her legs were oddly cold.

T-Rex! If he wasn't by her side helping her, something horrible must have happened to him.

Remi pawed at the curtains draped over her, pushing the particleboard off her chest. Glass flying, Remi lifted her head.

She could see nothing in the darkness. Fingers fiddling in her utility belt, she grasped at the plastic length of a chem-light. Snapping it, a halo of yellow lit the densely particle-filled air.

I have to find T-Rex, her mind repeated on a loop.

Do not leap into action. Remi had learned the hard way over her years in war zones. Yet there she was, pawing and struggling. "Stop," she shouted aloud.

Her first task was to acclimate to the situation. Check.

Second, self-assess. Lifting and flinging debris off her body, Remi found herself for the third time this trip palpating joints and bones, checking to see that her bleeding was a trickle and not a spurt. Remi realized that her legs from the thighs draped downward from a small hole in fallen beams. The front of the building was gone. Blown away. The exterior wall had vanished. Her naked legs were exposed to the cool early morning air.

Her head seemed to swell as her brain tried to focus, think, act correctly. A dull thud. A rock beat pulsing around her eyes.

Screams and sirens erupted around her as if the world had suddenly woken from a nightmare.

Remi slid backward, unsure of how stable her spot was.

Turning and getting on all fours, then up in a bear crawl, the chem-light held between her teeth, Remi inched through the building material.

She made it to the bed and the senator, an island amongst the wreckage. The senator seemed unconscious.

Dead?

Remi's stomach sloshed as a wave of nausea hit her. She stilled and panted until she regained control.

Lowering her ear to Blankenship's chest, hearing a constant beat, feeling the steady rise and fall of Blankenship's lungs, Remi felt little relief.

Remi pulled a pillowcase off the pillow and used it to remove the chalky white powder from Blankenship's face, lest it fill the woman's lungs and suffocate her.

Holding the light up, she searched for T-Rex. "As big as he is, this shouldn't be hard," she said out loud. But he was nowhere.

Panic gripped her throat. Her hands buzzed. Normally, this was the time when adrenaline receded. She could think with crystal clarity. But this time, someone she loved was in danger.

Loved?

She'd revisit that thought later. Because right now, she saw the sole of T-Rex's boot.

Remi fought against her system that wanted to freeze, to hold her captive, to keep her from moving over to that boot and find it had been severed from T-Rex's leg. That he had bled out. That she'd lost him within moments of finding him.

Inch by inch, she struggled forward.

Breath by breath, she forced herself to lift ceiling plaster.

Squatting and grabbing hold of the beam, sobs swelling and catching in her throat, she power lifted with an adrenaline surge she had never experienced before. It was less than a foot, but she was able to sidestep and get the beam to the side.

"Remi," T-Rex called.

"I'm here. I'm here. I'll get you out. Cover your face if you can." She worked for long minutes, fear sweat making her hands slick. Plaster caked in the web of her fingers.

She uncovered him inch by inch until he reached out his arms to her, and she collapsed into them. "Good god, you scared me." She indulged in an outburst of tears. They cleaned her eyes of debris, and she honestly couldn't control these sensations. She had to work through them. Her hands patted over T-Rex's body, looking for wounds or breaks.

"Stop. Remi, look at me."

She blinked, recovering her equilibrium.

"Are you okay?" he asked. "You're bleeding." His calm and steady seeped into her skin, soothing the prickly heat of her limbic system's gushing survival hormones.

"So are you." Her voice was hoarse. "Let's get you out of there."

What they discovered wasn't good.

While the three occupants had come through the blast in fair shape, the building had not.

They were sealed into the room. The structure wasn't stable. They were on the sixteenth floor with ten stories above them, the façade was destroyed, making the building's collapse seem inevitable.

Remi's mind went to the hospital. What about the people in those beds? Jean Baptiste.

They checked the landline. Remi and T-Rex tried their cell phones. Nothing.

"The cell tower probably fell," T-Rex said. "Or maybe everyone's jamming the lines by making calls at the same time." He couldn't raise Winner on his comms.

"Here's what we know," T-Rex reviewed. "The three of us are alive, and our injuries are not life-threatening. The senator seems to have lost consciousness. Not from the blast, from whatever was going on with her health before these circumstances."

"Right." Remi nodded.

Had the senator not gone nuts, he would have been in the hall and probably dead. Remi would be in her room, no idea what that looked like, alone. So if there were a miracle, it was that T-Rex was with Remi, and they could work as a team to survive.

"We're together." He caught her hand. "That's a plus."

"For sure," Remi said.

"We're going to be on our own for hours if not days," T-Rex said. "The first responders were heading to the wharf fire. I doubt they could have survived that blast."

Remi clutched at her chest. *My god, all of those people!*

"Winner, Havoc, Ty and Rory, people with skills know exactly where we were at the time of the blast. They'll come for us."

"Ty and Rory were on foot out there. Dear god. They were out there!"

T-Rex squeezed her hand. "We can't help them. They were seven miles out when I was on comms with them. They were southwest of our location, out throwing ball on a ballfield. Okay? Chances are good that they're fine. Havoc was even farther away, protected in an armored embassy car. They will move mountains to get to us."

"We can't get out on our own and send rescue in for the senator? No. Sorry. There probably aren't any rescue workers in the area. They all would have been over working the fire at the time of the blast. So..." Remi sighed as she let that thought sink in. It's what happened to the first responders in New York on 9-11. "They'll need to come in from surrounding areas. And you would leave me before you left the senator because you're on a mission.

"We're here for the duration. There's a beam holding the door in place. And honestly, we have no idea what's happening on the other side of that door."

"Hunker down." She nodded.

He took both her hands. "We're going to be fine, Remi. We're going to work the problem."

"Okay." She had no idea what that could mean in this set of circumstances.

"Show me what you have in your utility belt."

Remi carefully folded the dust-covered comforter out of the way, trying to preserve any spots of cleanliness. She unclasped the bag and laid each item carefully onto the sheet.

T-Rex held the glow stick.

"Mata Hari, you're a genius," he said, fingering the items.

He touched the water pouches. "This could be lifesaving. What's this purple thing?"

"It's a device that lets me pee standing up like a man does."

"That'll come in handy. The bathroom collapsed."

"Collapsed, collapsed? There's no water?" Remi thought they could probably snake an arm over to the tap. If the pipes were broken, there was always water in the back of a toilet tank.

"It's gone."

Remi's knees buckled, and T-Rex grabbed her by the elbows, holding her until she steadied again. "We're careful with what we have. The team is coming for us."

She nodded.

T-Rex checked the senator's vitals and documented the stats and the time in Remi's waterproof notebook.

Then they started on the room, working methodically together to find what resources they could. There was a bottle of vodka in the senator's suitcase. They used it to clean off their skin and their cuts. They staunched the blood and tied on bandages that T-Rex cut from a cotton T-shirt in one of the senator's drawers.

They piled what construction pieces they could to brace the ceiling and walls and stabilize their space. It was like being in a cave.

"No exterior light, but you have three light sticks. Each will last about eight hours. Two today, none while we sleep, another tomorrow."

Her hand shot out. "Wait, how long do you think it will take to get us out of here?"

Chapter 32

T-Rex

Saturday, Beirut, Lebanon

They sat on the floor with their backs to the bed. With chores done, as much as possible, they needed to sit still. Remi had enough water pouches in her belt to keep them from dehydrating for about twenty-four hours, though what they could do about hydrating the senator, he wasn't sure.

When they added in the minibar juices and a couple of sodas, that survival clock could tick a little longer.

There was a few days' worth of survival calories available. But T-Rex had seen these things go on far beyond a few days. They needed to be conservative in everything they did to stretch their resources out as far as possible. Resting, sleeping, keeping their movements to a minimum…

"Do you always sleep in that pack, or did you have women's intuition that something bad was going to happen?" T-Rex asked.

She leaned in for a kiss. "I went to bed thoroughly contented from our being together. I slept better last night than I remember sleeping in my life until the senator showed up on my balcony."

"I can't imagine what that scene was like to wake up to."

"Startling, to say the least. About my utility belt, with the places I report from, yes, I sleep with my gear around my waist and my shoes on my feet. I never know when I have to leap from my bed and survive the night."

"There's a story there."

Remi was using her tweezers to pick splinters out of T-Rex's bicep. "There's a story everywhere."

"You've done this before?" he asked, nodding toward his arm.

"Sure. I've had to help my colleagues and myself on occasion."

"The scars on your leg?"

"Shrapnel. I got off easy with the scarring. Others… well, it was a bad night." She put a shard onto the tissue and went back to her task. "I took a class in combat first aid to help myself or my friends if one of the crew goes down."

Wincing as she dragged out a piece of metal an inch long, T-Rex focused on Remi instead of the pain.

Man, is she pretty.

He'd like to pull that elastic from her hair and feel the silken strands.

"Sorry about this, but something's in there. I can just feel it with the tips of the tweezers. There. Don't move." Remi trapped the object in the tweezers and gently pulled it. "There. I think that's it for this cut." She poured a capful of the vodka over the wound.

Not the best thing to do, but under the circumstances, there weren't better choices.

T-Rex needed to bring this episode up with his team when they got out of here. From now on, there should be a survival pack in each of their principal's rooms with a minimum of seventy-two hours of supplies. Having them in his own room ready to grab and bring on site was a mistake.

Remi was smart to wear her tennis shoes and survival bag to bed. In her line of work, in the dangerous places she traveled, she knew that she could just stand up and run in an emergency.

That was too much to ask of anyone they were guarding but having everything prepped and within easy grasp would be good.

"Top of the hour," T-Rex said. "I need to pause your brutality to write down the senator's vitals." He stood and rounded onto the bed. "I wish I knew what we were dealing with here," he said, peeling back the senator's eyelids to check pupil constriction, making sure the senator wasn't brain dead.

"Yeah, you know, I was taping her in London when we were all down at the bar with Diamond. Diamond is so lucky that she was relegated to the robotics team and sent to Jordan. She's going to go home unscathed," Remi said.

T-Rex counted the senator's pulse in her right then left wrists and at both of her ankles, documenting the numbers.

"Diamond seemed pretty uncomfortable around the senator. She and I both knew that night that something was off." Remi pulled her phone from the end of the bed. The cell phone wasn't connecting to the Internet or to a cell tower.

She was scrolling and tapping, grateful she always charged her phone before falling asleep. "At the time I took this video, I thought that I'd hand this off to Liu. He's my managing editor. This kind of reporting isn't my strength. It probably needs a great deal more attention than I could give it. Maybe my colleague Jasmine whom I displaced on this trip."

T-Rex was now counting Senator Blankenship's breaths per minute. "You said you taped a video? Give me a second, and we can watch it together. Maybe there's a clue to help us figure this out."

"It wasn't just about the senator's health. This video was thickly seeded with information that hadn't been in the public domain. It seemed to answer some questions my friends had been pondering."

"Your wombats?"

"Some are wombats. Not everyone can be a wombat."

"Right, some have to be the koalas." T-Rex stood, placing the pad and pen on the table by the senator's head. "Okay. What have you got there?"

"I wanted to watch this again, this time looking for a clue about her present condition."

"Catatonic?"

"I'm not going there. *Not.*" She stopped and sucked in a lungful of air.

"What were you thinking just then?"

Remi caught T-Rex's gaze and whispered, "What if she dies? And we're in here in the heat with her body for days."

"Yeah, let's not go there." T-Rex rounded the bed and sat down on the ground with her. "Will you show me your video?"

Remi turned and cuddled into T-Rex's arms, allowing them to watch the screen at the same time. Remi oriented him, "I'm at the bar. Ty had taken Rory up to sniff the senator's room. Havoc is over there in the corner. I'm not sure where you were at this point."

The tape played of the senator slurring over her scotch. Though Winner's advanced prep told T-Rex that the senator had a high alcohol tolerance, Blankenship's bar tab that night only showed three drinks.

Blankenship flourished the glass toward Remi. "I am the only woman on my committee. You know why?"

"There aren't many women in the Senate, and they're spread thin?"

"There aren't many of us broads around. And you know what? That's a darned shame. I mean, look at the men I serve with. Look at Senator Chuck Billings, falling in love with a whistleblower, having an affair. Then that self-centered son of a gun dragged his poor wife out to stand beside him while he gave a press conference. 'See? If my wife can stand with me after I screwed her over—'" She swirled her glass through the air. "'Then you too can get screwed over by me and appreciate my being honest about it.'" Blankenship sneered. "Did you see his wife's face when he was extolling the virtues of his dead mistress? Dead. Probably his fault, though. I can't say that for sure. Something snaky about that whole story. Got himself re-elected, though. I've got a running theory on why that happened."

The camera jostled.

"Can you share that theory?" Remi asked.

"I'm trying to picture…picture *myself* in that guy's shoes. Senator Billings. They think, 'Man, I want to have an affair with a woman half my age with huge boobs like that woman had.'" Senator Blankenship shook her head with a tsk tsk tsk. "How she walked upright, I have no idea. If I had boobs like that—" The senator put her hands under her C cup breasts, lifted, and juggled them for a moment.

Remi paused the video. "She's not drunk unless she pre-drank before I saw her. That's her first glass that I saw. Just seconds prior to this, she seemed—not fine, but better than this. I think she forgot she was talking in front of her aide and a reporter. Diamond was trying to warn her off and wasn't successful." She tapped the video back on.

"Yeah, if I had boobs like that, I'd need a wheelbarrow." She looped her finger through the air like she was prepping a lasso for a throw. "But men think, 'I'd like to have an affair and have my wife suffer in silence.' Well…that's probably unfair. They probably don't want their wives to actually suffer. Just be silent. And accepting. Let the man dip his dick in any slick spot he'd like to stick it, and then the wife towels it off and pats him on the head."

The three fell silent as the bartender swiped a rag over the bar then stepped back out of the frame.

Remi shifted on her thighs back and forth. "The bent of the conversation was uncomfortable," Remi told T-Rex. "Not so much the substance, the substance had… substance. For someone who was a political reporter, studying the women in Congress's views on their male counterparts' unethical behaviors would be interesting. Liu would know whom to hand that story to. But the delivery was off. Strange. I didn't put it together with a medical crisis. I'm not sure, other than showing you this video, how I could have helped her. I mean…what could you have done?"

"Not much," T-Rex whispered as Blankenship spoke on the video again.

"Then there's the other one. Senator St. Clair. Ethical by comparison. But still a hot mess. They blew up the prep school where his grandkids went."

"Wait. What?" Diamond said, leaning forward.

"The terrorists blew up that grade school in Maryland," Senator Blankenship clarified.

"St. Basil's Preparatory School in Bethesda?" Remi asked. T-Rex could hear excitement inch into her voice. Like she'd hooked a fish and now needed to reel it in.

"That's the one."

"I know there was a terror attack there. I didn't know it was tied to the senator. Could you tell me about that?" Remi asked. Open-ended like the CIA had taught Echo Force to use in interrogations.

"It's not classified. But it would be a strain to find the information. Nobody knows to go looking for it because of St. Clair's grandkids. It's called a what…a lion's kidnapping?"

"Tiger kidnapping?" The angle of the phone changed. Remi had pitched forward with concentration.

"That's the one."

"I knew that the children went missing—there was the AMBER Alert," Diamond said.

"But the story I read was that the children had been ill, and because there was a miscommunication, they thought the kids were missing, but it wasn't so. They were found fine. Senator Blankenship, those children weren't kidnapped. Perhaps you're conflating—"

"Nope. That's not the story. The kids were kidnapped to force St. Clair to vote a certain way on a bill to get it out of Senate Arms Committee—which it failed to do because it was crap legislation. They kidnapped the schoolteacher too. Suzy-Q. No. Suzy…"

"The one that was on vacation to get away from the news feeds after she saved her students?" Diamond asked. "Suz Molloy. She was on vacation, Senator."

Blankenship shook her head. "They went to her house and kidnapped Molloy to go take care of the kids. Some ploy to draw everyone in the wrong direction. Six-year-old twins. They're down there in some jungle near Brazil. The teacher, Suz Molloy…" Blankenship stared unblinking for an overly long time. Like she was stuck and needed to reboot. Remi must have been thinking the same thing at the time. She reached out and touched the senator's arm.

"South America," the senator continued on as if nothing bizarre had just happened. "Lucky for all of them, the teacher was dating an ex-SEAL, now working for a group called Iniquus. Heard of them?"

"Yes," Remi whispered.

"He went looking for her. Found them. Saved them. Brought the kids back. Having convinced the kids that they had been on a great adventure with 'Captain Jack.'" She waggled jazz hands in the air. "The kids are hunky-dory. Even with the kids' lives on the line, their grandpa voted against what the terrorists told him to vote 'yes' for. Cajones. Maybe. Not sure what to make of that." Blankenship swallowed down her drink. "But before that SEAL guy found them and saved the three, I asked the Secret Service about the likelihood that they'd come home again. They said the kids were dead one way or the other. Lion kidnappings never end well. You do what you're told, and they dispose of their victims. Damned if you do. Damned if you don't. Personally, I might consider a bullet in my brain before I had to make a choice about my grandbabies that way." She held her hand like a gun and said, "Pckew," when she put it under her chin.

"You have grandkids?" Remi asked, confused.

"Dogs. I've got a passel of dogs, and horses, and cows. The cows, they're good eats." She froze again.

"That's about it." Remi turned off the phone. "She sat there in silence, and I couldn't get her talking again."

"That could be in a script for some thriller."

"I don't write for entertainment value."

"I know that." His words were meant to be a balm.

She sighed. "I'm thinking about my dear friends, Marie-Claude and Éloïse, captured and held in Syria. These are people. Real people with real hopes and real dreams. They feel pain and horror. They are mourning and desperate. I write the stories to bring a spotlight to the dark recesses of humanity. The hope is that we will try to do better." She caught T-Rex's gaze and let it just hold.

He hoped Remi knew he was listening deeply.

"You heard what she was saying about St. Clair? It all can just seem dirty and desperate. Corrupt. Insane. Angry. Smelling of feces, blowflies, and death."

"And yet you're not deterred."

"Hope floats." She shrugged. "I keep hoping. I don't have a choice about doing my job—any more than you do."

Chapter 33

Remi

Sunday, Beirut, Lebanon

T-Rex had told her they should sleep as much as possible. Conservation of bodily resources blah, blah, blah.

Remi thought about the stories she'd read of submariners who were trapped and waiting for rescue, how they'd lay very still and breathe as slowly as possible, trying to conserve what air was available. People pant when they're terrified, and it sucks up the air quickly.

That was not her problem. Air was available. It made her nervous for T-Rex to say that they were reserving liquids and calories. How long did he think rescue might take? Right or wrong, they were with a United States senator. Surely, there would be extra effort paid to get her out fast.

Remi had napped off and on throughout the day.

She was awake in the dim yellow glow of her chem-light. She was surprised the light was still useful almost thirteen hours after she snapped it on.

She and T-Rex were lying on their sides, staring at each other.

He swiped his fingers through her hair. "What are you thinking about?"

"Adrenaline," she whispered. "I'm so used to it flowing through my veins that when I try to stop. Just stop. Just..." She shook her head. "I was thinking about what I'd like to do when I'm out of here. Where I might like to go. I was considering a vacation. Normal feels odd. Uncomfortable. Sitting on a beach and drinking a mai tai—what a strange thing to do. Unless a great white shark is going to rear up on his tail and saunter out of the waves, then that cocktail and the sand between my toes would be fine. My system, my biology, has learned to run on a different fuel."

"Adrenaline."

T-Rex had said they should keep their talking to a minimum to preserve the water in their systems. Remi guessed that the body humidified the vocal cords to speak or some such thing. Talking calmed her. So she'd have to risk dry-mouth. "I don't feel adrenaline anymore. What I feel is when it's not there."

"You need to detox."

"Like with a kale shake?"

"If you'd said spinach, I'd say that would counter the detoxification process."

"What? This sounds vaguely like our wombat conversation."

He lifted his brows.

They paused for a long moment. "I get it," Remi finally said. "It's a Popeye reference. If I was downing the spinach, it was so I could pop a muscle and go fight. Kale it is."

Another long pause.

"Remi, I know these circumstances would be hard for anyone, but you have it worse. You told me this is one of your issues."

"*One* of them."

"Stop. I guess I'd feel like I could help better if I knew where your claustrophobia came from and what to avoid."

"Oh, easy. Avoid getting trapped." She barked out a cough. The dust in the room was pervasive. "I'm all right telling you. I've told a few people, and it didn't make anything worse." She let her gaze take in what she could of the room. "Of course, I was never in a situation like this."

She picked up the glow stick and gave it a waggle. In her imagination, that excited the chemical reaction, and it glowed a little brighter. "I don't tell stories for free."

"Okay, what's the price?"

"My painful memory for one of yours. Only, you go first."

"All right. Here we go. When my wife was killed, I was off-grid. We'd dropped into the area via parachutes, and we were supposed to hump ourselves back out. Three weeks. My commander decided not to tell me about her death because they couldn't get us out, and I needed to lead my men. When I got back to base, they called me in and told me they'd arranged for me to fly home and deal with the circumstances. My wife had been in a refrigerator drawer all that time." He was staring at his hands. "Jess never wanted to be a body. She'd made me promise her that the second she was declared deceased, I'd head her straight over for cremation. There was something about her being a corpse that wigged her out. So I swore to her, I'd protect her. And yet, it was the worst thing that could happen. She was autopsied and then the drawer."

"Does it haunt you?"

"Does she haunt me?" T-Rex asked back.

Remi sat still—the void was where people revealed themselves.

"We used to like to go out to the fields and park, lay in the back of my truck, look up at the stars and just hold hands and feel peace. We had some beautiful nights exploring each other out there. I see her in the stars. Feel her out there watching me."

"I'm sorry for your loss."

"Thank you. A deal is a deal."

"Yup, you told me yours. Here's mine: A Furniture Story. When I was little, we had gone up north to upstate New York to visit my grandmother. One of grandma's friends had passed away, and the family wanted to get rid of the dining room set. My parents bought it and decided that they wouldn't shell out any more money to rent some kind of trailer or something to bring that dining set home. Instead, they were just going to put it in the back of my dad's van. This wasn't a family minivan. To understand this story, you have to picture a commercial van with no windows in the back. My dad had figured out a way to make it dual purpose. He needed it for work to carry paint and ladders, wood, and construction materials. But it was also a family vehicle."

T-Rex pinched at his nose, focusing on her with a wrinkled brow.

"He went to the junkyard and got an old bench seat from a car that had wrecked. He made a wooden base for it, and he stuck it in the van. My older sister had a lot of mental health issues. She was a violent kid on lots of medications. I tried to just keep out of her way. She was the one who got that bench seat to herself."

"The bench seat on the wooden base. How did your dad attach it into the van to make it safe?"

"He didn't," Remi said.

"What?"

"He didn't. It was just set inside the van. And strangely, they insisted that she buckle herself to it. If there were to be an accident, that bench with my sister would fly around the interior of the van. I was always very nervous about that."

"Where did you sit?"

"Normally? Dad had these metal brackets on either side of the van. A piece of plywood fit between them. He put a foam pad on top of that and a carpet to make a van-wide sized bed, reaching from the back doors to just behind the bench seat. My brother and I were to lie on that bed."

"With no restraints."

"None. And it was gross. My dad had a bunch of affairs. Apparently, they'd just screw around in the van. I found spermicidal cream canisters back there all the time. Just gross to think of my dad back there humping."

"I'd imagine. How old are you in this story?"

"Somewhere around eight or nine. So my cheapskate father put the board for the bed down on the floor of the van. Then he figured out how to get all of the various dining set pieces in there. When we were loading up, there were still pieces out on the driveway. Dad said, 'that's your space in there.' He pointed at a little cave on the left. 'No,' I told him. 'I'm not getting in there.' That didn't go over well with my dad." Remi thought back to the physical altercation and how he'd picked her up and shoved her into the space while she screamed for help. People had shown up to stare, but no one did anything.

"In order to fit into the space, I had to curl up in the fetal position. Then, my dad packed in the rest of the furniture. My brother got in. And dad closed the back doors."

"How long was the ride?"

"Nine hours."

"What?"

"Nine hours. My legs had gone numb. I was hot and sweating. There was so little air. I kept thinking that no one would think to look for me in the middle of the furniture puzzle if there were an accident. I'd be towed off and put in one of those metal crushers." Remi gave a whole-body convulsion.

T-Rex grabbed her and pulled her into his arms.

"My brother's spot was a lot more open and comfortable. He thought it was funny that I was crying. He kept poking his finger into the only gap—the one I thought of as my breathing hole. I asked him to stop. Begged him to. He kept poking. Poking. Poking. Finally, I balled up my fist and punched my hand through the hole. I hit him square in the nose, and blood shot out everywhere."

T-Rex was rocking her like a baby as she whispered her story.

"My dad yanked the van over to the side of the road. The furniture shifted, and my space was even smaller. He came around back and opened the doors, pulled out the chairs, grabbed my ankle, and dragged me out too. I was so relieved to be out of there, though I couldn't stand because I had no circulation in my legs. Dad was beating me on the side of the road. A punishment for punching my brother. I thought someone's going to pull over and rescue me. They're going to put me in their car and drive me off, and my dad will never hit me again." She took in a breath. "But naw. No one stopped, or honked, or anything. He shoved me back into the space, loaded up the furniture, and we started home. I plotted. When we traveled, we were allowed to go to the bathroom while my dad filled the tank with gas. I thought, 'I'll go to the bathroom and ask someone for help.' But when we stopped, my dad didn't let me out."

"But, surely you needed to pee over a nine-hour time frame."

"I held it as long as I could, then I just peed my pants. That was another punishment when we got home, and they discovered it. Apparently, the wood was damaged by the moisture."

"Remi…"

"You went through worse," she said.

"Me? No."

"SERE training? Don't they torture you to see what makes you break?"

"In SERE, you can tap out. It has ramifications, but that has to be part of your mindset. Here? You had no choices. You were a little kid getting rolled like some rogue wave in the ocean."

"I don't like getting myself into places I can't get out of—elevators, airplanes, and now I guess hotel rooms."

"How did you work it out that you're able to cope? I've seen you struggle. You seem… You seem determined."

"I was worse. I found my phobia to be debilitating. Then I read about Seligman's Theory on learned helplessness. A dog was fine. But he was put through this experiment where they shocked the dog. It was a complicated research project, some of which is being debunked, if you will. But the theory helped."

"Go on."

"The gist is that this dog learned that he was going to get shocked, so he stopped trying. And I thought, 'that's not going to be me.' I'm not going to lay down out of fear I'll be shocked, punished, what have you. I'm going to go about my life as if it's okay. And if I get shocked, punched, stabbed, bombed…well, I'll deal with it. That mindset means I can force myself onto the plane or elevator. It doesn't mean that my body and brain aren't punishing me the entire time. I just push through it to the other side." She pressed her forehead against T-Rex's. "I need to believe that there's another side to this."

T-Rex tipped his head and kissed her. "We're not helpless, Remi. We're together in these trying circumstances. Do you know what that means?"

Remi shook her head.

"It means we have to keep trying."

Chapter 34

T-Rex

Sunday, Beirut, Lebanon

They lay there too hot and sweaty to even hold hands. It was pitch black. They'd decided to guard the phone batteries and the chem-lights for necessity. They'd been trapped for nearly thirty hours.

They'd eaten the hotel snacks. They each had a meal bar from Remi's pack. There were two more bars that they set aside for tomorrow, but then they'd be down to a roll of breath mints.

T-Rex wasn't holding out much hope for the senator. Remi had found an oil dropper in the senator's makeup kit. They'd cleaned it with vodka and had used it to get some fluids into the senator.

If she expired, tragic in its own sense, it would also be a psychological hit. And T-Rex didn't know what they'd do with the body. Lying here in survival mode with a corpse decomposing on the bed was a nightmare scenario. There wasn't any place else to put a body, should it come to that. They were trapped.

Remi had had her moments. The fear had grown too big, and she stood there and screamed until she was hoarse.

He was dealing with his own demons. After Remi's story of being crumpled up and trapped, beaten and trapped again, he was worried for her sanity in this situation. Though the pockets of time when she lost control were short-lived.

As T-Rex lay there, careful not to touch her skin, he raked his fingers through her hair. It soothed him, and she was asleep. To finally find her. To have hope in his life for love and connection again. To have it snatched away just as quickly seemed like the heavens were mocking him.

There was a sudden sound of shifting building materials that sent a flash of fear through his veins. Any minute, the weight above them could come crashing down. He'd pressed those fears away. But lying here in the dark, he could hear the screeching beams, the thunks and…scrambles?

On a lark, T-Rex licked his lips then whistled a shrill "come here" whistle that they sometimes used with the military K9s.

He paused. Could rescue be at hand?

Remi stirred, then shot upright. "What?"

T-Rex reached out in the dark for the chem-light they'd been saving and snapped it on. They were bathed in an eerie green light. "I thought I heard something." He whistled again.

This time he was answered with barks.

"Ty and Rory?" Remi asked.

"No idea." T-Rex pursed his lips a third time when Remi reached onto the mattress where their supplies were laid out for easy access. She had a flat orange hurricane whistle. She blew it three times.

The barks were closer.

There was scrambling and clawing above where the bathroom had been.

T-Rex and Remi moved underneath. "Get me up there, T-Rex," Remi said, sticking the chem-light into her mouth and holding it between her teeth.

He squatted, and she flung her leg over his shoulders like a cheerleader at a game. Holding her thighs, he pressed up from his squat.

There, she worked to pull pieces free. With the last piece that she handed down to T-Rex, he heard, "Beautiful. Oh, you are so beautiful!" Her body rocked on his shoulders as she cried. T-Rex couldn't see what she did. He figured she'd give him more information as she could.

"Miss Taleb?" a voice asked.

"Yes. Yes!"

"I'm Bear MacIntosh, Cerberus Tactical K9. This is Truffles, my search and rescue dog."

Remi was crying too hard to speak.

"Ma'am, I can see you on the video camera. Are you alone in that room?"

She gulped down her sob, dragged in a hitched breath, and said, "No. I'm here with Senator Barb Blankenship and with Master Chief T-Rex Landry." Off to the side, T-Rex heard, "All accounted for." Then, "Ma'am, can you reach Truffle's collar? She's wearing two comms units, one for me to direct her, one for you to maintain communications with us."

"Yes. Does it matter which one I take off?" Remi asked, her voice thick with emotion.

"If you can see color, choose the orange collar."

Remi worked to hand that down to T-Rex. "Thank you, ma'am," Bear said as Remi scrubbed her fingers into the blonde coat of the British lab. "Ma'am, I'm going to recall Truffles now if you can pull your hands free."

The "No!" that rose up her throat sounded primal. Like her last hope was being ripped from her.

Bear waited her out. When Remi calmed, he said, "We have your location. I've plotted the path Truffles took. We have communications open."

"Please!" Remi said.

"We need Truffles to come out so we can assess your needs and get equipment into you. You have the comms. You'll be talking to Bob, our chief tactical operations commander. We've got you."

With a sigh and a blown kiss, Remi let go of Truffles. Over the comms, they heard, "Truffles, back to me." And the lab wriggled herself out of sight.

T-Rex got Remi onto the ground before he said, "T-Rex Landry."

"Hey, T-Rex, Bob here. I see you have a chem-light. Can you take me through your situation?"

Remi sat on the floor out of his way as T-Rex walked Bob over to see Senator Blankenship. "We've made diapers for her. But she hasn't voided in a while now. We're down to a single packet of emergency water."

"We'll send in a hose."

T-Rex held the camera to the notebook of vitals information. He described as best he could what had happened with the senator.

"No unusual foods, contacts with animals, anything that would help explain her behaviors?"

"Nothing."

"I need you to slowly move in a grid pattern clockwise ceiling to floor, move the camera over two feet, slowly sweep ceiling to floor. We need our engineers to understand the stability of that room."

"When is Truffles coming back?" Remi called out.

"Ma'am, our team is putting together a rescue pack based on this information. Food, water, air, medical supplies. Truffle's job is to find people in urban disasters. She'll keep searching for other victims since you have your own K9 out here."

"Rory's coming?" Her voice sparked with hope.

"Yes, ma'am. He's been trained in tunneling work. He'll be to you soon. T-Rex, if you would finish your surveil?"

As Remi and T-Rex waited for Rory, Bob played a book on tape for them over the comms.

That wasn't something that T-Rex had heard of before, but he'd admit it was a great distraction. It seemed to help Remi settle.

By the time they got to chapter eight. Ty came over the comms. "T-Rex, man, you holding up?"

"Affirmative." He sent a wink to Remi. "Four syllables." He hoped to lighten the mood.

She tried to smile.

"Rory is almost to you. You should hear him coming through the hole in a moment. If you'd catch him when he jumps, that'd be good."

Remi held the light high. T-Rex reached his arms out as Rory's black nose poked out of the hole and looked around. T-Rex patted his hands on his chest and reached out again, taking the full brunt of Rory and his packs.

After T-Rex unhooked the two hoses from his side

clasps, and unsnapped the bags, Remi took over Rory, talking baby talk and whole body hugging him, scratching between his ears, letting him roll over for a belly rub.

Dogs are good medicine.

"Water in the clear hose," Ty said. "Air supply in the black hose. Check them both, please."

"They're functioning," T-Rex said.

"In the pack on the left is an IV for the senator. The doctor wants it on a slow drip."

T-Rex pulled out the equipment and went to work. She was so dehydrated that he was having trouble finding a vein even using all the tips and tricks he'd learned along the way.

It was a good thing the senator was blacked out and couldn't feel this.

T-Rex conferred with the doctor and ended up running a line into her foot.

He looked up to see Remi watching him with her eyes filled with warmth. He sent her a wink, and she smiled over Rory's head.

"Got it," T-Rex said.

"Okay, next, you need to insert a catheter. You'll find the catheter and void bag on the right side of Rory's packs."

T-Rex lifted his thumb off the comms button. "Remi?"

"Yes."

"The senator needs a catheter."

"Yes."

"I think you should probably do that part."

"Why? I don't have your level of medical training."

"But you're a woman."

"I'm not following."

"You're a woman. You have female parts."

"Yes, we established that in your room a while back."

T-Rex spread his arms wide. "I've never done female catheter training."

"They'll talk you through it."

"Remi, *please*."

"Agh. No. I don't know how to do that. I've not been trained like you have."

"You have the same parts. You'll know best how to work things," T-Rex tried.

"I beg to differ. I've never been up close and personal with any other woman's body parts. You have. You are much better equipped in every sense of the word to do this."

Remi was probably right. He just felt all kinds of awkward about touching a woman's private body while she was passed out. But following the doctor's instructions, he did it.

And now he was glad it was in his rearview.

Pulling out a packet of hospital wipes, Remi and T-Rex gave the senator a bath and dressed her in one of the oversized T-shirts from Rory's pack. They moved her onto a sterile sheet. She was clean and hopefully comfortable if she could feel anything at all.

Once the doctor had okayed their work, Ty told them Rory needed to come out of there. That was going to be a trick.

Remi obviously found solace from the rescue dogs.

Rory leaned against Remi when she stood and sat in her lap when Remi was on the floor. Rory was always good around people in distress. It was as if he absorbed their pain and then shook it off.

When Ty was recalling Rory, T-Rex watched Remi gird her loins for this loss of fur compassion.

T-Rex draped Rory over Remi's shoulders, then put Remi back in her cheerleader pose on his shoulders.

Standing under the hole, Remi ducked her head and shoved Rory forward. Rory disappeared with a final wag of his tail.

When T-Rex lowered Remi back to the ground, they wrapped into each other's arms.

"We have light. Food. Water. And air," Remi said. "We have comms. We've helped the senator. We're in such a better place than we were a few hours ago."

T-Rex was too relieved to speak. He just needed a minute to let go of the bleak pictures that had been forming in his head before Truffles showed up.

"It's hard to let the dogs leave," she whispered.

"Rory will be back if we need him," T-Rex soothed. "So now we get cleaned up with our own wipes. We put on the fresh shirts. We have a clean place to sit on this tarp."

She stepped out of his arms. "What happens next?"

"The engineering team will look at our situation and plan for a way out."

"Which could take days. Weeks."

"It could." He wasn't going to lie. "But we have what it takes to survive. That's what we'll do, survive to tell the tale."

Chapter 35

T-Rex

Monday, Beirut, Lebanon

"Okay, here it is," Bob said. "Our engineers are looking at the videos that the dogs are bringing out. Humans can get as far as the west stairwell on your floor. From there, we simply don't have a way to get you out. They're talking about bringing in a crane and starting to offload the building materials from the top."

"How long would that take?" Remi asked.

"Weeks to do it in a way that the building doesn't collapse on you."

"T-Rex and I could survive that with provisions coming in. So, I'm not freaking out about this information. For me, I know we can survive it. But Senator Blankenship. Weeks? I just don't see her living that long without medical help. I'm just wondering if..."

"Anything you've got would be helpful, Remi," Bob said. "We have the military engineers in there working on this."

"When the blast first happened, my legs were outside."

"Wait, say that again."

"When I woke up from the blast, my legs were dangling outside of the building."

Bob called out to someone. "Hey, hand me those pictures there would you? Thanks." His voice came back strong. "Okay Remi, I'm looking at the close ups of the exterior of your room. I don't see any cavities into your space. Where were you standing during the blast?"

"I was looking out the left corner of the window. I saw the blast go up. I screamed. I knew that the concussion was the thing that was most dangerous. I threw myself to the ground. When I revived enough to assess my situation, I was outside of the building from my thighs down. I was covered in debris that weighted me down or I might have just slipped out the hole."

T-Rex's hand squeezed her arm as if keeping her from that fall.

"I don't see it," Bob said.

"T-Rex and I moved things around to try to stabilize the room. The hole was covered up. I could try to find it and signal you."

"Hang on before you move anything and put yourself in danger of getting cut or moving the wrong thing. Give us some time to see if that would be at all useful. We need to consult with the engineers. Things are difficult out here on the ground in terms of space to organize a rescue. And that building isn't stable."

"Okay," Remi said her gaze holding on T-Rex's.

"We need to find the hole," he said. "Slow and

smooth. Extra care that we don't make anything unstable."

It didn't take long.

A half hour of effort gave them a four-by-four hole. T-Rex imagined Remi waking up dangling halfway out the way she'd described, and his body slicked with the cold sweat of fear. T-Rex pushed those sensations down. Remi's emotions had calmed, and he'd do nothing to put her back in the dark place she'd been battling.

She handed him the red bedspread, and he pushed it through the hole, letting it dangle so the rescuers could see it.

"Red fabric. We've got you," Bob said over the comms. "Okay. Let's try to come up with a way to use that to our advantage. A helicopter is going to be a no-go, we can't risk the down draft collapsing the structure or degrading it further. There are other folks like you in the pockets. Truffles is finding them and getting them survival equipment."

"Good girl, Truffles," Remi said. "When I get out of here, it's steaks for the rest of her life."

The paramedic from Israel was the one who rode the basket on the crane cable to their hole.

He slid into their room, and then he and T-Rex wrestled the senator onto the backboard where she was strapped in tight.

Her vitals were erratic, and that was concerning, but soon she'd be on the ground, into an ambulance, and out of the country.

It took the rescuers most of the day.

And now it was night.

"It's going to be okay," T-Rex said.

"That basket. Tied. Dangling. Oh my god. They need to medicate the shit out of me."

"It's better that they don't. You're going to be fine."

"I'm going to be tied down."

"Okay. I get your point. Besides medication, what would help."

"You. Can we go down together? Would the basket hold us both?"

"We're going to have to leave it up to the rescue folks."

"Okay." She exhaled vehemently. "Can you be the one who straps me in?"

"That I can do."

"Will you go first so you're there to get me out?"

"Are you okay being in here by yourself? If I go first, I can't strap you in."

"True." They sat, holding hands, saying nothing for a long time. Then she said, "I'm not letting go of you. We're going to talk to all of our friends with traveling jobs, all our friends who live on different continents than their spouses. We're going to come up with a game plan. We're going to make this work."

"We are." T-Rex brought her hand to his lips. Then stood to help the paramedic get the stretcher back in the hole.

They got a nervous Remi strapped in, he kissed her hard. "I'll see you real soon. We're going to be fine. I promise."

Shoving her out that hole, and away from him—though he knew she was heading for safety—was one of the hardest things T-Rex had ever done.

Epilogue

Remi sat on the stage, holding Senator Barb Blankenship's hand under the hot studio lights for the Wake Up with a Smile, America! morning show.

Barb had her ubiquitous red cowboy hat covering her chemo snood. She'd whittled down to about a hundred pounds.

"Such an exciting day today, Senator," the host began. "For everyone who didn't happen to read about the harrowing true-life survival story last summer, I want to introduce you to Remi Taleb, war correspondent for the Washington News-Herald, last year's recipient of the prestigious Excellence in International Journalism Award. And she just found out last night that she has been awarded a Pulitzer for her reporting on their harrowing survival story in Beirut."

The applause was loud and long.

Remi ducked her head in a seated bow and smiled graciously.

"Senator, you had no idea at the time you left on that trip to take the two girls' robotics teams to their home countries that you had uterine cancer. How are you doing?"

"Remarkably well," the senator said. "I'm happy I wasn't awake through the days we were trapped in the hotel. I'm so grateful to my dear friend, Remi, and her husband—now husband, for taking such good care of me. You know, when Remi showed me the videos of my behavior on that trip, I was horrified. I had no idea I was speaking or acting that way. But apparently, women who have uterine cancer have a small chance of developing anti-NMDA receptor Encephalitis like I did. Once the rescuers pulled me from the building—did you all see me swinging out over the debris in a basket, dangling from the crane?"

The audience clapped.

"I suggest if you try that, you be catatonic like I was."

The hostess leaned forward. "How are you doing now? Any updates?"

"The docs say I'm in remission. I need to eat my healthy diet. Work on building up my muscles again. Do my meditations, and get back on my horse, slowly." She adjusted her cowboy hat. "But I'll be saddling up here in no time at all."

"Not every story out of the Beirut blast had a happy ending. In particular, I know you dedicated your article to your friend Jean Baptiste Rujean. He survived being kidnapped and tortured by ISIS and was in the hospital where he was killed with so many others in the blast."

Remi swallowed and nodded.

"News though about his two colleagues," she looked down at the notes in her lap, "Éloïse Marquette and Marie-Claude de Nimoux were ransomed by their television station and are now home recuperating. Have you seen them?"

"We've spoken on the phone. They're receiving the medical attention they need. I hope to see them very soon."

"Just before arriving in Beirut, your group had already been attacked in London. Any update on who was behind the attack?" The host asked. "Why it happened?"

"Mostly, that's being held tight to the vest by Scotland Yard and our own intelligence agencies," Senator Blankenship said.

"We do know," Remi added, "that arrests are ongoing, and the first three men, the ones who were involved in the elevator debacle, are scheduled for trial in two months. Senator Blankenship, her aide, Diamond Johnson, and I will be traveling to London to give witness testimony."

"Remi, the senator mentioned your now husband. We, of course, wanted him to be here on stage with you to accept our appreciation to both of you for your efforts during that crisis. But your husband works in the security world and can't have his image on the screen. Please convey to him our best wishes."

"Thank you, I will."

"When was the wedding?"

Remi smiled. "Last month."

"Is it hard for you, out and about the way you are, going all over the world to report on hot spots, to make a marriage like that work? Are you two able to ride off into your happily ever after together?"

"Not in our line of work, but when we come home from a long ride, we have support and love, and that is one of the many miracles that emerged from the Beirut blast."

"Nothing better." Senator Blankenship patted Remi's knee.

"No, ma'am, there is nothing better."

"We need to cut to our commercial break, but when we come back, you're going to meet Truffles, the wonder dog. Truffles and her handler, Bear MacIntosh, from Iniquus's Cerberus Tactical K9 Team Bravo, will be here to talk about their charitable work, flying on a moment's notice to natural disasters to save lives. All that and more after this break."

When they cut to commercial, the hostess thanked them.

T-Rex came out of the wings to push the senator's wheelchair.

"There you are," Senator Blankenship said. "Such a good-looking man you found yourself, Remi. A happily ever after story."

"Oh, I'd say that after the events in Beirut, we're entitled to a little joy," T-Rex said.

Remi lifted her lips, and T-Rex softly kissed her.

Joy, absolutely.

*****